FIGHT WITH THE HEART

CITY OF VIRTUE AND VICE
BOOK 6

SUSANNAH WELCH

Cover Concept and Design by Art Muse (Patrisha E. Badalo)
Editing by Red Loop Editing (Victoria Basnuevo)

eISBN: 978-1-958568-05-7
Paperback ISBN: 978-1-958568-06-4
Hardback ISBN: 978-1-958568-07-1

www.susannahwelch.com

ALSO BY SUSANNAH WELCH

City of Virtue and Vice Series

Dance with the Wind

Dance with the Night

Dance with the Dawn

Fight with the Wind

Fight with the Dark

Fight with the Heart

Heart of the Queendom Series

A Spark of Storms (Coming Soon)

Don't let the darkness win

The Shining City

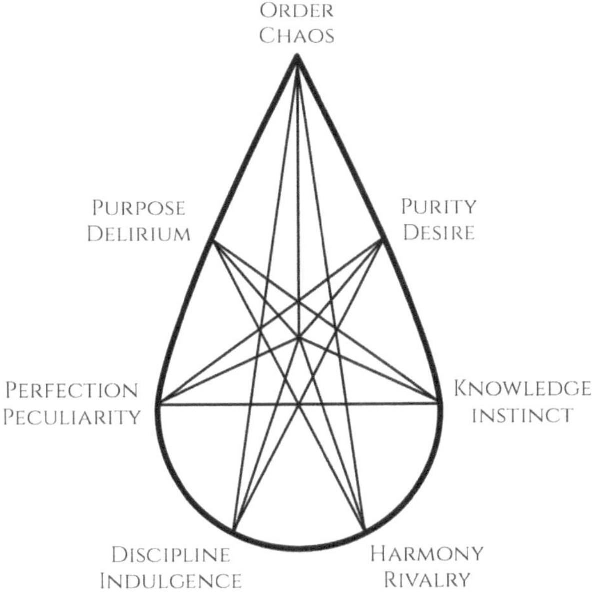

The Heart

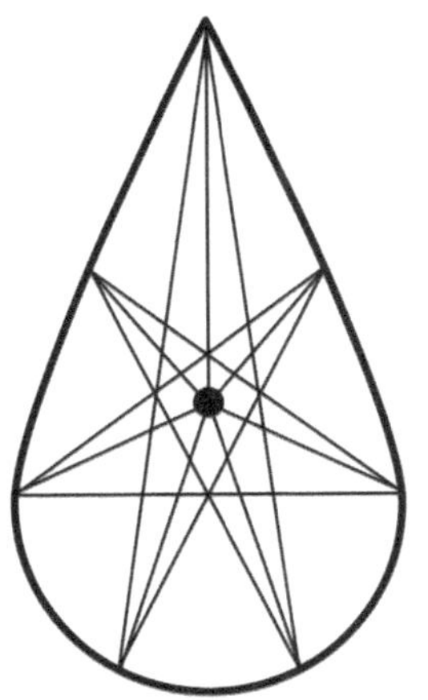

1

———

The stairway to the Underneath dripped with crystalline. Rose walked directly in the center of the stone steps, her arms tight to her body to avoid the glowing rivulets trickling on either side. Her stiff posture caused Vaylan's fingerprint on her collarbone to rub painfully against her dress. The only thing giving her the courage to enter Vaylan's lair was the mantra she repeated over and over in her mind.

Kill Vaylan. Save the crew. Return to Wilder.

Two Sentinels waited at the bottom of the stairs. Despite her burning anger, they still sent a spike of fear through her heart. Sentinels had terrorized the City at the High Priests' command for two hundred years. Rose wondered if Vaylan had recruited all new Sentinels or if some had stepped back into their matte black armor like nothing had changed.

Everything was so different and yet exactly the same.

As Rose approached, the pair nodded and turned to the side, revealing the scene at the bottom of the stairs. She had heard about the giant cavern called the Heart of the Grottos, but this was nothing like she expected. The roof of the cavern arched high above, but Vaylan had divided the space into rooms separated by walls of crystalline and fabric. Crystalline hung in tendrils from the top of the cavern, flowing down like dripping molasses, and the sight made her shiver with unease.

Giant swaths of white fabric billowed gently between the shining strands. The room created by the fabric and crystalline was fanciful—a luminous refuge underground. The only thing marring the beauty were the rows of Sentinels.

They stood at stiff attention, their armor absorbing the light from the crystalline. As she walked through the rows, the Sentinels angled inward, then fell back into formation. She had told Wilder that she wasn't in danger from Vaylan, but as she walked past dozens of Sentinels with only a few blades strapped to her side, she pushed down the embarrassing fear that still pounded through her veins.

"Rose!" Vaylan stood up from his silver throne with arms outstretched. "I'm so glad you made it!"

She studied his wide smile. There was no hint of the somewhat crazed expression from earlier that night when he had realized Wilder possessed more than one Gift. His face was just as open and friendly as she remembered.

But his warm expression was a mask to hide his depravity. And the sight of her crew was the proof.

They kneeled to the right of his throne and wore the same clothes she had seen them in the day before, though now torn and disheveled. The only one with injuries appeared to be Tayeh. One of her eyes was swollen, and she held her right arm as if she couldn't move it. Other than that, it was if they were among the penitent Adopted kneeling near them. Except floating above each crew member's head was a glowing crown like the High Priests used to wear.

But these crowns were made of crystalline.

The burning liquid flowed along the floor behind the

crew and snaked over their backs into a shiny crown hovering over each head. If they tried to rise from their kneeling position, the crystalline would burn them.

Anger flared in her chest, and she suddenly felt strong enough to fight the dozens of Sentinels around her. The only thing stopping her was the warning look on Kai's face. He had given her the same look many times during their childhood, so she knew exactly what he was saying.

Calm down. Think. Don't just react.

But she didn't want to calm down. Rose wanted to test what the Goddess said about her having a Spark. Could she truly control fire? She looked around for a flame. Even though she had never practiced, if she could find a flame, she would burn Vaylan and his entire lair to the ground.

As the fury built inside her, Kai's warning look intensified, and he shook his head sharply. A strand of his messy hair touched the crystalline crown and disintegrated in a little puff.

She inhaled sharply. If she called fire, there was no way her crew would make it out alive.

Her shoulders drooped, and she took a deep breath before turning to Vaylan.

"Crystalline crowns, Vaylan? The Sentinels are bad enough, and now you are adopting more of the High Priests' dramatics."

His grin revealed the dimple on his cheek. "The High Priests weren't responsible for all the drama in this City. Some of us come by it naturally."

She wasn't in the mood for his playful attitude. Not when her friends were in danger.

"What do you want from them?" she growled.

"The Chosen are perfectly fine. In fact, once you fulfill the prophecy, I will release them."

"How about you release them now, and I will consider

your prophecy?"

He smiled in the patronizing way that grated on her nerves. "Rose, you have no need for your friends anymore. You are here with me. You will darken the crystals, then watch as I remake this City, free from the Goddess's control. That's why you walked down those stairs. What else is there to accomplish?"

Kill you. But luckily, she kept that thought to herself. She wanted to laugh at his idea that she would darken the crystals, that she had any idea how to accomplish such a thing. It was as ridiculous as it was terrifying.

And yet, the Goddess had commanded her to do it.

The Goddess believed Rose could shut down the crystals and, as a result, save the dying Companion. But Rose had touched the crystal spires before many times in her life, and nothing, not a flicker, had occurred. What would be different now?

The only difference was that she now knew she had a Spark. But how would that knowledge help her with the crystal? She had too many questions and wasn't sure where to begin.

"What did you do to them?" she hissed.

Vaylan stared at the captured crew with pride. "Since they thought you stormed the Heart on your own, they fought fiercely. But eventually, my troops overpowered them. They drank some tea to still their Gifts, and they've been here calmly waiting for you to arrive." He gave her a warm smile. "I'm merciful, Rose. You should know that by now."

Heat flared in her throat, and her hands floated to the knives at her waist.

Vaylan sighed. "You are lucky I believe in the prophecy so deeply. A man with less faith would have been forced to kill you long before now."

"You wouldn't be the first to try," she growled.

"It's disappointing that you still lack faith, but I'm prepared to wait for you to believe." He raised a hand, and the crystalline crowns slithered into tendrils that reformed into a glowing cage. The sight of her crew trapped behind burning silver bars turned her stomach, but they each relaxed from their kneeling position with a small sigh.

Vaylan watched them stretch stiff legs with a warm smile. "If anything happens to me, I'm unsure what the crystalline will do. I've twisted it in some very unnatural ways around your friends. If I lose control of it, they could end up with a mark as painful as your own." His voice dropped to a low whisper, but his smile remained. "Or they could be scarred much, much worse."

She looked beyond her brother to the rest of her crew. She would give anything to protect them, and Vaylan knew it. He knew she was under his control. She couldn't win this in a direct attack. She needed to bide her time and make a plan.

Her hands unclenched, and she adopted a relaxed stance. "May I speak to them?"

He gave her a benevolent smile and waved her ahead.

Quinn studied the crystalline bars and Fitz's head was bowed in prayer, but they both looked up as Rose drew near. As she approached their glittering cage, she could see Tayeh's injuries more clearly and the pain she was trying to hide. Rev wore a brave face, her arm wrapped around Feather, though Rose could see the exhaustion in her eyes. Kieran lounged as if he wasn't a prisoner, but his trembling hands disproved his performance.

At the sight of the tears in her brother's eyes, her voice caught in her throat. "Kai ... I'm so sorry," she whispered. "This is all my fault."

"It's not your fault," said Kai quietly. "Vaylan is to blame."

"Is Tayeh okay?" asked Rose. Tayeh slumped over, and Fitz moved closer to hold her up.

Kai gave Tayeh a concerned look. "She healed each of us quickly before they forced us to drink the tea that smothered our Gifts. Unfortunately, there was no one who could heal her."

Rose imagined Wilder somewhere up in the City with the power to heal in his hands. She had to get Tayeh to him.

Kai lifted a hand as if he might reach through the bars. "I'm so glad to see you are okay. After the Sentinels appeared, we didn't know what happened to you."

"I'm okay," she choked out. "So is Wilder."

The closest Sentinel was several feet away, but Rose wasn't sure how much they could hear. She wanted to tell the crew everything the Goddess said and that she had a Spark, but she didn't want Vaylan to find out.

She spoke slowly, choosing her words carefully. "Vaylan asked me to darken the crystals by touching them one by one." They each gave her mixed looks of incredulity and confusion. "I know it seems odd, but I need you to trust me. It's … necessary for the City to survive."

Quinn cocked his head as he considered her words, but the rest of the crew still looked confused.

It was Rev who spoke the words Rose needed to hear. "We trust you."

Rose bit her lip to keep it from shaking. "You have little reason to trust me, considering your circumstances, but I swear I will get you out of here."

Kieran raised an eyebrow. "Don't do anything stupid. You won't do us any good if you end up in a cage like us."

She sighed. Stupid ideas were the only ones she had.

2

———

Rose turned away from the crew in their shiny cage and returned to Vaylan's side.

He grinned. "You look tired. Let me show you to your room."

"You have a room for me? Not a cage like theirs?"

He looked at her with surprise. "A cage? You came here of your own free will. You aren't a prisoner. You are the Marked One."

"Ah, I see. You believe I will eventually rule at your side."

He chuckled. "Well, I wouldn't say you will *rule* with me. But you will definitely be the first among my followers."

He turned around in a swish of midnight-blue robes, expecting her to follow. She looked back at the crew but had no idea what to do. Tayeh gave her a sharp nod, as a soldier would to a commander. Rev's piercing blue eye met hers with a glare that told Rose to behave. And in Feather's open face, Rose found complete trust. She swallowed the lump in her throat and bowed her head in acceptance of their request.

Rose would free them all.

Vaylan walked confidently at the head of his Sentinels,

and Rose hurried to catch up. They walked down a billowing hallway until they reached a red tent among the white. Vaylan lifted the red fabric and ushered her inside.

Her room was furnished with a bed piled with pillows and luxurious quilts of red and gold. The dark burgundy rug stretched the length of the tent, which was larger than her former room in Temple Discipline. The desk in the corner held a stack of books and a bowl of fresh fruit. In the other corner was a rack of clothing.

All in white.

Vaylan noticed her narrowed eyes and smiled. "It looks like the Adopted who prepared your room want you to wear white like they do."

She bared her teeth as she spoke. "I'm sure they do nothing without your approval."

"They want to please you as much as they want to please me. They must have assumed you had already switched to white." He studied her dress with a raised eyebrow.

She was still in her white showgirl costume. Rose grumbled quietly in irritation. She hadn't picked the short dress for herself. The costume designer, Hazel, had chosen it for her to match Wilder. And Hazel had picked Wilder's costume just to see him in those white leather pants.

"I hope you sleep well, Rose." Vaylan backed to the curtained door, his Sentinels still at his side. "We have a busy day tomorrow. We will head to Grotto Peculiarity, and you will darken the crystal there. It's the first step to the City being remade."

She wondered briefly if he would take all the Sentinels with him on the trip. Maybe it would be easier to kill him once they were outside the Heart?

She kicked off her turquoise boots and sank onto the bed with an exhausted sigh. He'd be much easier to kill after she had rested. "I'll see you in the morning, Vaylan. I'm looking forward to it."

He chuckled softly and closed the curtain behind him as he left.

The next morning, the Sentinels wouldn't let her leave her room until she removed her weapons. She was relieved they didn't pat her down; she didn't want them finding the blades concealed under her clothes. A part of her wondered if they only made her remove her outer blades because the black sheaths clashed against her white clothes.

She had a lot of clothing to choose from but settled on a cropped white leather jacket with inner pockets and white boots with interesting straps and buckles, which had the added benefit of concealing weapons securely. The outfit was like an all-black ensemble she used to wear as a Priest. She felt a strange sense of comfort pulling on the jacket as long as she ignored the color.

As she exited her tent, it surprised her that the Sentinels didn't stop her from exploring. She had assumed she really was a prisoner, but they let her walk down the strange hallways of fabric and crystalline, staying just a few steps behind.

She thought she would find rooms filled with signs of Vaylan's nefarious plans, but everything seemed mundane. After peeking inside several rooms with neatly made beds, she found a kitchen with a dozen men and women stirring large pots and three teens in white sweeping the stone floor. A gray-haired woman brought Rose a bowl of porridge with a smile and bowed head.

Rose sat down to eat at one of the long wooden tables and stared at the flames inside the cookstoves. Could she really control the fire? She longed to reach out like she used to with the wind to see what she could do, but the nearness of the cooks held her back. They were victims of Vaylan's manipulation and didn't deserve to be hurt during her experiments with fire.

Because knowing her, someone was bound to get hurt.

A young boy moved between tables with quick steps, collecting dishes. She handed him her empty bowl, and he grinned, revealing two missing front teeth. He took careful hold of the bowl and spoon and ran it up to a man with his hands in wash water. The man ruffled the boy's hair with a smile, and the boy ran off to the next person with an empty bowl.

How had Vaylan convinced these people to follow him? Could they not see how manipulative he was?

She continued her walk through the hallways as she thought back to when she first met Vaylan. He had irritated her from the very beginning, but she found many people irritating, so that meant little. She didn't trust him, but she could find nothing to fault him for. Even after she knew he was responsible for Brother Owyn's death and set her up to get the new High Priests killed, he denied it, and she couldn't prove it. Vaylan slid away from all her accusations and left her feeling as if she had imagined it all.

Until he took the crew. He couldn't hide from that.

She walked down the draped passageways until she reached the bright center of the Heart. Seven stone pillars directed a central pool of crystalline up into the City above, and a large tent faced the pool, its soft fabric entrance draped open to the light. The crystalline was so bright it lit up the white tent with a diffused glow. A dozen Adopted sat at desks, writing carefully on little strips of paper, then placing them in neat stacks.

"Good morning, Rose." Vaylan's quiet voice at her back

made her jump. He smirked at her reaction. "Are you enjoying your exploration?"

She straightened her jacket needlessly and cleared her throat. "You said I wasn't a prisoner, so I thought to test that out."

"And you haven't been detained, have you?" At her quick head shake, he said, "Perhaps you will trust me now?"

"You still believe I will trust you? After everything you've done?"

He shrugged. "I've only done what Brother Owyn prophesied, as I will continue to do." He walked to a desk and picked up a strip of paper. "None of us can resist the pull of prophecy. It's what led you to this tent."

He handed her the paper, but she hesitated before reading it. "I don't believe in your prophecies, Vaylan. You just twist his words to mean whatever you want."

He grinned. "You don't have to believe in prophecy for it to come true." He nodded at the strip of paper in her hand. "Wouldn't you rather know in advance?"

She didn't want him to think she believed in the prophecies, but it would be helpful to know what goals Vaylan was working toward, so she reluctantly read the words.

The Marked will bow and beg for mercy.

She choked. "You believe I will bow before you?"

He chuckled. "There's no need to be embarrassed, Rose. You are first among my Adopted, and you've seen how they bow before me all the time. No one will think less of you for it."

She opened her mouth to respond but couldn't put together any words.

A woman with wire glasses approached Vaylan and lowered her head.

He gave her a benevolent smile. "Yes, child?"

She handed Vaylan a strip of paper. "I don't think our

newest Adopted will work in this position. Sometimes he can copy out the prophecies clearly, but other times, he just scribbles and draws pictures."

Vaylan looked at the paper with a nod. "Not all Adopted are suited for every position. I'm sure we will find somewhere for him to serve well."

The woman's face lit in a warm smile as she bowed. "You are very kind, Lord Founder."

Rose opened her mouth to express her distaste at his new title, but her eyes landed on the piece of paper, and the words froze on her tongue.

Those weren't scribbles. The symbols were the old language she had only seen one other person write. She snapped her head around to study every face in the room with a sense of dread.

Walter sat at a desk in the back of the tent, his gray head bent over his paper. He looked up, caught Rose's eye, and winked.

She bit her lips to keep a gasp from escaping. When she had first met Walter, she thought he was just an odd elderly man in a home for people who couldn't care for themselves. It wasn't until Quinn interpreted the piece of paper Walter had given her that she realized who he was.

He had the Spark of granting long life. He was the reason the former High Priests had lived so long they could terrorize the City with Sentinels and create the Underneath. If Vaylan discovered Walter's Spark ...

She turned to find Vaylan studying her. She cursed the fact that her emotions were always written clearly on her face.

"You don't have to be afraid," said Vaylan. "I'm not a monster. He won't be harmed."

She tried to slow her breathing and refused to look at Walter again. "What do you mean?"

"I don't hurt people just because they are different, and I don't hide them away to be forgotten. He will find a place to serve and will live as one of the Adopted."

"Oh ... that's good." She cleared her throat and tried to speak in her usual confident tone. "I will check on him later to make sure you're telling the truth."

His smile didn't falter, but irritation flashed in his eyes. "I would expect nothing less from you."

A cool hand took hold of hers, and she turned to find Walter. His face was lined, but there was no way to tell he was hundreds of years old. He had seen the High Priests come and go and now stood in the headquarters of a man who would use him in the same way they did.

Walter nodded. "You see more than you did before. That's good. There is so much to be seen by those who are looking."

The woman with glasses took Walter's other hand, and he released Rose to follow the woman out of the room.

Rose relaxed her face before turning back to Vaylan. "I guess I've seen enough here for now."

Vaylan's eyes narrowed as he studied her, but he relaxed into his usual smile. "Good, because it's time to begin. We are heading to darken the first crystal spire."

"Sure." She gestured to the tent opening. "Lead the way."

When he turned, she glanced at the strip of paper Walter had put into her hand. She couldn't read the old language, but she knew it was for her. The rose he had drawn had many thorns.

Perfection

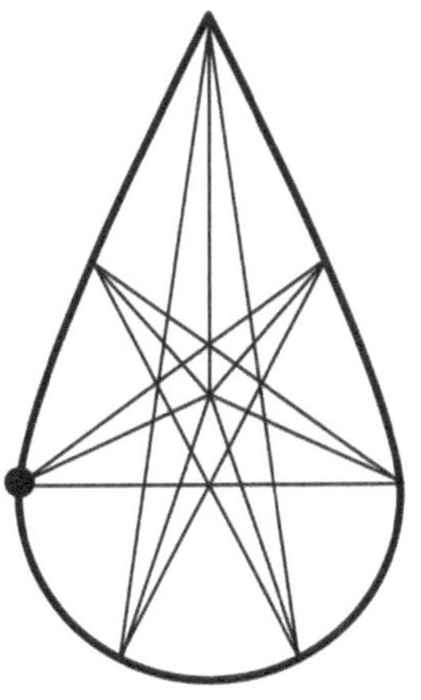

Peculiarity

3

Vaylan and the Sentinels led her through the confusing curtained hallways back to the throne room. More Sentinels lined the perimeter, and the crew stood in the center of the room.

They wore simple black robes, and their hands were bound with ropes of bright white. The ropes would prevent the skilled fighters like Tayeh and Kai from injuring too many, but Rose knew the main restraint was the Gift-restricting tea still in their system.

She didn't notice the low growl in her throat until Vaylan spoke.

"They're strong, Rose. They'll be fine." He patted her on the arm, and she realized belatedly that he was close enough to attack. He walked away before she could react.

Vaylan strode down a curtained hallway, and a dozen Sentinels fell into step behind him. Another dozen surrounded the prisoners and took hold of their ropes, pulling them along. Anger flared in Rose's chest, and she ran forward to join the procession.

She looked up to see Vaylan standing at a dark entrance cut into the wall of the cave. Her mouth went dry as she imagined walking through a long, dark tunnel. The entrance to the Underneath had been that dark, and she wasn't interested in trying that again. However, Vaylan raised both arms overhead, then pushed them forward as if moving a boulder.

Crystalline flowed down the walls of the cave and poured along the top of the tunnel, bathing it in bright light. A Sentinel at her side grabbed hold of Tayeh's rope and pulled her forward roughly, causing her to stumble.

Tayeh was at the back of the line and slower than the others because of a limp. Some of the other crew members had a single Sentinel holding the rope around their hands, but Tayeh was surrounded by three Sentinels of her own. The rope cut into her wrists, and her body was twisted as she held her arm protectively at her waist.

Despite Rose's instinctive fear of the Sentinels, she yelled at the one holding Tayeh's rope. "Let go of her! What are you afraid of? She's injured. It's not like she can hurt you."

The Sentinel laughed.

Rose blinked, trying to comprehend the sound. She had never considered the possibility that a Sentinel *could* laugh. She barely considered them human.

The Sentinel nodded and handed the rope to Rose with a bow. Tayeh's three guards gave them space but stayed in perfect formation, surrounding her as they walked through the tunnel leading to Grotto Peculiarity.

"Are you okay?" whispered Rose.

"I've been better." Tayeh's voice was strained, but she sighed as Rose put some slack on the rope. "Thanks for stepping in."

"Did you hear that Sentinel laugh?"

Tayeh chuckled softly. "I have a bit of a reputation after taking down several Sentinels on my own."

Rose frowned. "I wish I would have been there."

Tayeh gave her a hard look. "I wish none of us had been there."

Rose swallowed the lump in her throat. "Tayeh, I'm—"

"It's not your fault."

"Yes, it is! If I didn't rush into places without thinking, this never would have happened."

Tayeh nodded. "It's true that you charge into danger without thinking about the consequences."

Rose's shoulders sagged, and she nodded meekly.

"And what did we do?" asked Tayeh.

"You thought I had done it again and ran after the person you thought was me."

"Exactly. We charged into danger without thinking about the consequences."

Rose spoke slowly as she considered. "Yes, I guess you did."

"We followed our leader a little too accurately, don't you think?" A small smirk curled the edge of her lips.

Rose snorted. "I'm not a good role model."

Tayeh chuckled, then winced. "I took down several Sentinels, but they definitely left a mark."

Rose looked up as they approached the entrance to Grotto Peculiarity. The bright crystalline of the tunnel fell into a thin sheet, closing the entrance, and Vaylan led the procession toward the crystal. Grotto Peculiarity was just as quirky and colorful as Rose remembered, but all she could see was the base of the crystal spire looming closer.

"I need to darken the crystal," she said to Tayeh without removing her eyes from the glowing shape.

"I know," said Tayeh.

"I don't know what will happen to your Gift," she whispered.

"I can imagine."

"I'm so sorry, Tayeh. If there was another way—"

"I'll be okay. I haven't had the Gift long enough to suffer its loss."

The words "as much as you did" remained unspoken.

"Besides, it will make it easier to fight again." Tayeh's eyes unfocused as she stared blankly ahead. "There is something distinctly disturbing about feeling the moment someone's heart stops, especially when I'm the cause." She shook her head, as if shaking loose a memory. "But it was nice being able to heal. I'm usually the one taking life, not protecting it."

"Don't say that!" snapped Rose. "You always protect life. The crew is alive because you protected them. I'm sure none of them took out as many Sentinels as you did, and I'm also sure the only reason you surrendered was to save their lives. If you were only interested in taking lives, you would have fought until you were all dead."

Tayeh didn't speak for a while, but when she did, her voice was rough with emotion. "Thanks, Rose. I'm glad to be in your crew."

Rose couldn't answer without tears, so instead, she took gentle hold of Tayeh's hand as they walked the rest of the way to the crystal together.

4

———————

Rose stood in front of the glowing crystal and rubbed her sweaty hands against her pants. Dozens of people surrounded her, watching to see what she would do. Because of the Havens, Vaylan had become a well-known figure, and their procession had picked up curious onlookers as they walked through Grotto Peculiarity. People wanted to see where Vaylan led a troop of Sentinels and seven bound figures in black robes. When they stopped at the crystal, Vaylan's Adopted flooded out of the Haven to join the crowd.

And now all their eyes were on Rose.

She raised her hand but hesitated, her shaking fingers highlighted by the crystal's glow. The Goddess said Rose could darken the crystal with her Spark, but since she didn't even realize she had a Spark until the Goddess told her, Rose had no idea how to use it. What if she touched the crystal and nothing happened? Maybe that would be for the best. Vaylan believed she could do it, and if she failed, all his plans would fall apart.

Except that the Companion was dying, and the Goddess

believed this could heal him. If Rose had the power to save the City, she had to try.

She took a deep breath and slowly placed her hand on the crystal.

Nothing happened.

Rose frowned. She had seen Ylena darken the crystals by simply placing her hand on them. But, of course, Rose shouldn't have imagined it would be that easy.

She blew out her breath and focused on the crystal. Perhaps it required a tear? Sparks weren't supposed to need a tear to work, but since the City was founded on tears, maybe this time it did? She blinked a tear from her eye, then pressed it into the crystal.

The crystal mocked her with its light.

The surrounding crowd shuffled nervously, unsure of what was supposed to happen. Vaylan hadn't given a speech. He had just walked to the crystal and ushered her forward. The crowd didn't know what they were waiting for.

Tayeh knew. She gave Rose a determined nod.

Rose took strength from Tayeh's calm confidence, so she removed her hand and shook out her shoulders to relax, as if preparing for another round in a sparring match. She flexed her fingers, then rested her hand on the crystal again.

She closed her eyes and pictured the fire of her Spark residing deep within. Even though she hadn't used her Spark yet, she reached out for the flame as she had for the wind. She imagined her Spark smothering the crystal's glow, plunging the entire Grotto into darkness. Without the crystals, the Underneath would be as dark as a tomb. The thought of the unrelenting darkness constricted her lungs, and her eyes shot open.

The crystal still shone a bright white.

Before she could let loose a string of curses, Vaylan stepped smoothly to her side. "There's no need to try so hard, Rose. You are destined to darken the crystals. Just believe, and it will happen."

"Just believe?" she asked incredulously. "That's all? Maybe you could do something helpful and tell me how you control the crystalline? Do you *just believe*? Or is there something else you *do*?"

His face tightened. "What does my ability to control crystalline have to do with this?"

Rose realized that calling his ability to control crystalline a Spark might not be wise. Especially since she didn't want to mention her own.

"Um ... I don't know what I'm doing. I thought controlling crystalline might be similar."

Rose saw the briefest flash of anger pass behind his eyes before they settled into their normal twinkling glow. "My ability to control crystalline is the sign that I am the true ruler of this City. It's nothing like what you will do here. You will darken the crystal because I have marked you. I gave you the strength to do this. All you must do is obey."

A wildfire burst to life in Rose's chest. "Just obey?" She ground out the words between clenched teeth.

He gave her his most fatherly smile and patted her on the arm. "Exactly. Just use the ability I gave you and darken the crystal. It's that simple."

He thought he *gave* her the ability to darken the crystal? She wanted to strangle him. She wanted to scream that she had a Spark that might equal his own. She wanted to do anything but attempt to shut off the crystal.

But instead, she took everything in her heart and shoved it deep within the crystal.

White light flared, and Rose stood inside the Goddess's glittering jewel cave.

The Goddess stood before her in a long white dress with

sleeves that touched the floor. Her eyes were closed in concentration, then they shot open. "You did it."

Rose blinked, trying to shake off the disorientation from suddenly being somewhere else.

"You shut off the first crystal." The Goddess did not sound pleased. "You must continue."

"I'm not sure what I did."

"You will figure it out. This is the only way to save his life." Not pleased, just resolved.

"What do I do about—?"

The Goddess shut her eyes, and Rose stood in the dark.

People screamed in the sudden darkness, and Rose gasped as panic squeezed her chest. The cool crystal against her palm was her only frame of reference. She looked up at the faint light that trickled in from the bridge leading into the City and used that as a beacon to remind herself she was not trapped in the dark. Escape was possible.

She breathed through her nose to calm herself and blinked as her eyes slowly adjusted. With each blink, another flickering window came into view as people lit candles throughout the Grotto.

Flames.

Her panic receded as she watched the lights spring to life. She wanted to reach out for the flames and test her Spark, but they were too far away.

Vaylan's laugh alerted her to his presence at her side. "I told you I gave you the ability to do it!" he said triumphantly. She turned to the sound of his voice and could barely make out his shape in the dark. He raised both hands above his head and pulled downward sharply.

Crystalline flared to life around them. She had somehow also stilled the crystalline, but Vaylan forced it to flow again. Windows throughout the Grotto brightened as the crystalline lamps relit. Soon the Underneath shone with a faint glow, darker than before, but the screaming had stopped.

Vaylan spoke loudly to address the crowd still gathered around. "The Goddess abandoned her City long ago, leaving only traces of her power behind. I will cleanse this City of her presence, and then you will finally be free."

He looked pleased at his announcement, but the crowd whispered with various levels of alarm. They didn't seem happy to lose their primary source of light. They probably would be less than thrilled to learn he planned to withdraw the crystalline as well.

"One crystal down," she said. "Are we heading straight to the next Grotto?"

He chuckled. "No. This is only the first step. Now we head to the actual target. Temple Perfection."

Vaylan gestured to the Sentinels, and they nudged the members of the crew forward. Rose was glad to head toward the bridge, where the faint glow promised daylight, but her stomach churned as she wondered what Vaylan had planned.

5

Rose stepped into the sunshine and shivered. The City had always been warm, no matter the time of year. The only exception had been when Ylena disabled all the crystals at once and snow fell inside the City. Each time the crystals flickered off, the icy wind from the mountains flowed inside the City walls, but the temperature always returned to normal as soon as the crystals relit.

Vaylan's dark City would be cold.

He marched purposefully toward the temple. Gone was the humble attitude she had seen on display in the Havens. He walked as if he owned the City already.

Judging by the rapturous faces of the people they passed, maybe he did.

Rose knew there had been growing tension between the Priests and the people Upstairs. Factions had unashamedly called for the removal of the Priests, sometimes calling for murder. Rose had been afraid to go out at night wearing all black.

Now she wore white and marched with Vaylan, leading a group of seven prisoners dressed like Priests.

She ground her teeth at the thought of being Vaylan's pawn again and reconsidered her plan to just kill Vaylan and be done with it. But as she stared at the angry faces of the people they passed, she realized killing him would probably start a riot that ended with every Priest dead. She clenched her fists and continued the walk to the temple.

They arrived to find a line of Priests guarding the entrance. "Guarding" was too strong of a word, though, considering that most of these Priests had formerly been healers and hair stylists. More than a dozen strong young men circled the inner courtyard while more Priests peeked out of the arches and doorways. They murmured anxiously to one another, and Rose saw a look in their eyes that she hadn't seen since Ylena had stripped away all their Gifts at once.

Doubt.

The crystal in the center of Temple Perfection was a dull gray. It wasn't the first time it had happened, but this time, only the single crystal was dark, and the rest of the crystals still shone a bright white. Rose could read the questions on their faces. Why had only their temple gone dark? Did they displease the Goddess? Why would she remove her light from only them?

Rose had a shadow of an answer, but it wouldn't be enough to erase the doubt from their minds. It would not comfort them if she said this was part of the Goddess's plan. She had struggled with those dark feelings of doubt and knew there was nothing she could say to reassure them. They would have to wrestle with those questions on their own.

Vaylan stopped directly in front of the temple and looked up at the dark crystal with satisfaction. He turned to face the gathered crowd. "The Goddess abandoned you but left her crystal prison to lock you away. I have come to set you free."

He pointed at Rose's crew. "These seven were the Goddess's so-called Chosen. They were the last gasp of her power as she tried to imprison all of you again. But my Marked One delivered them into my hands." He smiled warmly at Rose, and all eyes turned to her.

There were too many faces for her to interpret everything they felt about her, but she saw enough. From the Adopted, she saw pride. From the angry crowd, vindication. From the Priests, betrayal.

She shrank back from them all, confused and angry at the misunderstanding. This was spiraling out of control, but she had no idea how to fix it. Maybe she needed to make a speech of her own? But she looked at all those faces and realized there was nothing she could say to convince them all. Everyone wanted something different, and she had nothing to give.

Vaylan faced the temple and the Priests who had gathered in the courtyard. A sense of foreboding shivered down her spine.

She stepped in front of him. "I darkened the crystal like I said I would. Can we just leave now?"

The Sentinels moved to pull her back, but Vaylan held up a hand, and they halted.

"Rose, the Priests inside oppose my plan to rebuild this City. I can't let their disobedience stand. They've made their choice. I'll cleanse this temple, then fill it with true believers."

He lifted his hands and circled his fingers as if he was gathering up strands of wool. Then he held his clenched fists straight before him, softening his hands as if honey trailed along his fingers.

That's when the screaming began.

Even though the crystal was a dull gray, crystalline shone through the open arches and windows throughout the temple. As Vaylan moved his fingers, the light shifted. Every lamp and curving thread of crystalline had suddenly become a weapon. Priests screamed and ran for the doors, but Vaylan moved his palm in a wiping motion, and a thin sheet of crystalline covered each arch leading out to the courtyard.

"Vaylan! Stop! They'll die in there." She stepped toward him, but his Sentinels blocked her path.

The screams grew louder and more panicked. She heard voices pleading for mercy and begging for their lives. And not just their own life. Now that the temples had been opened to those without Gifts, that meant there were parents inside, begging him to save their children's lives.

She wanted to run to help, but she wouldn't make it through the crystalline-covered doorways, and killing Vaylan might not stop the crystalline from rampaging. Her Gift was gone, and her Spark couldn't save them. She was completely helpless and could do nothing. She screamed in frustration, then did the most desperate thing she could think of.

She dropped to the ground before Vaylan and begged.

"Please, Vaylan! Show mercy!" She ducked her head in the penitent posture he had forced her crew into. "Please, I beg you."

The screams didn't stop, but she saw his midnight-blue robes move into the edge of her vision. She didn't know how to convince him to change his mind, so she just chanted "Please, Vaylan, I beg you," over and over again. As the screaming inside became desperate sobs, her tears streamed from her eyes directly into the rough dirt under her face.

Vaylan reached down and lifted her chin to look him in

the eye. "You are begging me to show them mercy?" he asked softly.

"Yes, Vaylan, please!" She hated herself for being so weak, for having no power to stop him other than kneeling before him as one of his faithful Adopted.

His lips curled into a grin with his dimple on full display. "I knew you would submit to me, Rose. The prophecy foretold it. And to prove to you I am merciful, I will relent." He pulled his fingers into fists, and slowly, the screams halted. Sobbing could still be heard from inside, but the panicked cries had stopped.

Rose sat stunned, her dirt-filled tears dropping onto her bright white clothes. She watched as the crystalline pulled back from the edges of the doorways, and fearful Priests peeked outside hesitantly. They weren't sure if it was safer inside or out.

Rose wasn't sure of that herself.

Vaylan nodded at the Sentinels who held Tayeh, and they led her forward. He spoke as if he already had his words prepared. "These seven Chosen had each of the Gifts, and this girl had the Gift of Perfection. I say *had* because when the crystal went dark, she lost hers. I know this from Brother Owyn's prophecy."

Murmurs arose from the crowd. Brother Owyn may have been martyred, but his prophecies continued to spread. Rose hadn't heard that prophecy, but some in the crowd apparently had.

"She no longer has the Gift. I removed it from her, like I will remove it from the other six."

Rose opened her mouth to say that actually *she* had removed the Gift but didn't think that would be helpful.

An Adopted had gone inside the temple and led out a woman clutching a child of around three years. The child's arm from his hand to his shoulder was burned. Rose still felt the burn at her collarbone as strong as the first day Vaylan had given it to her, and she expected the child to be screaming in pain. Instead, the child was strangely silent. His eyes looked like glass, as if his mind had broken from the pain.

Vaylan summoned the woman forward with a warm smile. She moved forward numbly, unable to resist his gentle kindness.

He looked at the child's arm with sad eyes. "What a terrible burn ... The Goddess created a dangerous City, then abandoned it. And where are her Gifts now?" He gestured to Tayeh. "She gave you the Gift of healing, correct? Use it."

Tayeh was always so confident and strong, but she stared at the child with helplessness written on her face. Rose found the expression terrifying.

Vaylan gently lifted Tayeh's hands and untied the ropes around her wrists. Rose longed to see her tackle Vaylan to the ground, but instead, Tayeh raised a shaking hand to the child's cheek. She closed her eyes gently, and a tear fell from her lashes. Her eyes opened, and she bit her trembling lip. Tears continued to fall, but the child remained unchanged.

Vaylan stepped behind her and whispered in her ear, "Say 'The Goddess has abandoned us.' Say it, and they will be free to go."

Rose stopped breathing. She felt trapped between one moment and the next, unable to say a word.

Tayeh closed her eyes and whispered, "The Goddess has abandoned us."

Vaylan nodded wisely and whispered, "Yes, she has. But I am here to pick up the pieces." Then he unfastened the top of Tayeh's black robe, revealing a white dress underneath.

Vaylan raised the black robe above his head and spoke to the silent crowd. "She is no longer Chosen. No longer a Priest." He turned to look at the terrified Priests huddled in the temple courtyard. "As a result, she is no longer an enemy of mine. She is free to go."

Tayeh's eyes were still locked on the child's face, unaware of his pronouncement.

His words weren't for her, though; they were for the other Priests. "And if you renounce the Goddess, you won't be my enemy either."

Rose stared at Vaylan with wide eyes.

He raised his arms in a benevolent offering. "You are all free to go. The Goddess has no claim on you anymore. I offer you the freedom to decide what you want."

The Priests stared at him without moving a muscle. Without breathing.

Vaylan chuckled. "Don't worry. My Sentinels will let you pass. You can leave here today without fear. But tomorrow, if I discover you worshipping the Goddess or still wearing black, I will pronounce a swift judgment."

He signaled to his Sentinels, and they cleared a pathway through the crowd. The Priests still hadn't moved, so Vaylan walked up and did a shooing motion to the Priests on the bottom step. "Go on. This temple is mine now."

A Priest stumbled down the steps and looked up at the gray crystal with tears in his eyes. He turned around, walked through the crowd, and didn't look back.

After that, the rest of the Priests calmly filed out behind him.

6

———

After the Priests wandered off, Vaylan led the rest of the crew inside the temple but left Rose and Tayeh where they were. Rose tried to get Tayeh to leave with the Priests, but the Sentinels blocked her way. Instead of fighting her way out, Tayeh slumped onto the bottom step of the temple in defeat.

"I'm sorry, Rose." Tayeh closed her eyes.

"Sorry for what? None of this is your fault."

"I never understood." She stared off at the other lit spires of the City. "I thought you were overly emotional when you lost your Gift, but I didn't understand. I only had my Gift for a short time. I don't know how you and the other Priests survived after losing the Gifts you had for a lifetime."

Rose ducked her head to hide the emotion on her face. "You had no way to know, but thank you for saying it."

Tayeh sighed. "Losing my Gift is sad, but I'm more upset about Wilder's loss. I was really looking forward to seeing him."

Rose's eyes widened as she realized what that meant. Tayeh wouldn't be healed immediately. Her injuries would be with her for a long time.

They sat in silence, watching the sun slide further down the horizon.

"Do you think he really plans to let me go?" asked Tayeh.

"He must," Rose said forcefully.

Tayeh turned to face her. "He has no reason to release me. I wouldn't release me if I were him. You should prepare for the worst."

"Worse than Vaylan burning children?"

Tayeh just gave her a flat stare.

Rose shook her head sharply. "No, I will not consider it. He will release you. I will do whatever it takes."

Tayeh's whisper was surprisingly kind. "Even beg?"

Rose looked away, her shame at war with the fierce protectiveness she felt for Tayeh. She pulled in an unsteady breath and whispered, "Yes, I'll beg him to release you if that's what it takes."

Rose felt Tayeh's callused hand take her own. They lapsed into silence again.

As the last trace of sunlight slid beyond the horizon, Vaylan and his Sentinels led the crew out of the temple. The Sentinels stopped the crew at the top of the steps, and Vaylan walked toward Rose and Tayeh with arms open wide.

"Good evening, ladies!"

Rose was always surprised how he could sound so kind when she knew how evil he was. "Good evening, Vaylan." She helped Tayeh to her feet. "Isn't it time to release her now?"

Vaylan looked at the horizon and nodded. "Yes, the time is right, but there is still one more thing to be done. I thought you would instinctively know what to do since the prophecy is about you."

She clenched her fists and swallowed a string of angry curses. Instead, she answered calmly, "I've already fulfilled multiple prophecies today. I'm at my limit."

He grinned. "Everything we do is prophecy fulfilled, Rose. And tonight, you will fulfill it once again."

"Fine," she huffed. "What must I do so Tayeh walks out of here alive?"

"The prophecy says, 'The Chosen will suffer at the hands of the Marked before disappearing into the dark.' Thanks to the crystal going out, the dark is here. Now all we need is for the Chosen to suffer."

Fire burned in Rose's chest, and she wanted to murder Vaylan more than ever. She choked out, "I think Tayeh has suffered enough."

Vaylan clicked his tongue. "That's not what the prophecy says. It must be at your hands."

Rose crossed her arms in front of her chest. "I'm not hurting her. You can take your prophecy and shove it—"

The Sentinels took a menacing step toward Tayeh, and Rose stilled her tongue.

Vaylan pulled a dagger from inside his robes. The handle was mother-of-pearl and, without the light of the crystal, only shone dimly in the moonlight. He held it out to Rose as if giving her a gift.

"I will see the prophecy fulfilled," he said. "It only says you will cause her to suffer. It doesn't say that my Sentinels can't hurt her for a while before you finally do what needs to be done."

Tayeh took her hand. "You said you'd do whatever it takes." Her eyes were fierce and unafraid. "This is what it takes."

Rose looked at the dagger in Vaylan's hand and imagined hurting Tayeh with it, and bile threatened to rise in her throat. Tayeh was already bruised and battered, and Rose couldn't bear the thought of adding to her pain. The crew stood silently on the top step. She expected them to erupt in fury at Vaylan, but they fixed their eyes on Tayeh with a mixture of respect and encouragement.

Tayeh's eyes were still swollen and bruised, and the white dress that had been under her black robes made her look vulnerable in a way that was jarring to her usually tough exterior. Tayeh was strong, but Rose had seen how gentle her heart could be. "I can't do it," she whispered.

Vaylan's voice was warm yet remorseless. "Yes, you can." He placed the blade in her numb hands. "Suffering is a part of life. Do as you must, then release her into the dark."

Rose looked at the blade in her hand. She could spin around and use it on Vaylan. Tayeh was too weak to be much help against the four Sentinels surrounding them, but maybe Rose could take out one before the others killed her and Tayeh.

But only one crystal had been darkened. If Rose didn't darken them all, the Companion would die. The City would grow cold, and without Gifts, there wouldn't be enough food. Everyone would die a slow death.

Rose reached out a shaking hand, and Tayeh held hers out in return. Her face held no trace of fear, only trust.

Rose swiped the blade across Tayeh's palm. Blood spilled out, but Tayeh never made a sound. The cut was deep; Rose didn't want Vaylan to say she didn't cause enough suffering. She couldn't turn her head, because she was afraid to see the look of betrayal on the faces of her crew.

Tayeh bowed her head to Rose, as if in thanks, then pulled her bleeding hand to her chest. Blood dripped down the front of her white dress, but she stood calmly, waiting to be released.

Rose stared at the blade in her hand in revulsion. She turned to Vaylan and found him grinning like a proud parent. She held the blade out to him, unable to look at Tayeh's blood on the surface, but he shook his head.

"Keep it. You'll need it again soon." And with a final nod to the rest of the crew, he strode back inside the temple.

Rose stood unmoving as the Sentinels ushered her crew back inside. The blade was a weight in her hands, locking her in place.

The sound of Tayeh ripping a strip off her dress woke Rose from her paralysis.

"What are you doing?" asked Rose.

"I'm going to find Wilder," said Tayeh. The words held no bite, only exhaustion. She wrapped the fabric tightly around her hand, and it immediately turned red.

Rose stripped off her jacket and placed it on Tayeh's shoulders. Rose's bare arms tingled, but Tayeh's cotton dress and thin slippers offered no protection from the frigid air pouring down from the mountains. She put her arm under Tayeh's, and they walked away from the temple, further into Perfection Diocese.

Tayeh's lips curled slightly. "I don't need you to come with me. You should probably stay with the rest of the crew."

"The crew is fine for now. Vaylan obviously plans for me to hurt them one by one." Rose stared at the ground, but her mind was imagining a similar scene at the next six temples. The thought of hurting each member of her crew, one after another, caused her stomach to churn.

Tayeh stopped walking abruptly. "Don't be selfish and make this about you, Rose."

Rose stared at her in surprise. "But I hurt you. You're bleeding because of me."

Tayeh held out her hand. "Do you think this wound hurts the most right now? I've got a lot bigger problems internally. This cut is actually a nice distraction."

Rose's eyes widened, trying to imagine what other injuries Tayeh was dealing with in silence. "Vaylan is manipulating all of us to fulfill prophecies only he knows. He's going to force me to hurt the rest of the crew and make all of you suffer. I don't have any choice here."

"No, we don't have a lot of choices here, but we do have the choice about how we will respond to what is handed to us. And when Vaylan orders you to hurt again, the crew will each decide how they will respond. Will they shrink in fear, or will they stand tall? That's the choice they have. So, if you want to feel sorry for yourself around me, fine. I'm used to being the strong one. But when Feather marches up to you with no fear and offers you her hand, you better show some respect and honor her choice by keeping your silly guilt to yourself."

Rose bowed her head in response to the correction. "Yes, Tayeh. I will remember that."

Tayeh nodded once in acknowledgment, then adjusted the jacket over her shoulders with an awkward shrug. Rose watched as her face tightened in pain, then relaxed into a grin.

"What is it?" asked Rose.

Tayeh pointed down the street, past the little shops closed for the night.

Calmly sitting at the corner was a white wolf.

7

Rose and Tayeh followed the wolf down an alley to a small archway cut into the back of a building. Storm Fang walked through easily, but the two of them had to duck to fit inside. The storage room they entered was dark, but they saw white fur heading up a staircase ahead. Rose helped Tayeh limp up the steps until they emerged in a bright hallway.

Wilder was bent down, petting Storm Fang's neck with his head cocked as if listening. Who knows what gossip a wolf tells a man, especially a man the wolf considers her boyfriend?

Instead of the tight leather pants she had seen him in last, he was wearing simple trousers with a thick-woven cream sweater slightly tighter than was necessary. Wilder lifted his eyes to Rose, and a jolt of lightning seared through her. She had just seen him the night before, but the time she had spent in the Heart and then at the temple felt like a lifetime away from him. He stared at her like dry ground soaking up the rain.

Tayeh cleared her throat.

At the sound, Wilder glanced at Tayeh, then jumped to his feet and ran to her side. "Tayeh, you are—"

"Yeah, I'm not doing so great," she forced out. "I could really use a place to rest if you've got one."

"Yes, of course." Wilder let her lean on him as he pushed open the door to a modest bedroom. He lowered her to the bed, then sat down beside her. He touched a gentle hand to her shoulder, then to her stomach, and drew in a sharp breath.

"How are you still walking?" he asked.

"I'm stubborn." She sank her head into the soft pillow and closed her eyes. "I wish Vaylan had started with one of the other crystals. Both of us losing the ability to heal is a real shame. The apothecaries don't have enough remedies to patch me up this time."

Wilder lifted his head and looked at Rose in surprise. She saw tears in his eyes as he turned back to Tayeh and gently lifted her bandaged hand.

A tear dropped onto her finger.

Tayeh's eyes shot open, and her other hand reached tentatively to her stomach. "You didn't lose your Gift?" She looked up at him with wonder. "I should have known you wouldn't follow the rules, you magnificent scoundrel."

He grinned as he unwrapped the bandage from her perfectly healed hand. "Sorry I didn't heal you immediately. Seeing your injuries after a brawl is so common that it was strange to summon up a tear."

She laughed with her whole body, and Rose sighed in relief to see that Tayeh didn't flinch from the movement.

Tayeh sank back into the pillow again and closed her eyes. "I feel much better, but I haven't slept for two days. If you don't mind, I think I'll rest now." She opened one eye to peer at Wilder. "As long as this location is secure?"

He smiled and took hold of her hand again. She closed

both eyes, then nodded. "That is acceptable." She kicked off her slippers and rolled onto her side. Wilder covered her with a blanket, shuttered the lamp, then led Rose into a cozy living room across the hall.

Rose sank down onto the well-worn couch with a sigh. "What did she say was acceptable?" Her eyes snagged on the lantern illuminating the room with a flickering light, but she focused on Wilder as he sat down beside her.

"I used Knowledge to show her what I had done to make this apartment safe. I used my Gift to seal the entrance Storm Fang led you through, and I showed her where the wolves were stationed to keep guard. I knew she wouldn't sleep until she agreed we didn't need her protection."

Rose looked down at her hands. "Wilder, the cut on her hand ... I did that. There is a prophecy that says I must cause the Chosen to suffer, so he forced me to hurt her before he would let her go. She's my crew, and I hurt her."

Wilder took her hand, and she looked up to find him barely holding back a smile. "Rose, considering the rest of her injuries, she probably didn't even notice the scratch you gave her."

She pulled her hand away and glared at him. "I'm serious, Wilder. I hurt her, even though I didn't know you could heal her."

Wilder's voice was grim. "Tayeh was bleeding internally and probably wouldn't have survived the night. I'm glad you got her out of there. No matter what you had to do."

She leaned back into the cushions with a sigh. "I don't know if I can do this six more times."

He took hold of her hand again. "You will."

Her voice dropped to a whisper. "I had to beg him for mercy, on my knees, as if I was one of his Adopted. Another one of his prophecies fulfilled."

"I heard," he said quietly.

She looked up at him hesitantly, unsure how he might react to her begging Vaylan for anything.

His dark eyes looked haunted. "When the crystal went out, I knew where to find you. By the time I made it to Perfection, Vaylan had already cleared the temple. I found groups of Priests wandering through the Diocese, looking for a safe place to go. I healed those I could and found places for them to stay. They told me how you begged for their lives, how Vaylan only relented because of you. When they saw you in white, they initially believed you a traitor, but by the end, they believed the Goddess sent you to save them."

Tears slid down her cheeks. "But I couldn't save them. Vaylan hurt children, and I couldn't save them."

He wiped away her tears with a soft hand. "I healed every child I found. It will take time for them to recover emotionally, but thankfully, their burns healed in a way that yours hasn't."

"But they have no home. The temple belongs to Vaylan now, and he intends to occupy them all."

"He can have the temples until all the crystals go out, but once the City is reborn, we will take them all back." His voice was fierce and stirred something in her chest.

"You believe that?" she asked.

"Yes." His eyes were intense and held no doubt. "I don't believe in Vaylan's prophecies, but I do believe this City and its people are on a path to a new era. It will get much darker before the end, but I believe the City will be born anew."

She pulled in a deep breath, savoring the hope Wilder radiated. He made her feel strong—that with him by her side, they could defeat anyone who stood in their way.

"We have to be proactive," he said thoughtfully. "Even if we know how it will end, we are always one step behind

Vaylan. We need to find out what the prophecies say. Then we can guess at his plans."

Her eyes widened as she remembered something important. "He has Walter."

Wilder drew back abruptly, and she gave him a moment to consider the implications.

"Vaylan doesn't know what he can do," she said. "At least, he doesn't appear to. I think Walter is just one of the many people Vaylan has tricked into being his Adopted. I have to get him out of there before Vaylan figures it out."

"You can't do anything that will draw attention to Walter. Vaylan might not know, but if you act suspicious, he will assume Walter is important to you. And that automatically puts Walter at risk."

Rose frowned. "So, I should just leave him wandering around the Heart? He's like a trap prepared to spring."

Wilder nodded. "Yes, and it is one small piece of information we have that Vaylan doesn't."

Rose bit her lip as she considered. "True, and he also doesn't know you can still heal, even though Tayeh can't."

"He won't be happy to hear that. It doesn't fit into his prophecies." His face was solemn. "He also doesn't know about your Spark. That will be equally surprising to him."

A vicious smile curled her lips. "We must keep my Spark a secret. It's clearly not in Vaylan's plans, so we have to use it to our advantage."

Rose considered the perfect time to tell him. The knowledge would certainly wreck his beliefs. She would hold on to her secret until she could stab him in the heart with it.

8

____

Once they made all the plans they could, Wilder carefully lifted the flickering lantern and sat on the ground. He patted the floor beside him, as if summoning her.

"Show me what can you do." His face was hopeful, and he leaned forward in anticipation.

"Um, this is the first flame I've seen since I found out, so I'm not exactly sure what to do." She felt strangely embarrassed with him watching her. Even as a child, she hadn't liked to practice using her Gift in front of others until she was good at it. The thought of disappointment on his face caused her stomach to clench.

She still sat on the couch, but he reached for her hand. "There's nothing to be embarrassed about. You've seen me practice using my Gifts. I'm still learning."

She twisted her lips wryly. "You summoned a hurricane the first day you got your Gifts. You haven't exactly struggled to catch on."

"I had an excellent teacher." His voice dropped to a low rumble. "Let me teach you."

Her eyes never left his face, but the fire flickered wildly in the lantern.

His lips curled in a smug grin, and she swatted his arm.

"Fine. I'll try." She sat down on the floor across from him and looked at the lantern between them. The flickering had stopped, and the flame burned with a slow and steady light.

Her sense of the fire wasn't the same as her sense of the wind. With the wind, there was never anything to see, but if she was still enough, she could sense the airflows through the room. It was almost as if she could hear them, and she could reach out with a sense beyond her eyes to point a direct line at each current. She had used that sense to coax each breeze into the path she wanted it to go.

The flame was different, though. It blazed in front of her eyes with no subtlety. It moved with no discernible pattern, fluctuating based on the tiniest trickle of airflow. She had no idea how she would coax it to do anything.

She huffed in irritation, and the flame jumped away from her puff of air. Perhaps that was the most she would ever accomplish.

"Are you getting discouraged this quickly?" asked Wilder. He leaned back on his hands to study her with a raised eyebrow. "I assumed that with all your training to be a fighter, you would have gained a little more stamina for handling a challenge."

She narrowed her eyes. "That was different. I had instructors who knew what they were doing. I followed the lessons and improved."

"Oh, really? You always did everything exactly as your instructors told you?" By the knowing look in his eye, he had correctly guessed that she did not.

"I occasionally devised alternative methods that produced better results." She was pleased she could say it with a straight face.

"I bet you did," he said with a grin. "We just need to figure out what produces results."

"The only time I've done anything with my Spark was when we were dancing in Peculiarity. All the candles went crazy when we kissed."

His grin caused her heart to flutter as wildly as the candles above the dance floor had. He nudged the lantern to the side, then leaned toward her.

"Consider this my contribution to your education."

He placed his hand gently on her cheek and pulled her into a kiss. She pressed her hands against the floor as she leaned forward to meet his lips. Even though it wasn't the most comfortable position, she wanted to freeze this moment and never move again. Wilder had reordered her life almost as much as losing her Gift had. She vowed to learn how to use her Spark and to defeat Vaylan so she could spend the rest of her life kissing Wilder whenever she pleased.

The wolves darted into the room, sending her and Wilder sprawling across the floor.

After a glare of irritation at both wolves, Rose realized the fire had jumped from the lantern and tiny flames were scattered across the room. A flame curled around the leg of the end table, slowly moving upward. A couch pillow was burning, the rest not far behind, and the edge of the curtain dripped with a flame that looked like fringe.

Wilder dove for a blanket and smothered the flames on the end table while Rose threw the pillow off the couch and stomped out the flames. But when Wilder moved to extinguish the curtain, he instead studied it with a curious expression.

"What are you doing?" snapped Rose. "Put it out before I accidentally burn the whole place down."

Wilder stretched out his hand and ran gentle fingers through the flames.

Rose lunged forward to stop him, but at his calm expression, she stopped. The flames licked across his fingers, bathing his deep brown skin in a warm glow.

Her eyes widened in awe, then swiftly narrowed in irritation.

"What good is fire if it doesn't burn?" She huffed angrily and grabbed hold of the glowing curtain. She pulled back with a sharp hiss and stared at her hand. Her skin had turned an angry red, and blisters bubbled on her wrist.

Tears of pain sprang to her eyes, quickly followed by tears of shame. "I can't burn anything but myself?"

Wilder took hold of her hand. As a tear fell from his eye, he placed a soft kiss on her wrist. A cool blast of healing emanated from his lips, across her skin, and through her whole body. She hadn't realized how sore she was from the last few days until all her aches were suddenly gone.

"Maybe you shouldn't practice without me," he whispered.

His smile was sweet, but the words sent a ripple of embarrassment down her spine. The feeling of helplessness she experienced while watching Vaylan at the temple sprang back to life in her chest. She thought she had come to grips with those emotions, but she couldn't stop them from flooding back over her. And looking at her perfectly healed hand caused feelings of jealousy, followed immediately by guilt.

She ducked her head and turned to leave. "I should get back to the temple to check on the crew."

Wilder pulled her back to him with a gentle tug on her hand. "Rose, look at me."

Rose reluctantly lifted her face. The love in his dark eyes warmed her but also made her guilt even stronger.

"Your Spark is new, but you will learn to use it." His voice was gentle as he tried to comfort her. "Your Spark is just as valuable as a Gift, maybe even more valuable since it is completely unique. Give yourself time. I'll be with you through it all."

She only nodded in silent agreement, because she couldn't voice the overwhelming feeling strangling her heart once again.

Doubt.

9

Rose paced inside her room in the temple. Her collar was so tight it irritated her mark, but the other shirts in the wardrobe were just as bad. Being inside a temple with a closet filled with white clothing was jarring, so she slammed the door and kept pacing.

After she had left Wilder with Tayeh still asleep last night, she headed back to the temple. An Adopted led her to a room that previously belonged to a Priest and wished her a good night. Rose had tossed and turned, wondering where the previous occupant was now sleeping. The temples had always been buzzing with life, but now it was silent other than the quiet shuffling feet of Adopted and the boot clicks of Sentinels.

Rose opened her door and examined the inner courtyard. The only light was from the crystalline Vaylan had formed along the top of the ceiling. There had never been a need for crystalline lamps in the courtyard before, but since the crystal was now a dull gray, the space looked empty and sad.

As she stepped into the courtyard, two Sentinels fell in at her sides.

"You are going to follow me around in here as well?" she asked them. "Vaylan hasn't lived here long enough to have secrets to hide."

They said nothing, and their masked faces gave nothing away.

She sighed. "Do I have his permission to go find a room to run through some katas? I need to get out some of my nervous energy." She gave them a significant look. "It will be safer for everyone that way."

The Sentinel on her right shrugged, then headed out of the courtyard, expecting Rose to follow.

Rose paused for a moment, considering the image of a Sentinel *shrugging,* then followed them. They led her to one of the temple's large training rooms. Inside, she found over a dozen people already training.

As she stepped inside, they all stopped their movements to look at her. A teenage boy looked at her mark, then gave her a slight bow. After that, the rest bowed, then went back to what they were doing without a word.

She was relieved they had traded their white clothing for simple gray tunics and pants and looked around until she found a shelf with a matching outfit in her size. After she changed, she looked at everyone sparring around the room. Most of the people were Rose's age or younger, but there were a few older men and women scattered throughout.

She considered asking one of them to spar with her, then reconsidered. The Adopted always acted strange around her, bowing and apologizing to her. She assumed Vaylan had given them specific instructions about how to treat her and wondered if he allowed them to spar with her. The Adopted made her feel awkward, but she didn't want to get them in trouble if they accidentally injured her while sparring.

Instead, she found an open space in front of a mirror and began working through her katas. She had started almost every morning of her life with katas, followed by stretching and sparring with Kai and Caed. But since the Uprising, her life had been such chaos that she often just woke up and started her day without even considering it.

As she watched herself in the mirror, she was shocked at how different she looked. When had her posture completely changed? Her shoulders were raised, and her neck hunched over, as if in self-protection. Her hands kept forming into fists, even when the kata didn't call for it, and a scowl seemed permanently frozen between her eyebrows.

She found the image jarring, so she closed her eyes as she worked through the familiar patterns of movement. Without the distraction of watching herself in the mirror, she paid closer attention to what she felt inside.

Muscles in her neck and shoulders tingled, and she realized she had been clenching those muscles for weeks, so she adapted the kata until her shoulders loosened. She sensed a tightness along her spine, as if holding herself rigid would protect her from the storms blowing around her. So, she flowed into an exercise her instructors taught her about how to move with the wind instead of against it.

As she took a mental inventory of her body, she adapted each of her movements to bring life into the neglected parts of her. Eventually, she wasn't doing official katas at all, but something between katas and dance, something created only for her at this exact moment.

She became aware that the noise had faded away and opened her eyes to find everyone staring at her. When they realized she had opened her eyes, they went back to their sparring but kept peeking at her when they thought she wasn't looking. Only one boy was brave enough to approach her.

"What kata was that?" He was tall, but by his boyish face, Rose guessed him to be around fifteen years old. He twisted his dark brown hands nervously before combing them anxiously through his messy black hair.

"It wasn't a kata there at the end, I guess. I was just making it up as I went."

He looked intrigued. "My instructors would never have allowed something like that. They would have assumed I would ruin all my training if I didn't stick to the way they taught me."

Rose's lips quirked in a smile. "I had a few instructors like that. Luckily, I had plenty of dance instructors who outranked them."

His mouth fell open in shock. "Dance?"

She laughed. "Sure!" She demonstrated the steps as she talked. "A little step-ball-change to be fast on your feet. A quick twirl to spin away from your opponent. Then a pivot and a lunge to evade and attack." She straightened from her demonstration. "At the end of the day, it's all dance."

The boy stared at her in fascination. His words came out in a breathless rush. "Will you teach me that?"

She took a step back, unsure what to do. "Um ... I don't know—"

"Please," he begged. "I would love to learn. I ... never had the chance."

She tried to imagine the life of a young boy growing up in the Underneath. If he had a natural talent, the headmaster at the school Wilder attended would have snatched him up in an instant, but beyond that stroke of luck, it was unlikely he would ever have the freedom to dance for enjoyment. But she had a lot on her plate right now, and teaching dance lessons was not high on the list.

"I'm really not the best one to teach you. There are a lot of teachers more skilled than me at—" She cut off abruptly.

The skilled dance teachers were all at Temple Discipline. She didn't want to think about what Vaylan might do to them when he arrived.

"Please," he said. "I promise I'll be a good student. Even if you just teach me a few of those moves, I'll be happy."

She sighed. "Okay. If I have time."

His face lit up, and he bit his lips to hide his smile.

"But only if I have time. I can't promise I will have much time at all. I don't know when we are leaving for the next temple."

His face turned serious. "Yes, I understand. You are the Marked. You have a job to do."

"Yes, I guess I do." She squirmed awkwardly. Honestly, she would much rather teach a random boy to dance than to do what needed to be done.

"I really appreciate it," he said. "I'm going to talk to the others and see who else will join us!"

"What? No—" She tried to stop him, but he ran off to recruit more dancers.

She sighed, then changed back into her white clothes. They felt even tighter than before, but she didn't think she could get away with wearing the gray training clothes the rest of the day.

She walked back to where her two Sentinels stood by the door. "Nice of you to wait for me to finish," she said dryly. "Or are you waiting for your own invitation to dance class?"

The Sentinel to her right laughed.

Rose's eyes widened. She had never seen one of the High Priests' Sentinels express a single emotion, but now she had heard a Sentinel laugh on two separate occasions. Then the Sentinel did something even more shocking.

She removed her mask.

The Sentinel shook out golden blond curls as she held

her mask under one arm. A few curls stuck to her cheek, and she wiped off the sweat with a black gloved hand. Rose had never considered the faces of anyone behind a Sentinel's mask, but if she had, this girl's round face with pink cheeks would not have been it. She couldn't be over seventeen years old, yet wearing the Sentinel's armor, she appeared as intimidating as the rest.

"Do you realize what you did?" asked the Sentinel.

"Uh ..." Rose couldn't formulate words, much less coherent thoughts.

The girl snorted. "Yeah, I didn't think so." She raised an eyebrow at the other Sentinel, who stayed masked, but Rose could still detect a muffled chuckle.

"That boy's mouth never stops running. Before the end of the day, I guarantee you'll have half this room signed up for your class."

"I ... I don't know if I will have time ..." Rose mumbled.

"He will harass you until you make the time, so you better figure it out," she said sharply.

Rose's mouth dropped open. It was one thing to have a Sentinel be demanding, but to have a young girl boss her around hurt her pride, so she took on the haughty voice she used as a Priest.

"I have important things to do, and he can find other ways to amuse himself. There are plenty of ways for the Adopted to serve."

The girl turned to the still-masked Sentinel, and they both burst into howls of laughter. The masked Sentinel leaned against the wall to catch his ... or her ... breath.

"You really have no clue what you did," said the curly-haired girl as she wiped tears from her eyes.

Some of the younger teens had stopped sparring to watch the Sentinels laugh, but the few older people in the room just ignored them.

The girl gestured at them all. "Who do you think these people are?"

Rose clung to her dignity and answered quietly. "The Adopted?" It was difficult to keep the question out of her voice.

The girl's mouth curled up in a smirk. "Nope. We're all Sentinels. And it appears you've offered to teach us to dance."

ORDER

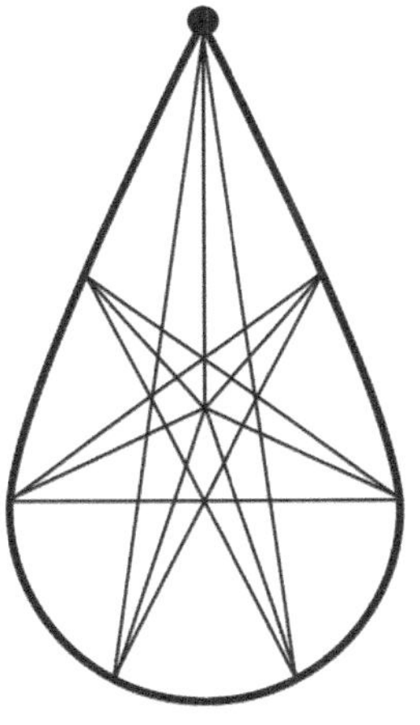

CHAOS

10

―――――

When Vaylan heard Rose had unwittingly invited all the Sentinels to a dance lesson, he burst into laughter. Rose was not amused at being the butt of the joke.

"I think it's a wonderful idea, Rose!" Vaylan said cheerfully. "The Sentinels will benefit from your excellent training; plus, it will give you something to occupy your time so you aren't moping about like a lovesick puppy."

A lovesick—? She opened her mouth to protest, but he ignored her.

"I will make sure you have plenty of room available wherever we go so you can instruct as many Sentinels that are interested."

After Vaylan was confident Temple Perfection was fully under his control, he left a contingent of Adopted and Sentinels to transform it into another Haven. The rest of them, including Rose and the crew, headed back to the Heart.

Rose walked in silence on the long walk back down the looping bridge, through the Grotto, and into the tunnel leading to the Heart, stealing glances at the Sentinels surrounding the crew. Was one of them the girl with the golden curls? Was one of them the young boy who'd asked to dance? Now that she had seen their faces, she found the Sentinels disturbing in a whole new way.

When they arrived at the Heart, Vaylan led Rose and the crew down a pathway she hadn't been down before. He stopped in front of a black tent.

"What is this?" she asked.

"A gift," he said with a smile. A Sentinel held back the edge of the tent and ushered them inside.

The tent was dark. Most of the tents were lit by the Heart's constant glow of crystalline shining through the fabric, but since these walls were black, it was dark inside. She could just make out the shape of six bedrolls on the ground.

"This is where the Chosen will stay until their individual trips Upstairs. Since you've been so obedient, Rose, I will let them out of their crystalline cage."

Her mind raged at the word *obedient*, but she bit her tongue to keep from screaming. Instead, through clenched teeth, she calmly said, "You are so merciful."

He raised an eyebrow. "Yes, I am. But I can easily put them back in the cage if there is any unacceptable behavior. On anyone's part."

She knew he meant her. He was holding their comfort and safety as leverage. But she had begged before, so she could play along now if necessary.

"Thank you, Vaylan. I'm sure everyone will be very well-behaved."

He nodded as if she had honored him, then left them alone in the tent. Rose peeked outside to see Sentinels calmly stationed around the perimeter, but none moved to come inside.

The crew sagged in relief. She removed Kai's ropes first,

and he hugged her fiercely before moving to help untie the others. After they were all free, they gathered the bedrolls and sat in a tight circle in the middle of the tent.

Rev was the first to whisper, "Is Tayeh okay? She was severely hurt."

"She's fine." Rose worried about someone listening outside the tent, but the crew was so upset that she had to ease their minds with the truth. They gathered close, and she whispered as quietly as she could, "Wilder can still heal."

Feather covered her mouth as she gasped, and Kieran rocked back on his heels. Fitz, Rev, and Kai all gave the sign of the Goddess.

"Interesting ..." said Quinn. "When the crystal went dark, I wasn't sure if all our Gifts would disappear at once or if it would just be the one. I didn't expect Wilder's Gifts to react differently."

Rose twisted her lips wryly. "As he is fond of telling us, he is exceptional."

Quinn nodded as if that were a given. "It's also interesting that even without Tayeh, the six of us can still use our Gifts."

"You can?" said Rose out loud. She caught herself, then whispered, "You can use your Gifts right now?"

Rev shook her head. "They've still been giving us tea, except ..."

"Except me," said Kieran.

"Why?" she asked. "That seems sloppy."

Kieran's jaw tensed. "They don't think my Gift is dangerous enough to waste the tea on me."

Rose blinked at the bitterness in his voice. Then she chuckled quietly. "That's their mistake, then. I've seen you turn your Gift to an advantage before, and you're clever enough to do it again."

Kieran's face softened, and he gave her a slight bow of respect.

Quinn explained more, excited about the news. "Their sloppiness helped us make the discovery about our Gifts. Even after Tayeh walked away, Kieran could still use his Gift. We didn't expect that."

Fitz shrugged. "I'm not sure how it helps us much right now, though. They keep the rest of us so drugged that I can only feel a hint of my Gift before they pour more tea down my throat."

Feather patted him on the arm. "It's okay. At least Rose got us out of our cage."

Rev studied Rose's face. "How are you? Are you okay?"

Rose snorted. "You're the ones being held prisoner, not me."

Rev's voice was gentle. "We weren't alone, and we worried you were."

Her throat threatened to close, but she said, "I haven't been completely alone. I've seen Wilder."

"Wilder does like to be seen." Rev gave a sly grin that made her laugh.

Rose sighed. "I wish my plan was to get you all to stop drinking the tea and help you escape, but unfortunately, the Goddess had other plans."

Quinn nodded knowingly. "She asked you to darken the crystals to save the Companion."

Her mouth opened in shock. "How do you know that?"

Quinn shrugged as if it was obvious. "You said it was necessary for the City to survive. I assumed that meant she was hoping the City could be reborn like last time."

"Well, yes ... I just didn't think it was obvious."

Fitz laughed. "It wasn't obvious to anyone but Quinn! And honestly, I'm still not sure what he's talking about. How did you shut down the crystal at all?"

Rose looked at Quinn with a raised eyebrow.

He shrugged. "I haven't figured that one out yet."

She dropped her voice even lower. "Because I have a Spark."

The crew's eyes lit up in delight, but she had to squash their expectations quickly. "The Goddess said I can control fire, but so far, the only thing I can burn is myself. I don't know how much help it will be."

"If it will save the Companion, I think it's pretty helpful," said Rev.

"And now it makes sense," said Fitz with a sigh.

"What does?" asked Rose.

"Why she didn't return your Gift," he said. "It's the answer to the question all of us were too scared to ask."

"Yes, she admitted it." Rose avoided their eyes. "When she told me, I may have reacted poorly."

Rev laughed. "I can just imagine you trying to murder a goddess."

When Rose ducked her head, Rev's laughter ended abruptly. "Rose ... tell me you didn't—"

Rose stood and headed for the tent flap. "I should probably go."

Kieran smirked. "Is it time for dance class so soon?"

"Funny," she said drily. "This isn't exactly how I planned to spend my time."

Kai's lips twisted to disguise a grin. "I hope they're well-behaved students like you were."

She rolled her eyes as he started laughing. Before she stepped out, she asked to speak to Quinn for a moment. The crack leading out of the tent lit up his face with crystalline, and his eyes sparkled as she handed him the note from Walter.

"What does this say?" she asked.

He traced a finger along the strange lines, and his lips curled into a warm smile. "It says, 'Don't worry.'" He handed the note back to her. "That's comforting, isn't it?"

She frowned. "Not nearly enough."

11

Even though the crew assumed Rose was headed to dance class, she instead went to seek prophecies. Two Sentinels outside the crew's tent followed her, while the rest stayed in their positions. She wondered if these two Sentinels were the same as before but couldn't think of a good way to ask.

They didn't stop her as she entered the white tent near the center of the Heart. Rose surveyed the room quickly, looking for Walter, but wasn't surprised he was gone. The woman with the wire-frame glasses approached her with a bow.

"Welcome, Marked One. The Lord Founder said you might come by."

Rose's lip curled in irritation, but she tried to stay polite. "Yes, he always seems to know what I will do. That's the benefit of knowing all those prophecies, I suppose."

The woman smiled warmly, unaware of Rose's sarcasm. "Wise of you to say so, Marked One."

Rose sighed. It was difficult to be rude to someone who was truly kind. "Please call me Rose. What's your name?"

"You can call me Sister Bria, but you will have to forgive

me for not calling you other than the Marked. I'm afraid I have spent too much time reading prophecies to refer to you in such a casual manner." She bowed her head to hide the embarrassment on her face.

Rose frowned. "Yes, that is the reason I am here. It seems like everyone knows these prophecies except me. May I read them?"

Sister Bria's face lit up. "Of course! I have a book where many of Brother Owyn's prophecies have been compiled, and you are welcome to read it. It must stay in this tent so the Adopted can make copies, but you can sit here and read as much as you like."

She cleared off a desk for Rose to sit and reverently laid a thick, leather-bound book in front of her. "Would you like me to explain the different passages to you?"

Rose touched a hand to the book that held all of Vaylan's strange beliefs about her. "No, thank you. I'd like some time to study alone."

Sister Bria nodded in understanding, bowed, then left Rose alone to read.

Rose had only read a few pages when she wondered if she should have accepted Sister Bria's assistance. She had heard the prophecies quoted in neat little sentences, so she thought Brother Owyn had simply created lists of prophecies that Vaylan picked from. The reality was much more complicated.

The book was not just a single book, but a collection of writings. She didn't know the time period that his thoughts had been written, but it wasn't all in one sitting. She found a poem, followed by a short story, followed by a list of non-connected ideas. The handwriting on each page was different, and Rose wondered who had listened to Brother Owyn's words and then written them down. Did they write it down immediately as he spoke, or did they try to remember what he said days later?

She thought she would find the prophecies about her listed out on a single page but found it hard to find anything about the Marked at all. She couldn't find the prophecy about her delivering the Chosen into Vaylan's hands or the prophecy he had shown her the other day saying she would bow before him and beg for mercy. Was there more than one book? Or did Vaylan keep some prophecies to himself?

She was about to give up and assume this was just a collection of Brother Owyn's ramblings when she read a sentence that froze her to the spot.

The Marked will watch me die and will weep.

Brother Owyn's dying words to her were "I saw you weep." It didn't seem strange at the time since she really had been weeping. He'd died in her arms, and she could do nothing to stop it. But now, in the light of this prophecy, his words took on new meaning.

He knew she would watch him die and would weep.

She shivered as she thought about him having a vision like that and writing it down. He saw his own death and believed in it enough that he smiled when it came true.

She turned the page quickly to escape the words. The next page was a poem, but her thoughts wandered as she skimmed lines that didn't make sense. Vaylan had convinced himself that Rose delivered the Chosen to him when he was the one who manipulated the situation to capture them. Maybe she was like him, making connections that weren't really there.

The last two stanzas of the poem lingered in her mind and wouldn't shake free.

Her words save farmers.
Her heart sets them free.

The poem didn't mention the Marked, but Rose had the sense this poem was about her. The words rattled around in her mind, and she wondered if she was going crazy. She shouldn't have opened the book at all, because now she would see connections in everything that happened.

She snapped the book closed and stood quickly. Sister Bria appeared at her side with a bow.

"Are you finished for the day? You can come back at any time." Her smile was warm, but it didn't soothe Rose.

"Do you believe everything in here?" Rose asked suddenly. "Does it all come true?"

Sister Bria sighed as if Rose had asked a very complicated question. "I believe everything in there has happened or will happen. However, I don't always believe the first interpretation I hear." She gave a wry smile.

Rose tilted her head as she considered. "So, it doesn't always mean what we think it means?"

"No, it doesn't," she said softly. "But that's why I've committed the rest of my life to studying it. I can't wait to see how each prophecy actually unfolds."

"Thank you for your time, Sister Bria." Rose gave a little bow and turned to leave but suddenly spun back around. "I wanted to check in on the man that was in here yesterday to make sure he's doing okay. Do you know where he's serving now?"

Sister Bria patted Rose's hand. "You're sweet for checking on him. I heard he was going to assist with the laundry. You might find him there."

Rose bowed again and asked her Sentinels where she might find the laundry. They led her to an area on the opposite side of the Heart where men and women sat scrubbing clothes in large vats of soapy water. Rose examined all their faces but didn't see Walter among them.

Rose was in the middle of a conversation with a woman

about how she kept the Adopted's white clothing clean when Vaylan entered the room. The people washing clothes immediately bowed their heads, but Rose only gave him a forced smile.

"You are such an explorer, Rose. I always find you in unusual places," he said.

"This isn't unusual for me. I'm always friends with the people who wash my clothes. I take fashion very seriously." She said the words by rote but realized they hadn't been true for some time. Since she had stopped wearing the black clothing of the Priests, she had struggled to find a new fashion. The costume designer, Hazel, at the burlesque show had made that realization shockingly clear when she'd psychoanalyzed Rose based on her clothing choices.

"How charming," he said. "I'm too busy to be overly concerned with fashion, but it's adorable that you take the time."

She laughed. "You obviously concern yourself with fashion, Vaylan. Your dark blue robes make quite a statement, seeing as they are so close to black as to be heretical."

Vaylan smiled, but it didn't reach his eyes. "It's time you cease your exploring for the day and get some rest. Tomorrow, you will darken the next crystal, so you need your strength."

She considered telling him that since she had no idea how she darkened the first crystal, she wasn't sure it required much strength, but instead, she asked, "Which temple are we headed to?"

He smiled enigmatically. "I'll keep that information to myself until tomorrow. I think it's best if no one knows where to expect us. Keeps it exciting, you know?"

Burning Priests and children with crystalline wasn't her idea of excitement, but she bared her teeth in a forced smile, then walked back to her tent, two Sentinels trailing behind.

12

———

Rose wasn't surprised when the Sentinels summoned her to the throne room, but she was surprised to only see Feather. She expected Vaylan to take the whole crew on each of his expeditions, but Feather stood alone in the center of the room, wearing a set of black robes and looking very small.

Her face lit up when Rose approached. "I'm so glad to see you." Feather reached for Rose with bound hands. "I can be brave if I have you with me."

Rose swallowed down her fear about what would happen at the next temple and smiled. She had shown some of her insecurities to Tayeh, but Feather wasn't strong like Tayeh. Rose would have to be the strong one today.

She patted Feather's hand. "Vaylan is a terrible person, but he did let Tayeh go. You will be free once the sun goes down tonight."

"I believe that, but I'm just worried about what he is going to do to the Priests in Temple Order. Do you think it will be as bad as last time?"

Rose watched Vaylan start the procession of Sentinels

and Adopted into the tunnel leading to Grotto Chaos. "I will do whatever it takes to make sure that doesn't happen again."

Feather smiled and held Rose's hand as the Sentinels prodded them forward.

~

When they arrived at the bright crystal, Vaylan held out his arms as if summoning Rose forward. She wanted to yell that she was darkening the crystals for the Goddess, not for him. Instead, she put on the most obedient smile she could manage and strode forward to join him next to the crystal.

"Do it exactly like last time, then we can be on our way," he said cheerfully.

Her fingers twitched with the fantasy of slapping the smug look off his face. She covered the movement by placing both palms flat against the crystal. She still wasn't sure what she did the last time to shut off the crystal, only that she had been angry at Vaylan.

Anger at him was easy to summon, so she stirred the wildfire in her chest, then plunged it into the crystal.

Rose blinked in the bright interior of the Goddess's sanctuary. The Goddess sat with a regal posture at the long table, sipping tea. Rose would have said she looked peaceful if it weren't for the dark circles under her sad eyes.

"Thank you, Rose. You must keep going, all the way to the last crystal."

"I will."

"Even if I'm unable to appear like this again, you must continue." The Goddess turned back to her tea.

Before the Goddess could dismiss her, Rose grabbed her arm across the table. "Wait! Why won't you be able to appear?"

The Goddess sighed tiredly and fidgeted with the teacup in her hand. "I'm exhausted, Rose. I don't know how much longer I can watch."

"So you're abandoning us again?" asked Rose. "You will leave your City for Vaylan to destroy in a way the High Priests never could!"

"I'm not abandoning the City." Her voice had lost the anger it had held before. "I'm cursed to never die, no matter what happens to the City. But maybe I can just fall asleep for a while." Tears pooled in her eyes, and she closed them as if the darkness would offer relief.

Rose grabbed her arm again and shook her awake. "That *is* abandoning us! We need you to fight for us! Are you our goddess or not?"

She sighed. "I told you, I've never been a very good goddess."

Rose smacked a hand down on the table. "Well, too bad! If you wanted to give up the position of Goddess, why did you let the only person with a Spark like yours leave the City?"

A hint of life stirred in the Goddess's green eyes, and her lips curled in a faint, rueful smile. "Would you prefer if Ylena and Caed were here ruling the City instead?"

Rose ground her teeth together, unable to give an honest answer.

The Goddess shook her head. "It would never have worked with them as rulers. Caed is a child of the City above, and Ylena was born outside the walls. They could never bring the balance you and Wilder can."

Rose's anger dissipated into confusion. "What does that mean? What do you expect us to do?"

"You are my children from above and below ..." The Goddess's eyes unfocused, and she stared off into the distance. "You are doing what I asked," she whispered. "I hear it."

Rose could hear nothing in the completely silent cave. She studied the Goddess's face, wondering if this was a sign she was losing track of reality.

The Goddess turned to her with a beatific smile. "They are singing a song from the Pageant. I hear it."

Rose's eyes widened. Was it Wilder? He said the homeless Priests would assist with a Pageant, but if he was already rehearsing, he worked a lot faster than she expected.

The Goddess settled back into her chair and took a deep breath, as if drawing in strength. "It's not enough yet, of course. But it's a good start." She smiled warmly. "Wilder really is such a remarkable young man."

Rose rolled her eyes. "Yes, we all know he is your Chosen."

The Goddess rapped a hard fingernail on the smooth table, and her previously sleepy eyes turned sharp. "Don't be jealous, Rose. It's a nasty habit and will get you in trouble."

Rose squirmed under the Goddess's glare, but the feelings of jealousy lingered. She averted her eyes. "I should go."

The Goddess nodded regally. "Yes, you should. Finish darkening the crystals as quickly as you can, and assist Wilder in staging a large Pageant, preferably with the entire City in attendance. Then I can return my Gifts, and you can defeat Vaylan properly."

Rose clenched her fists. "Is that all? Is there any other job you want me to handle for you in my free time?"

She didn't see the Goddess move, but they were suddenly standing face to face.

The Goddess twitched her lips, as if holding back words. Then she snorted a laugh. "You are very lucky I like you,

Rose, because you are entirely too mouthy." She raised a fingertip to Rose's forehead. "Time to go, dear."

Rose blinked her eyes and found herself back in the dark Grotto.

13

———

Rose held her breath, waiting for the light to return. She heard Vaylan stir by her side, then the trickle of crystalline flowed again through the dark Grotto. It wasn't as bright as before, but she could once again breathe.

Vaylan patted her on the back as if she were a faithful dog, then swept to the front of the procession to lead them up the winding bridge. Rose calmed her angry heart, then ran to catch up to Feather and her Sentinels.

Feather's thoughtful voice was quiet enough that only Rose could hear. "He allows you to get so close. It's such a shame you can't kill him."

Rose studied Feather's long black ponytail and her sweet, pouty lips. "It's surprising to hear such bloodthirsty words come out of your mouth."

Feather shrugged. "It would solve a lot of problems if he was gone, but unfortunately, it would cause so many more."

Rose narrowed her eyes at Vaylan strutting proudly at the front of his adoring followers. "But maybe it would be worth it?"

Feather frowned. "Remember Brother Owyn?"

Rose drew in a sharp breath. "Of course I remember. I watched him die." And wept, like the prophecy foretold.

"Yes, and because you were there, the people believed Priests were responsible for his death. Imagine the riots that would take place if they saw you kill Vaylan. None of the Priests in the City would survive."

Rose touched the white leather of her jacket. "They might think it was one of his own that did it. They wouldn't know that I'm a Priest ... used to be a Priest."

Feather gave her a serious look. "They would know, Rose. They definitely would know."

As they approached Temple Order, they both fell silent. The crystal was gray, a twin to the crystal they could see in the distance at Temple Perfection. The cold wind blew stronger than before, and Rose shivered despite her leather jacket.

Priests lined the perimeter of the top step of the temple with watchful eyes. A crowd had gathered around, and they whispered, waiting to see what would happen. Surely the word from Temple Perfection had spread, and though there was a lot of ill will toward Priests, Rose was glad the crowd wasn't chanting for him to do it again.

Vaylan stepped onto the bottom step of the temple, always one to put on a show.

"My Marked One has stolen the light of this crystal away from the Goddess, and it now belongs to me. She has forsaken you, but I have pity and will save you. Leave this temple now, shed your black raiment, and live as equals with the rest of the City. If you swear to turn from the Goddess, you are free to go."

The crowd mumbled in a mixture of fear and sick fascination. The air felt heavy with the weight of his offer, but none of the Priests moved.

"As you will," said Vaylan matter-of-factly. He raised his hands above his head, and Rose lunged forward.

"Please, Vaylan, wait!" She had ducked out of the grasp of her Sentinels and landed directly at his feet. "Please, don't hurt them!"

Vaylan dropped his hands with a slight huff. "Rose, you can't just beg for mercy at each temple. These Priests are defying me, and I must make an example, or it will continue at every temple going forward. Isn't it better that I should only hurt a few Priests here instead of all of them?" He spoke as if his decision was the merciful one, and Rose shivered at his delusion.

"But maybe I can get them to change their mind? I will explain to them why they should leave peacefully. I used to be a Priest, so they will listen to me. Wouldn't it be better if they obeyed you because they chose to, not out of fear?"

Rose kept her head bowed at his feet but could feel him weighing her words.

"I will grant your request," he said formally.

Rose sat up with surprise.

"You have five minutes to convince them that following me is the right path. After that, the crystalline will flow where I choose, even if you are still inside. Understood?"

Rose nodded and came slowly to her feet. "Thank you for your mercy."

She started up the steps, and two Sentinels followed along at her heels. She halted. "I need to go in alone. They won't trust me if I bring Sentinels."

Vaylan opened his mouth, but Rose said quickly. "Am I a prisoner? There's nowhere for me to run."

He squeezed his lips together, then summoned the Sentinels to his side.

She bowed and went up the steps.

The Priests lining the perimeter let her pass and

followed her as she walked into a large common room where the rest of the Priests had all gathered. There were fewer of them than she expected, but they stood tall as she approached.

Even though most Priests hated the way the High Priests ruled the City, they all carried themselves with pride in being a Priest. Something about being given a Gift gave them a presence that set them apart. These Priests still stood with pride, but without Gifts, they seemed more vulnerable than before. Some Priests were believers from the Underneath like Fitz. They had never held a Gift but had sworn to the Goddess anyway.

She looked at the faces of dozens of proud Priests and their families. How would she convince them to give up everything they believed in?

In less than five minutes.

"Um ... Hi, my name is—"

"We know who you are, Priest Rose." The Priest's russet hair was untouched by gray, but Rose guessed he was a couple decades her senior. He held himself with a casual grace of someone familiar with hard work, and his clear blue eyes pierced hers. "Although we are unsure if you still call yourself Priest."

She smoothed her hands across her white clothing self-consciously. "I am perhaps not the best example of a Priest right now, but I still believe in the Goddess."

He crossed his arms and gave her an appraising look. "Have you come to deliver a message?"

She wanted to explain everything to them—about her Spark, speaking to the Goddess in her sanctuary, the Companion as the City dying and needing to be reborn—but it was too much, and she didn't even fully understand it herself. A lie might be more expedient, but to her fellow Priests, she owed the truth.

She forced her hands to stop fidgeting with her clothes and cleared her throat. "I believe in the Goddess now more than ever, though I understand her even less. She has given me a task which, on the outside, looks like I have betrayed her and all of you. If I had less faith, I would find somewhere in the City to hide and never show my face again. But instead, I'm walking down this path she set me on, praying that in the end, it will be worth it."

Their faces looked as hard as before, so she took a breath and plunged on. "I know I appear to be one of Vaylan's followers. Even he believes it's true. But I'm asking you to consider what it would be like to be me. Imagine you are trying to follow the Goddess the best way you know how. You want to use what she has given you to make the City a better place. But unfortunately, you follow someone with evil intentions. Someone who will kill you or those you love if you don't obey."

At this, a couple Priests shifted uncomfortably. She felt slightly guilty at stirring their emotions from their long service under the High Priests, but she had little time to be delicate.

"Imagine following a leader you know has murdered innocent people. Imagine the guilt you would feel wearing their color. Would it be better if you spoke out, even if it cost you and your family your lives? Or should you play along, doing good where you can? What would you feel as you stood before people who only saw the outside, not your heart? Guilty. Ashamed. Embarrassed."

She could plainly read those emotions written on each Priests' face but didn't relent.

"You would feel those things and more, but above them all, one thing would remain. Your devotion to the Goddess. Vaylan can't take that from me, as the High Priests never took it from you. And because of that truth, I beg you to listen to the message I bring."

The good thing about Priests is that they weren't ashamed when tears came to their eyes. The Priest who had spoken before wiped tears out his blue eyes and spoke. "What is your message?"

She took a deep breath. "Please leave this temple. Surrender it peacefully to Vaylan."

Despite the tears in their eyes, the Priests' faces hardened. Enough pride remained that they would not leave so easily.

"The Goddess is not in this temple or any of the others. You can serve her out there even more than you can in here."

"And how will we serve her out there?" asked the Priest. "We have no more Gifts to give. What else can we do for this City?"

Even though there were no Sentinels or Adopted in the room, she still dropped her voice to a whisper. "You can put on a Pageant."

The male Priest blinked at her in confusion. A couple Priests burst out in laughter before covering their mouths after receiving her glare.

"Yes, a Pageant," she said stiffly. "It's what the Goddess requires to return her Gifts, and it's the only way this City will survive."

"So, we should walk out of here peacefully, then get together and put on a secret Pageant?" he asked.

"You won't be alone. There are others already gathered. Once you leave here, find Wilder. Do you know who he is?"

A young blond girl grinned. "Oh, we know Wilder." A few girls giggled.

Rose gave her a flat look. "Of course you do. Find him

and the other Priests and put on a Pageant. Will do you that?"

The Priest ran fingers idly through his reddish-brown hair as he looked around the room, then he sighed. "Yes, we will do it. We have experience with the Pageant."

The woman at his side smacked him in the arm and whispered, "Reid!" Her face was hidden by her profusion of dark curls, but Rose gathered the man was getting silently reprimanded.

His lips quirked into a smile. "Priest Adhira and I will assist backstage, but we will make sure the show goes as planned."

14

F eather and Rose sat on the bottom step of the temple, waiting for the sun to set. Rose was trying not to think about the pearl dagger hidden under her jacket or imagine the sight of Feather's blood pouring down her white dress but was unsuccessful.

Feather didn't seem to be preoccupied with the thought. "I wonder how quickly Wilder found them. If he saw the crystal go dark, he would have headed this way, but I wonder if the Priests had to wander long."

"Wilder is resourceful. Plus, he has the wolves. I'm sure he gathered the Priests quickly." Rose wondered if Feather would cry out or be as stoic as Tayeh ...

Feather sighed. "I'm so glad you convinced them all to leave peacefully. We need farmers now more than ever."

"Farmers?" The strange word drew her out of her imaginings.

"Yes," said Feather. "The City is running out of food, and the Priests from Temple Order ... well, they're farmers, you know."

The word shook loose the prophecy she had read the

day before. She quoted, *"Her words save farmers ... Her heart sets them free."*

"That's pretty!" said Feather. "What is that?"

Rose's voice was a rough whisper. "It's a prophecy from Brother Owyn."

Feather's eyes glowed. "It's about you!"

As she spoke, the sun dipped below the horizon, and Vaylan walked out of the temple. Feather stood up with a straight back and waited for him to descend the steps.

"The sun has set," he said calmly. "I hope you'll make this as easy as you did with removing the Priests?"

"Yes, Vaylan. I always enjoy making your life easier." She turned around before he could read just how much sarcasm was on her face.

Feather stood with her hand outstretched. Rose wanted to throw a fit or to beg Vaylan to reconsider, but Tayeh's words came back to her. *Don't be selfish and make this about you.*

Rose took a deep breath, then held Feather's hand in hers. She whispered softly so Vaylan couldn't hear. "You are a brave woman, Feather, and I'm proud to have you as my crew."

Feather squared her shoulders, and Rose sliced the blade across her palm. She made a soft squeak of pain but bit her lip and didn't make another sound. Tears leaked from her eyes, but Rose had seen them form during her words of encouragement, and not just because of the pain.

Rose didn't let go of Feather's hand as she sheathed her dagger and pulled a bandage out of her pocket. She wrapped it around Feather's wound before a drop of blood could fall on her white dress. Feather smiled while Rose wrapped the bandage tight, then held her wounded hand in her other, as if it was a treasured gift.

Vaylan grunted. "Very touching. Off you go now. You are released to live free of the Goddess forever."

Rose put her arm around Feather and started to lead her away, but Vaylan called her back. "Rose, I think she can make it fine on her own. The other one was barely walking, but this one can see to herself. Come inside and relax with the other Adopted."

Rose drew in a deep breath and prepared to unleash a storm of words at him, but Feather stepped smoothly out of her grasp. The shock brought Rose up short.

"I'll be okay, Rose. Don't worry about me." She stood tall, cradling her injured hand. Rose didn't want Feather to think she found her weak and in need of protection. Even though the sight of Feather stirred a protectiveness in her heart that made her want to destroy everyone who even looked at her the wrong way.

She took a deep breath and kissed Feather on the cheek. Her whisper was just a breath of sound. "Goddess blessing upon you." As she pulled back, she saw the silent response in Feather's eyes.

Feather turned and walked away from the temple with her head held high. Rose hoped Wilder was close. She didn't want Feather wandering around the City alone. Even though Rose was just a couple of years older, she still saw the girl as much younger.

After Feather turned a corner, Rose walked up the steps of the temple, Vaylan and his Sentinels a looming presence at her back. She ignored him and went to the kitchen to find some food.

The kitchen was the same as every other temple she had been in yet different. Previously, there were many non-Priests who worked in the temples, but it was still strange to see no one in black other than a few scattered Sentinels. An older male Adopted bowed to Rose and handed her a bowl of stew.

She didn't know if the Adopted had brought food along or if this had been stolen from the Priests. She briefly wondered how Wilder would feed all the Priests he collected, then she laughed quietly to herself. Wilder had the Gift of Order. He could feed an entire army.

She hoped it wouldn't come to that.

A young man and woman sat down at the long dining table across from Rose, murmuring quietly to one another and looking so deep into each other's eyes that they didn't even notice her. Rose tried to pay close attention to her stew, but when the young man slid his elbow across the table, he pushed his own bowl to the edge. Rose lunged across the table and caught it before it hit the ground.

Her eyes instinctively shot to the Sentinels to see if they were watching. Then she realized these Sentinels were no longer controlled by High Priests. They didn't execute people for spilling their dinner.

They only killed people on Vaylan's whims.

Rose relaxed back in her seat with a sigh. Then she noticed the couple was watching her. "Sorry to react so strongly," she said. "I ... didn't want to see food go to waste."

The couple unfroze and bowed their heads.

"Thank you, Marked One," said the young woman, who was possibly only a few years Rose's senior. Her black hair was woven in a thick braid that slid over the shoulder of her white dress when she bowed deeper.

The young man bowed further, and his blond curls hid his blue eyes. "We're the ones who should apologize."

Rose sighed. She used to enjoy the deference she received as a Priest, but being Vaylan's Marked One made her feel like a freak. "There's no need to apologize. Just enjoy your meal and each other." She gave them a slight bow and returned to her stew.

"You are kind, Marked One," said the woman, brushing her braid over her shoulder. "Thank you."

"Call me Rose. The other name makes me uncomfortable." She continued eating her stew, thinking they would go back to their loving murmurs, but they both turned to look at her.

"Thank you for the honor, Rose," said the young man. "I'm Hunter, and this is Yasmine. It's nice to meet you in person."

Rose hoped that eating her stew would hide her bitter smile. "I'm sure you've heard all the prophecies about me."

"Yes," said Yasmine breathlessly. "It's so fascinating! I heard the prophecies, but it wasn't until the first crystal went out that I truly believed."

"Great," grumbled Rose. By trying to save the City, she was converting more followers for Vaylan. "But believed in what?" She kept eating and didn't expect an answer to her hypothetical question.

"Believed in you, of course," she said.

Rose looked up sharply. "In me? I think Vaylan is more interested in you believing in him."

Hunter laughed, then dropped his voice to a whisper. "The Lord Founder is great, but the prophecies about you are much more interesting. We have a group of friends that get together every night and discuss prophecies." He pointed at Rose with his spoon. "We have quite a few theological discussions about you," he said with a smile.

She thumped back in her chair. "You sit around with your friends discussing the theology of *me*?"

Hunter continued, blissfully unaware of Rose's outrage. "Yes, we're always debating our ideas about what you will do and what it all means."

Rose gave him a flat stare. "If you figure it out, please let me know. It would save me a lot of time."

Hunter and Yasmine chuckled awkwardly, unsure what to make of Rose. She found the topic of herself uncomfortable, so she decided to shift the conversation.

"Have the two of you been together long?" The question had the desired effect when they both took their eyes off Rose to stare at each other lovingly.

"A couple years," said Yasmine. "I met him when I moved to Grotto Indulgence when I turned eighteen, and we've been together ever since."

"Are you going to get married?" asked Rose.

They both broke eye contact to stare down at their bowls.

"We were," said Yasmine sadly.

Hunter sighed. "The Lord Founder thinks it's best if we focus on our tasks as Adopted. He said getting married is a distraction."

Rose's mouth dropped open. "Even the High Priests with all their rules never outlawed marriage. I can't believe he would try."

Yasmine looked at Hunter with shame-filled eyes. "It makes sense, though. When we are together, we're totally distracted. We only see each other."

How dare Vaylan make these people feel guilty for falling in love! He already worked his Adopted to the bone, and now they couldn't even be in a relationship?

She leaned across the table and whispered conspiratorially, "Here's a topic for your next meeting with your friends. Vaylan was married and had a child, so why does he command his people to stay single?"

Hunter and Yasmine both stared at her with wide eyes. Rose felt a little guilty about messing with their world but felt a jolt of glee when she considered them gossiping about Vaylan instead of her at their next meeting.

"The Lord Founder has a child?" whispered Yasmine.

"His son's name is Wilder," she said casually.

They both gasped.

"Wilder is his son?" asked Hunter, blue eyes wide.

"You know Wilder?" Rose asked.

Yasmine's voice was breathless. "Everyone knows Wilder."

Rose rubbed her forehead. "Yes, it seems they do. He's Vaylan's son, though I can't say they're on the best of terms." She stood and picked up her empty bowl. "It's been a long day, so I'm heading to bed. I wish you both well, and I hope you get married whenever you decide it's best." She bowed and left them staring after her with wide eyes.

Her Sentinels fell into step as she headed to her room. They pulled up short at the inner courtyard where the Priests used to sleep, but she continued up the stairs. They hurried to catch up, and she restrained a giggle at how undignified it made them look to scramble after her.

"I don't want to sleep in the inner courtyard. The darkened crystal is disturbing. I'll sleep up in the acolyte's quarters instead."

They both gave her a quick nod as she closed the door to one of the upstairs rooms. It was slightly smaller than a Priest's room but much better suited to her needs. She shuttered the crystalline lamp, plunging the room into darkness except for the light shining under the door.

Instead of her usual panic in the dark, this time, she smiled. She opened the window, shimmied down the trellis, and escaped into the night.

15

Rose breathed in the frosty night air, savoring her freedom. Even though it was much colder with another crystal dark, she found the chilled air invigorating. She wondered if she was the only one who enjoyed the feeling. As she walked past shops closed for the night, she realized how empty the streets were compared to the last time she was there. Considering that she had stood in the middle of an angry mob her last time in Order Diocese, she wasn't upset to be alone.

She had no idea how she was going to find Wilder but was determined to try. Feather had likely told him that Rose had gone meekly inside, and the two of them probably joined with all the renegade Priests. Wilder would have found a place to hide everyone, but she didn't know how or where. She didn't think he would hide them close to the temple, so she needed to make it further into the City and see if she could spot the wolves again.

A looming figure in black pulled her into the dark alley as she passed by. She leaned into their momentum and slammed her captor into the wall, holding her knife at the ready.

She recognized his scent before her eyes adjusted to the dark. He smelled like parchment from the little notebooks he always carried and fresh cedar. She savored the familiar scent before she slapped her hand against his chest.

"Goddess curse you, Wilder! Are you trying to get yourself accidentally murdered? You shouldn't—" She didn't get to finish her rant, because Wilder spun her and pushed her against the wall this time. His kiss was passionate and fierce and lovely and clearly intended to make her forget what she was ranting about.

What *was* she ranting about?

"I'm glad you escaped," he said with a grin.

"I've lived inside a temple my whole life. If Mims couldn't keep me from sneaking out, I don't think Vaylan will."

He gave her a long look up and down, and she suddenly didn't feel the cold air.

He raised an eyebrow. "It was probably easier to sneak out back then since you weren't dressed in bright white."

She ran a self-conscious hand across the front of her jacket, then looked at him and paused. "You're wearing all black."

"Oh ... Um ..." He adjusted the collar of his black leather jacket nervously. "When the Priests discovered I had the Gifts, they insisted I wear black."

She merely stared at him, unable to respond.

Wilder's voice took on an unusual sound of embarrassment. "I tried to talk them out of it. I wasn't sure ..." He cleared his throat and looked at her with a playful question in his eyes. "However, it *is* convenient for sneaking up on girls dressed in white."

She narrowed her eyes, unsure if she wanted to let him turn the conversation into a joke. She shrugged and flipped her ponytail over her shoulder. "It's just a color. It's not like wearing all white actually makes me an Adopted."

He flinched slightly. She bit her lip, angry at herself for being hurtful but still too hurt to apologize.

She started walking down the alley. "Where is everyone? Do you have a secret headquarters somewhere?"

He fell into step beside her. "Not yet, but we're working on it. Tonight, we are staying in a warehouse, then tomorrow, we'll head to the center of the City to find a safe place to stay. From there, I can see when you darken a crystal, then head that direction."

"I'm glad the Priests found you. I wasn't sure I convinced them."

He studied her out of the corner of his eye as they walked. "You convinced them. They spoke about you in reverent tones and believe the Goddess sent you to liberate them."

Rose snorted. "If they believe that, I know some Adopted that would love to discuss theology with them."

"What?"

"It's nothing," she sighed.

They had been wandering aimlessly, but when they came to one of the City's orchards, Rose walked inside. The normally fruit-laden trees were picked bare, and the orchard felt empty. The icy wind caused the leaves to shudder, and the sound made Rose unreasonably sad.

"Was the City destined to fall?" she asked.

Wilder stopped under the branches of an empty apple tree. "Why do you say that?"

She leaned against the trunk and stared at the moon through the branches. "Everyone around me discusses prophecy all day long. They believe Brother Owyn envisioned this and that we are just acting out everything that he foretold. Maybe he was just smart enough to see the natural conclusion of the City's demise."

"Rose, Brother Owyn's prophecies are vague predictions Vaylan has used to shape the present into what he wants. He believes you delivered the Chosen into his hands when you clearly did no such thing. He is the one forcing you to hurt the crew to fulfill his sick ideas. Vaylan is using people's belief in Brother Owyn to get what he wants."

"But what if some prophecies are true? Brother Owyn predicted I would watch him die and would weep. He said those words to me as he died. I saw them written in his book of prophecies. He believed it, and it happened."

Wilder shook his head. "But anyone would've wept as they watched him die."

"Yes, but his prophecy said the Marked would weep."

"And who decided you were the Marked? It was Vaylan, and only after Brother Owyn had died. It's all an illusion, Rose. Another way that Vaylan is manipulating you and the Adopted."

She crossed her arms on her chest. "You think I am weak and allowing him manipulate me."

He sighed. "I don't think you are weak, Rose. I think he is a master manipulator, used to getting what he wants. Vaylan wants you to question everything you've ever believed. He wants you to doubt me. He wants you to doubt yourself." His voice dropped to a whisper. "Please don't let him come between us."

His voice was so sweet and sad, and it nearly broke her heart. "No one will come between us," she whispered as she pulled him by his collar into a kiss.

He pressed her against the tree, kissing her like the storm that had always been between them. She melted into him, wrapping her fingers into his hair, pulling him close. One of his tears landed on her cheek, and she felt it sizzle as if she was the flame. His palm rested on the tree above her head, and all around her, she felt the sensation of *life.*

Flower petals bloomed, then fell to the ground as apples burst into existence above them. The scent of Wilder filled her nose, followed by apples. Then peaches. Then pears. The whole orchard was filled to the brim, bursting with the glory of him. She had vowed to be no longer jealous of his Gift, and when she opened her eyes and surveyed the beautiful orchard, she kept that promise.

"It's beautiful," she breathed.

He chuckled quietly. "I think it will be pretty obvious a Priest was here."

A familiar twist of pain.

The Priest was him.

Not her.

She had surrendered the Gift, but the title was still hard to lose. A burning shame consumed her, because she could not sacrifice the name *Priest* to him.

He still held her pressed close to the tree. His body was warm, but it was nothing compared to the heat of shame crawling across her cheeks. She was glad there was no flame nearby, because she knew it would blaze out of control.

Then suddenly, the fire was there.

A brushfire sprang up at her back, consuming the tree behind her. The two of them leaped back in surprise. The fire burned red and orange along the leaves, but at the trunk where she had stood, the flames were pure blue.

Wilder took a step closer, then reached a tentative hand toward the flames. After a moment, he plunged his hands into the leaves with a relieved sigh.

"It's not truly burning." His eyes trailed along the rows of trees in the distance. "That could have been a disaster."

Rose stared at the flames, unmoving.

"I didn't realize you could call fire without having it nearby. That's amazing!"

He was so proud of her. Her shame was mounting.

He noticed her silence and moved closer. "Rose, are you okay? Did it burn you?" His eyes turned playful. "Come here, and I will heal you with a kiss."

He grabbed her hand, and she hissed, "I don't need a Priest!"

Wilder pulled back with an abrupt gasp and looked at the blisters forming on his hand, then studied her face, still frozen after her shout. "Apparently, your fire *can* hurt others."

She clapped her hands over her mouth, angry at the words she had let escape. She wanted to touch his hand to examine the wound, but there was nothing she could do to fix it.

"I hurt you ..." she whispered, more to herself than him.

He pulled himself up taller, hiding his palm near his side. "I'm fine, Rose."

"You can't heal yourself." Her voice wouldn't raise above a whisper.

"No. But I can find an apothecary." His voice was clipped, and Rose felt the pain behind the words.

"You will suffer because of me."

"Don't be dramatic. I'll be—"

"You will suffer ..." The words rang inside of her like a gong. "How could I forget? I knew it, but I forgot ..."

"What are you talking about?"

"The crew isn't the Chosen. You are."

Wilder rolled his eyes. "Rose, the prophecies aren't real. Stop—"

"You are the Chosen. You're the one I will cause to suffer."

"Don't let him get to you! Listen to me! Rose ..." He held out both arms as if he might hold her but then hesitated.

Rose looked him in the eyes. "You think I might burn you again."

He grunted in irritation and reached for her, but she stepped out of his grasp. "Please, don't. I don't know how I burned you, and I don't want to do it again." She took another step back. "I need to go."

His voice returned to the gentle tone from before. "I'm not afraid of you, Rose. I'm strong enough to handle it. Please, don't leave."

She took another step back. "I'll find you at the next crystal. Good night, Wilder."

She left him standing by the unburning tree as she ran all the way back to the temple alone.

16

____

Rose lay on her bed in the Heart, avoiding her crew. She knew she should go check on them—they would wonder if Feather made it safely away—but she couldn't meet their eyes yet. Kai would know something was wrong, and Rev would see right through her. Rose wasn't prepared to answer their questions yet, so she hid.

She had no answers to give. She didn't know how she burned Wilder and wasn't sure if she could do it again. Not like she wanted to try, but she would rather know so she didn't accidentally burn anyone. Although knowing how she did it wouldn't prevent her from burning someone again. She was skilled at hurting people with her words and rarely did that on accident.

She sighed and rolled over, hiding her face against the wall of her tent. Why couldn't she keep her mouth shut? She couldn't count the number of times she had hurt Wilder with a stupid remark, apologized, and then done the same thing again. Why couldn't she stop? Maybe she was cursed. Or maybe she was destined to hurt him because of the prophecy.

Part of her clung to the idea. If it was because of a prophecy, she wouldn't feel the same guilt as if she did it all herself. But blaming everything on prophecy is what Vaylan did, and her mind recoiled at believing as he did. So that left her at fault. Brother Owyn just happened to be fantastic at predicting how terrible Rose would be.

"Pardon me for bothering you, Marked One."

The gentle voice caused Rose to sit upright.

Yasmine bowed at the waist near Rose's bed. "I apologize for disturbing your rest, but the Sentinels asked me to come find you. They were too scared to come on their own."

"Uh ... The Sentinels were too scared?"

"Yes, they were scared you changed your mind."

Rose scratched her head, then groaned as the realization hit. "Is this about dance lessons?"

Yasmine smiled. "It's very kind of you to offer. I always worry the Sentinels aren't cared for in the same way as the Adopted. It's so nice you would do something special for them."

Rose opened and closed her mouth, unable to respond.

Something special.

For Sentinels.

She thought the whole idea was ludicrous, but since she was still trying to avoid the crew, dance lessons seemed as good as any other excuse.

"Fine," she said. "Let's go."

Yasmine smiled and led Rose out of the tent.

Nine Sentinels stood outside of her door. She staggered back a step in surprise. "All of you?" she asked.

They didn't respond except to fall into a formation and lead her down the hallway. They curved around tents until they made it to an outer wall of the Heart, where a giant stage was erected.

Rose blinked her eyes in surprise. "Did Vaylan build this

for our class?" She didn't expect a response, but when she turned around, she saw a Sentinel had removed his mask, revealing the face of the boy who asked for the class.

"The Wardens built this stage for the Spectacle. Ylena and Wilder performed here, along with the Little Wardens," he said.

Rose studied the stage, irritated to have another memory of Ylena and unsure what to think about Wilder at the moment. She shook her head to clear her thoughts and turned to her class. "I hope you brought dance clothes, because I don't think your armor will be helpful here."

Her new students stripped out of their armor, revealing similar gray clothes she had seen them train in before. Watching them peel off masks and hoods and gloves was unnerving. On the surface, they all looked the same, but underneath, she found an odd collection of teenagers.

She started by learning all their names. The young boy who'd convinced her to teach dance classes was named Latham. Despite his silence when wearing armor, he never stopped talking once he removed it. It was as if he stored up his ideas underneath his armor, and when the mask came off, all the words spilled out.

The girl with the golden blond curls was named Dany. At seventeen, she was the oldest in the group, and she bossed them around like she was their commander or mother or both.

Rose asked them to space out on the stage so they could follow her movements, and they fell into an easy formation. She led through some simple stretches, then started with the kata Latham had seen her practice.

"Some dance styles are as strict as a traditional kata, calling for precise movements done exactly the same way each time. However, there are also dance styles that are totally improvised. Instead of throwing you into one of those two extremes, I thought we would start with something formulaic but not rigid. Since you appear to be familiar with the basic katas, we can use this one as a starting place."

She led them through the kata, showing them moves they could substitute as they went. Instead of a lunge with a quick jab, she demonstrated a move she called Petals on the Wind. She leaned down, trailing her fingers near the ground, then flung them forward. Instead of a simple pivot, she showed them a twisting move called Branch in a Storm. She showed them Bird on the Wing, Falling Leaf, and Fluttering Ribbon. She never realized how many of the simple dance steps she knew were named for the wind. It made sense, considering all her instructors had been skilled Discipline Priests.

She was pleased at how quickly her class caught on. Dany was especially good, taking to each movement like a natural. Rose knew that to become a Sentinel, they must have trained in the fighting arts, and those skills transferred over. It always made sense to her how closely dance related to the Discipline Priests' katas, so she was glad to see her theory pay off.

At the end of class, Latham ran up to Rose. "Thank you for the lesson! I can't wait for the next class. Are we practicing again tonight? If not, I wake up really early, so just tell me the time, and I will be there!"

Rose chuckled. "I'll need a day to think about what to teach you next. You picked up those moves so quickly that I need to consider what should come next."

"This isn't how you learned, is it? Do all dance teachers instruct the same? Maybe there's someone else who can teach us tonight, and you can teach us tomorrow morning?"

He always asked so many questions that she had to choose only one to answer before he moved on to the next.

"Not all teachers are the same. Just be grateful it wasn't my brother teaching you. The entire first lesson would just be how to stand properly. He would yell about your shoulders the entire class!"

Latham touched one of his shoulders. "What's wrong with my shoulders?"

"Nothing. Which is why I skipped you ahead a few lessons."

He sighed happily. "Thanks, Rose. For a minute there, I really felt like I was dancing. It's so strange. It's like the powerful feeling I get from sparring, except it just makes me smile."

"Me too," she said. Somewhere in the middle of the lesson, her stress about talking to the crew had melted away. She was grateful the Sentinels had convinced her get out of bed.

She shook her head at the strange thought and watched as Latham put his armor back on piece by piece. As he pulled on the same terrifying mask, she tried to imagine Latham's smiling face underneath, but it was difficult.

Dany approached her, thankfully with her mask in her hands and not on her head.

"You did a great job today, Dany," said Rose. "You're a natural."

She smiled, and her pink cheeks turned even rosier. "Thanks. It helped that all the moves had descriptive names. They're easy to remember."

"Yes, it also helped when we were training with the wind. Our fighting katas blend with dance moves, which blend with using our Gift. It's all very connected." She sighed, feeling the familiar sense of grief. "Well, it *was* very connected."

Dany nodded. "I understand what you mean. But since I

never danced before, I hope learning those moves will help me deal with the loss."

Rose stared at her dumbly. "What loss?"

Dany looked at her as if Rose were the strange one. "Losing the wind. I haven't been able to touch it since the Uprising, either."

Rose's mind was slowly processing her words. This girl, Dany, used to have the Gift of Discipline? If she had been a Discipline Priest, Rose would have known her. They would have taken classes together. But Rose had never met her before the day Dany removed her mask.

"Who are you?" whispered Rose.

"Oh ..." said Dany, realization slowly dawning on her face. "You don't know where he found us."

"Where who found you?" asked Rose, still confused.

"Vaylan ... um ... I mean the Lord Founder. I don't know where he found all the Sentinels. Some of the older guys might have been Sentinels in the past for all I know. But almost all the young people have the same story. We didn't have anywhere to go, but Vaylan showed up with food and a safe place to stay. Most of us have been with him ever since."

Rose's mind raced, trying to connect the dots, but Dany connected them for her.

"We were the Wardens' Champions, the children they kept drugged with tea to hide us from the Priests. We lost our Gifts on the same day you did."

Harmony

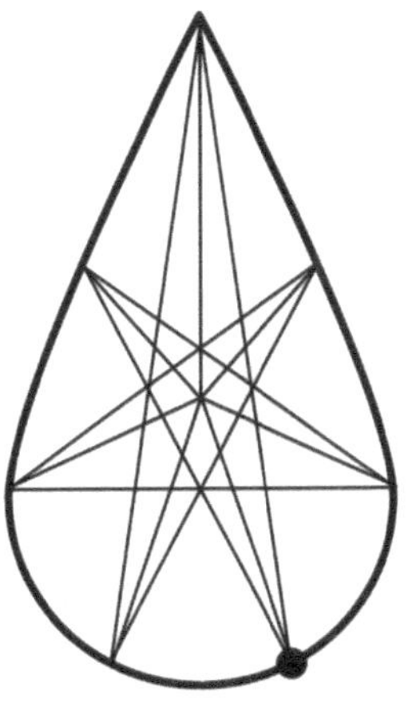

Rivalry

R ose wasn't ready to face the crew but hoped that the surprise of the Sentinels' identities would mask her guilt from what she did to Wilder.

Rev nodded as she listened to the story. "It makes sense why they would follow him. They lived their entire lives inside the Dens under the harsh training of the Wardens. I bet protecting Vaylan seems laughably easy compared to that."

Rose whispered so the Sentinels outside wouldn't hear. "But he's asked them to kill for him. Brother Owyn died at the hands of Sentinels. They killed Lark at the performing arts school. They almost killed me."

She only survived her fight with the Sentinels because Wilder healed her. He had hidden his Gifts because he didn't want to upset her. He was right. She had lashed out and hurt him when she found out. Another time she'd caused him to suffer ...

She realized she had lost track of the conversation. When she looked up, she saw Rev studying her with a narrowed eye.

Rose jumped in with another question as a distraction. "But how did Vaylan know about them? The High Priests held him as a prisoner along with Brother Owyn until the night the Goddess reshaped the City, cracking their prison open. How did Vaylan know to find them?"

Fitz shrugged. "Maybe there is a prophecy about them, too?"

Rose chewed on her lips as she mentally reread all the prophecies she'd seen.

"I'm not saying I believe in the prophecies," Fitz said quickly. "But if Vaylan believed strongly that someday he would be free and also believed he would find a group of people to bend to his will, he would have been searching for someone just like them."

Rose groaned. "He's always one step ahead of us. Because he knows the prophecies, he knows the future and is always prepared."

Kai gave her a look that meant he was speaking as a big brother, even though they were the same age. "Rose, Vaylan doesn't know the future. He's just twisting the words to mean what he wants."

"You sound like Wilder," she grumbled.

Rev shot her a look, but Rose turned quickly to Quinn. "Do any of the old books talk about someone with the Spark to see the future?"

Quinn shook his head. "Not that I've read yet. But there were Sparks both big and small. I never found a book that had an exhaustive list."

"Rose, it doesn't matter," said Kai. "We just have to follow our plan. You need to keep darkening the crystals, and we need to put on the Pageant to restore the Goddess's Gifts."

She waved him off. "By now, I'm sure Wilder has the

Pageant well in hand." Did he find a salve for his burns? Maybe she should visit an apothecary while she was in the Underneath. Or maybe she still had some of the remedy that helped numb her crystalline burn?

Rev stood from their circle in the center of the tent, picking up a bedroll. "Guess what time it is?" she asked.

Rose looked up, confused at what she had missed. The rest of the crew was suddenly not looking at her.

"What time?" Rose asked suspiciously.

Rev's blue eye sparkled. "Time for girl talk."

Rose groaned but obediently followed Rev away from the others. Rev laid out the bedroll, then patted the spot next to her. "Out with it."

Rose flopped onto the bedroll with a huff. "I don't have any coins to pay you for this confession."

"Since I'm not in a position to spend any money at the moment, this one's on the house."

Rose sighed. "It turns out I can burn someone other than myself."

"Ah." Rev nodded knowingly. "And was it intentional?"

Rose started to say a reflexive no but hesitated. Confessions were about being completely honest. "I'm not sure."

"And did he forgive you?"

"Um ... I ran away before I could ask him to." She bowed her head.

"Honestly, it's not surprising. Any serious training will result in some accidents, and considering the two of you are involved, I'm amazed you didn't burn down the building."

"It was an orchard," she said miserably.

Rev snorted. "Even so. Accidents happen. And if it wasn't an accident, but an instinct you couldn't control, it's good for you to ask yourself why it happened."

"It happened because of the prophecy. It says I am

destined to make the Chosen suffer. Vaylan thinks that's each of you, but Wilder is the Chosen. This is just one of the many times I've caused him to suffer."

Rev patted Rose's hand like a mother soothing a child. "Honey, you're being an absolute idiot."

Rose huffed as if Rev kicked her. "An idiot?"

"Yes, dear," said Rev patiently. "Of course you've caused Wilder to suffer. You're causing me to suffer right now." She sighed dramatically. "Here's a prophecy for you. Someday, you will hurt Wilder's feelings. And another prophecy ... Wilder will hurt your feelings. When those prophecies come true, please come back and tell me how brilliant I am."

Rose tightened her jaw. "It doesn't change the fact that I hurt him, and there's no one to heal him."

"Wilder will recover. The most important thing is that you stop blaming his injuries on a prophecy and get to the core of what triggered your response."

Rose didn't know how she did it, but she knew why. It was embarrassing to admit it out loud, so her voice was barely more than a whisper.

"Wilder was dressed as a Priest."

Rev made a humming sound deep in her throat. "Being a Priest was your identity for a long time."

Rose nodded, trying to bring her voice under control. "I'm not sure what I am anymore. I was finally wrapping my mind around not being a Priest, but if he's a Priest and I'm not, what does that mean?"

"It means that he is starting to embrace who the Goddess made him to be and that you still have some things to sort out."

Rose's voice leaped out of her control. "I don't have time to sort this out right now!"

The crew turned their heads at Rose's exclamation, then quickly went back to their own conversations.

Rev gave her a pointed look. "Make time. If you don't, you'll continue to hurt him and everyone around you."

Rose folded in on herself. "I became a Priest before I even knew what that meant. I never had to question my identity until everything fell apart. How do I figure it out now?"

"It turns out you are in the same situation as the rest of us non-Priests. We flail around hoping to figure it out on our own, or depending on your beliefs, we ask the Goddess for direction." Rev tapped her lip in thought. "I can't discover it for you, but here's a thought for you to consider. One thing I've noticed about you is that you instinctively see people's strengths. This is usually so you can be bossy and put them to work doing what you think is best, but you do see their strengths."

Rose studied Rev closely, trying to determine if she was giving a compliment or not.

Rev continued. "Perhaps you can use this ability on yourself. Turn it inward and see what strength lies within. Maybe it will reveal something to you."

Rose leaned back against her palms as she considered. "It's an interesting idea. I will think about it."

"Good," said Rev. "Because it's a prophecy, and I'm counting on you to make sure it comes true." Her lips curled in a playful smirk.

Rose rolled her eyes. "How about you direct some of your girl talk energy to them?" She pointed at the other members of the crew, who were trying to stay as quiet as possible.

"Don't worry. I've had plenty of time for girl talk with each of them. I think everyone is hoping they are the next one to leave so they can escape from me."

Rose laughed. "Maybe it will be you, and they'll all be off the hook." She stood to leave.

Rev studied her with a serious eye. "Take some time to think about what I said, Rose. It's one of the most important things you can do right now."

Rose nodded and bowed to her before she left.

18

Rose could have gone back to her room and considered what Rev told her, but instead, she went to the tent with the prophecies. Lying on her bed and considering her inner self was something she could do anytime. She could only examine the prophecies while in the Heart, and Vaylan would probably lead them to the next temple tomorrow. She had to go now.

Sister Bria was happy to see Rose and set the thick book on the desk in front of her. Rose flipped through the pages, unsure where to start. She wanted to ask Sister Bria questions about the prophecy but worried she would report back to Vaylan what she asked. So instead, she skimmed through the pages, looking for anything about Sentinels, the Marked One, or the Chosen.

She hoped passages about them would jump out at her and Vaylan's plans would suddenly become clear, but all the words jumbled together, as confusing as the thoughts in her head. How could these prophecies be so clear to Vaylan and the Adopted, while she struggled to make sense of them?

Her eyes fell on a short poem set apart on its own page.

Her finger traced the shape of the words, and she couldn't move on. The poem brushed against the feelings of shame that lingered in her heart. When she'd been a Priest, she felt like she belonged in the City. She was chosen by the Goddess, and her status was clear. Back then, she could get angry too easily or be mean, but those flaws hid comfortably behind a wall of self-righteousness. Small imperfections that fit neatly inside the box of her title.

But without the label of Priest, her identity was unmoored. All her faults stood out in sharp relief against a blank page. Her former shield of self-righteousness had been dismantled by crushing doubt. Even if she darkened all the crystals, somehow saving the City and defeating Vaylan, the Goddess's Gifts would return. But would she give one to Rose? She had the chance before and chose another. Would she return Rose's Gift as if nothing had happened?

Would Rose want her to?

She tried to imagine returning to Temple Discipline and taking up her old life but couldn't. The temples, which had once been her refuge, were now a source of confusion and regret. She had lived her whole life inside a temple, and yet her heart lost its home even before Vaylan arrived.

She belonged nowhere.

Was that how Brother Owyn felt? When she had seen

him speak, he appeared so confident. Crowds listened to him, in awe of him, and even after his death, his words were treasures and sold as commodities. Yet he wrote a poem about his imperfections and searching for a place to belong.

She turned the page with gentle fingers, as if the paper was as fragile as the words. The next page was a long paragraph she skimmed, but when she saw the word "marked," she went back and read it slowly.

Compassion is a mighty gift and a crushing burden. To feel what another feels, to understand another perspective, builds new cities inside a mind and entire societies inside a heart. Build an internal realm full of the other, the different, the wayward. This multitude of gathered souls brings insight, but also a responsibility. An obligation to listen to those whose voices are silent, those trapped in a prison not of their own making. The one who knows this best is the one marked by pain.

Brother Owyn's words were beautiful and not what she expected. Was this one of the prophecies Vaylan believed was about her? Vaylan hadn't mentioned it, but maybe that's because it didn't fit in with the rest of the prophecies he liked to quote. She hadn't found any of those prophecies yet, but if they were hidden inside passages like this, she wasn't sure how long it would take for her to find them.

She was about to give up for the day when her eyes fell on another poem, crammed in the margins of a page. One line stood out.

The one who has lived the longest grants long life.

Her hand flew to her mouth to cover a gasp. Walter. This prophecy was about Walter. She looked around the inside of the tent, wishing Walter was still there so she could smuggle him out of the Heart and hide him. She still hadn't been able to find him, even though she had casually gone back to visit the laundry a few more times. Had Vaylan already found him? Had Vaylan forced him to use his Spark to grant long life? If so, what would he do with Walter when he was finished with him? Rose shivered and read the short poem.

> *Is it better to be the first to leave the party*
> *Or the one who remains when everyone has gone?*
> *The one who has lived the longest grants long life*
> *But what kind of life will that be?*

"Find something interesting?" asked Vaylan.

Rose slammed the book shut with a snap. She tried to still her racing heart and act calm, but based on the question in Vaylan's eyes, he knew she was hiding something.

"I thought all the prophecies were interesting to you," she said, trying to find her usual mocking tone.

He smiled, but his eyes were still watching her every movement. "I find all the prophecies fascinating. I'm just surprised to find you studying them so closely."

She gave a haughty sniff and avoided looking him in the eye. "I can be a good student when I choose. As a Priest, it was my responsibility to study the liturgies."

His watchful eyes suddenly twinkled. "I get the impression you spent more time training than reading scripture, Rose."

He was entirely correct, but Rose didn't want to admit it. "I spent plenty of time in dance classes studying the Pageant, which is a part of the liturgy."

His grin froze on his lips. "But you haven't heard the music from the Pageant for some time."

She detected a slight question in his words. Did he know they planned to put on a secret Pageant? She tried to keep her response as neutral as possible.

"No, I haven't. It's a shame, because the music is quite beautiful."

He raised an eyebrow coolly. "Yes, if I'm forced to listen to religious propaganda, I prefer it has a catchy tune."

She gave him a flat look. "What do you want, Vaylan?"

"I thought you might be lonely. The Heart is a big place, so I want to make sure you feel at home here."

She nearly laughed. "You think this should be my home?"

He shrugged. "You're also welcome in any of the Havens, either Upstairs or in the Underneath. The Adopted will welcome you wherever you choose to live."

Vaylan's kindness jarred her, but she knew better than to relax her guard. "And where will you live when you finish converting all the temples to Havens? Will you stay here in the Heart?"

He looked up at the top of the tent, as if he could see the roof of the cave through the fabric. "I think I will leave the Heart as a training space for Sentinels and turn the amphitheater into my fortress."

She nearly choked on the sacrilege of desecrating the amphitheater but swallowed it down. "You believe you have a right to all of it? That everything in this City should belong to you?"

"It should, and it will." He rested his hand lovingly on the book of prophecy still closed on the desk between them. "It's so clear. Everything perfectly lined out in black and white. All we must do is believe, then be strong enough to do as we must."

She shook her head. "It's not clear. I've read what's written here. I don't know how you can say your vision for the City is the correct one. Brother Owyn's words are beautiful but vague. You are just forcing them to fit what you want to believe. I can read this and imagine a completely different City, one that doesn't include you controlling every Haven, temple, and amphitheater."

He chuckled as if listening to a small child's story. "You and I aren't so different, Rose. We are both passionate about what we believe and will do whatever it takes to achieve it."

She snarled. "I am nothing like you. You are angry and vicious and willing to hurt anyone who stands in the way of what you want."

He gave her a searching look that made her uncomfortable. As if he could detect the angry part of her soul that she was trying desperately to fix. "There are some things that should make us angry. Some things that are worth the pain we inflict. You only judge me because you hate that it's true. Once you embrace the part of you that's furious, the part of you that's enraged, it will become your strength."

He picked up the book of prophecies, bowed to her, then left the tent.

19

Grotto Rivalry was their destination the next day, and Quinn was her companion as they walked to the crystal. Despite his bound hands, his blue eyes glowed with questions.

"Tell me about your Spark," he said.

She shrugged. "The Goddess said I should be able to control fire, but so far, I have no control over it at all."

"I'm assuming you don't need tears to trigger your Spark since Vaylan doesn't. But does it feel the same as your Gift did? Can you sense a flame like you could the wind? Can you see it with your eyes closed?"

The personal questions would normally irritate Rose, but Quinn's innocent curiosity just made her smile.

"It's not the same. With my Gift, I always felt the wind's presence. It was impossible to ignore. I don't feel a flame at all unless I really concentrate. And honestly, I have no idea how I called a flame from nothing."

"Fascinating." He adjusted his glasses with his bound hands as he considered. "Perhaps you should experiment with how wind affects flame."

"What do you mean?" she asked.

"Remember how the candles in Peculiarity flared when you and Wilder kissed?" His voice was matter-of-fact, but a blush rose to her cheeks. He continued, "Wind can snuff out a flame, but it can also stoke one. Considering your previous affinity to wind, you might use it to understand fire."

She frowned. "But they're so different. I tried to control the flame like I did the wind, but they're nothing alike."

"You're right. They aren't the same. But despite their differences, the flame needs to work with the wind. Without wind, a flame can suffocate."

She pictured Wilder's blistered hand. "Maybe it's better that way. I think my fire is too dangerous."

"You said you only burned yourself last time. Did you discover how to make the flames burn others?"

She thought about the unburning tree and Wilder safely running his hand through the flames.

She sighed. "My flames don't wound. But I do."

"Fascinating ..." He lapsed into silence, lost in thought.

He was quiet for so long that she was surprised at his sudden question.

"Will it hurt?" he asked.

"Will what hurt?"

They had already been speaking quietly, but his voice dropped to a rough whisper. "Will it hurt ... when my Gift is taken away?"

Her throat clenched at the memory of losing her own Gift, and she didn't think she could respond. Quinn marched ahead bravely, but she could see the fear in his clear blue eyes. She swallowed down the grief again and gave her best answer.

"It doesn't hurt physically. But ... it felt like a piece of my consciousness was suddenly missing. It stopped me in my tracks. Suddenly, I was no longer myself. My mind kept reaching out for a sense that was no longer there. It was very disorienting." She sighed. "Sometimes it's still disorienting, but I don't feel the loss as strongly as I once did."

Quinn gave her a sad smile. "Thanks for sharing that with me. I know I've only had my Gift a short time, but I can't imagine not having it." He frowned. "I think my mind will be very lonely."

She gave him a confused look, and he cocked his head.

"I hear them all the time," he said. "There's a mouse eating crumbs by that trashcan. And in that window, a cat is looking down at us. Everywhere I go, I have their voices in my head. I can't imagine how silent it will be once you darken the crystal."

She took hold of his bound hands, which caused a Sentinel to look in their direction. She ignored the Sentinel and spoke clearly to Quinn.

"You and the rest of the crew were there for me when I was grieving the loss of my Gift, and you won't be alone either. When Vaylan lets you go, find Wilder and the others. I promise I will free the rest of the crew, and we will be together again, okay?"

He smiled as a tear trickled down his cheek. In her heart, she wished he would use his tear to summon the wolves to rip out Vaylan's throat. But the wolves didn't come and soon enough, they arrived at the crystal.

Vaylan raised his arms to summon her to do her duty. She touched Quinn's hand one more time and walked forward quietly to place her hands on the crystal. She built up the fire within her, then pushed it inside the heart of the glowing crystal.

The Goddess sat at her table, unmoving. Even though Rose stood just a few feet away, the Goddess didn't notice her. Her usually neat hair was disheveled, and her green eyes were dull and lifeless. There was a stillness about the Goddess's sanctuary, an emptiness that felt different from before. The Goddess lifted her right hand, and Rose thought she might speak, but her shaking fingers snapped.

Rose blinked her eyes open in the darkness of the Grotto.

∾

Quinn stayed close by Rose's side as they walked up the bridge to the City. Rose was grateful for his quiet presence but couldn't shake the uneasiness she felt about the Goddess. The plan Rose and the crew were following was based on the Goddess's directions, but Rose had no way to know if it was working.

And she wasn't sure the Goddess was still conscious.

Quinn gripped her arm tighter, and Rose realized she wasn't the only one struggling.

"Are you okay?" she asked him.

His usually amiable smile was forced, and his footsteps were unsteady. "It's strange. I lived most of my life without a Gift, but now that it's gone, I don't remember what it was like before."

She squeezed his arm to steady him. "I'm sorry, Quinn. I wish this wasn't the solution."

His forced smile became a little more natural. "It's okay. I have faith you'll fix the City and our Gifts will return."

She blinked at him in surprise. "You believe that? I ..." She wasn't sure how to voice her awkward question. "Umm ... I wasn't sure that you believed in the Goddess."

Luckily, he wasn't offended by her clumsy statement. "I was never one of her followers like Wilder, Fitz, and Rev, but that doesn't mean I don't have faith. I have faith all this change and upheaval is leading somewhere. And I have faith in you."

She ducked her head to hide her insecurities and fear.

115

Once again, she was the Priest with less faith than a non-believer.

When they arrived at Temple Harmony, Vaylan gave his usual speech about how the Goddess had forsaken them and that he was setting them free. Rose pictured the Goddess's unseeing eyes and wondered if he might be right. She cursed herself for the sacrilegious thought and tried to remember the Goddess as she was the night of the Uprising. She'd stood high above on the cliffs surrounding the amphitheater and reshaped the City, connecting above and below. Rose meditated on that image, then realized Vaylan had stopped talking.

He watched her as if it was her cue. She looked around, trying to guess what she had missed, when she noticed the Harmony Priests lined up in the temple courtyard, watching her. Vaylan turned to her with an eyebrow raised, asking a silent question.

He expected a similar show at each temple.

She sighed and sank to her knees in the dirt. "Please, Vaylan. Don't hurt them. Allow me to talk to them. Let me convince them to surrender peacefully." She took a deep breath, summoning the courage to once again grovel. "Please, Vaylan. Show mercy. I beg you."

She felt his hand on the top of her head, as if in blessing. "I have heard your plea, Marked One. Convince them to abandon the Goddess's temple, as she has already abandoned them."

Rose stood slowly, brushing the dirt off her white clothes. She didn't think she could convince them to leave with the idea the Goddess had abandoned them. Her plan was to use the same speech she used at Temple Order.

And if that didn't convince them to leave, she would beg.

~

Rose sat on the step with Quinn, eating a sandwich. After she had convinced the Priests to leave peacefully, she'd tried to bring Quinn inside so they could get something to eat. Vaylan refused to let Quinn enter, but he also wouldn't let him leave until sundown. One of the Adopted was kind enough to bring Rose a sandwich, and when she split it with Quinn, he smiled.

"Of course you share your meal with me. You're a good alpha." He winked as he said the title given to her by the wolves. He dropped his voice to a whisper the Sentinels couldn't hear. "And now their name for you makes complete sense."

Lady Fire Wolf. "Yes," she said with a slight eye roll. "Wilder thinks they're quite brilliant for being the first to figure it out."

"I'll miss talking to them," he said wistfully. "Their minds work in such an interesting way."

She squeezed his hand. "I'm sure it won't be the last time you get to hear them berate me for stealing Wilder from them."

He laughed, then studied her hand on his.

She felt the pearl blade heavy in her coat. "Quinn, I'm s—"

"I'm stronger than you think," he said suddenly.

She swallowed the apology on her lips and reprimanded herself for almost making this moment about her.

"Yes, I know." She looked him in the eyes. "You're brilliant and kind and able to handle massive amounts of conflicting information without getting overwhelmed. Despite the darkness all around, you still hold on to curiosity and wonder. I hope to one day be as strong as you."

The sun dipped below the horizon, and Vaylan started on his way out of the temple. Before he had descended the stairs, Rose had already cut a sharp line across Quinn's palm and then wrapped it up.

Vaylan frowned, irritated he didn't get to command her. He turned on his heel and walked back into the temple without saying a word.

Rose looked over Quinn's shoulder, then smiled. "It looks like you have friends waiting for you."

Quinn turned to find Storm Fang and Pickles watching him from across the street. He waved at them, and they sank down on their haunches to wait.

Rose gave him a hug and whispered in his ear, "Just know that if you hurt my brother, I will injure you far worse than this."

She pulled back and saw the twinkle in his eye that proved he knew she was joking, but his words were as serious as a vow. "I won't hurt him."

She nodded sharply and watched him go. When he was out of sight, she walked upstairs to the acolyte rooms and told her Sentinels she was going to bed early.

It was unfortunate the Sentinels wore masks, because she couldn't judge by their reaction if they knew she was lying.

20

———

Rose was not pleased with the selection of clothes she found in the wardrobe. She hated scavenging for clothes but refused to go out into the City wearing all white again. She tried to guess who had used this room last based on what she found, but it was a complete mishmash of styles, and she had no clue. Maybe it was someone like Fitz, who had come from the Underneath to become a Priest? Rose was always surprised at his strangely matched clothes but had never learned if he had chosen them out of necessity or preference.

Her choice tonight was all necessity. She kept her white pants and boots since none of the shoes fit and the City was getting so cold that she didn't want to wear a skirt. She found a soft gray sweater that was tight but warm and a velvet jacket in peacock blue that was long enough to cover most of her white pants. After she pulled her hair back into a knot, she climbed down the tree outside her window and escaped into the City.

She found Wilder outside a building across the street, leaning casually against the wall. He wore a smooth black

119

sweater and leather pants, and her heartbeat skipped at the sight of him.

His right hand was wrapped to the wrist in a black bandage that some might assume was a fashion statement, but Rose knew what lay beneath. She wanted to grab him and pull him into a savage kiss. And she wanted to run away to protect him from herself.

In the end, she wasn't strong enough to do either.

He stayed against the wall and spoke in his slow drawl. "I decided against jumping out at you tonight."

"Smart," she said. "I don't know how I did it, so I can't promise I won't burn you again."

"I'm not scared you'll burn me. I'm scared you'll hate yourself and run off again."

His eyes pierced her to the core, and she had to look away. "But I hurt you. You can't deny that."

He rolled his eyes. "Why are you being so dramatic about this? Don't you remember I broke your wrist when you taught me to fight with the wind? Injuries happen when you train."

"We weren't training," she said seriously.

He finally pushed himself away from the wall and stepped in front of her. In his nearness, she sensed the orchard—apples and peaches and falling petals and rustling leaves and *life*.

He raised his bandaged hand and trailed a soft finger down her cheek. "This is how we've always trained, Rose."

She closed her eyes, remembering the night in Peculiarity when he'd called a windstorm and the candles flared in response. She felt him inch closer, his breath warm against her cheek. His lips were only a heartbeat away, hovering in the air, waiting for her permission.

She wanted to trust herself and surrender to his kiss, knowing he would be safe, but doubt crept into her thoughts. She imagined him pulling back in pain with blistered lips and betrayal in his eyes.

But her actual fear had never been about burning him.

It was always about her words.

She had only injured him physically a few times, and it was always on accident. But she had lost count of the number of times she said something hurtful to him. That was the bigger fear and the true source of her guilt. If the prophecy was true and she was going to cause Wilder to suffer, she knew what the cause would be.

She would be cruel to him, as she had been before.

A dove cooed twice sharply, and Wilder pulled away from her and looked down. Flames licked the grass beside her, as if they'd dripped off her fingertips to fall at her feet. Wilder stomped at the curling flames until they went out, then looked at the roof above their head and gave the sign of the Goddess. A dove shot into the sky and landed on the building across the street.

He chuckled, unaware of Rose's dark thoughts. "Perhaps we should find a less flammable place to continue our *training*."

His grin was playful, but her smile was reserved as she put her hands in her pockets, still unsure if the flames he stomped out would have injured her or him.

Wilder led her down two curving streets until they arrived at a row of empty shops. She couldn't tell what they had once sold, but the windows were dirty with debris scattered in the window displays. He led her into the alley behind the shops and knocked in a very specific pattern.

Tayeh opened the door. "Glad to see you made it."

"Tayeh!" said Rose. "You look so good!"

She preened while touching her beautiful, full hair. "You're not the first to say so."

Rose rolled her eyes. "You were almost dead the last time I saw you, so it doesn't take much to be impressive."

Tayeh punched Rose in the arm with a laugh, then spoke to Wilder. "The others are still working in the rehearsal space."

Wilder Rose further into the building. What looked like empty shops from the front had been shaped into several large warehouses. The first room they walked through was filled with crates of dry food and what appeared to be medical supplies. The warehouse had a weird smell, and when she entered the next room, she realized why.

Animals crowded inside the second warehouse. A Priest had opened a crate of food and was serving portions to a couple of cows as some chickens ran around his feet. There were pens with goats and pigs and rabbits with Priests walking between the tight rows.

"When did you have time to do this?" she asked.

Wilder laughed. "I didn't. The Priests have kept this place a secret for weeks. Tomorrow, we'll move all the animals to a new location to keep them safe."

"Safe from what?"

He looked at her strangely, as if he was unsure if she was serious or not. "Safe from the Adopted."

She coughed. "The Adopted? What do they have to do with this?"

Wilder sighed. "I thought you knew what they do for him."

"For Vaylan?" she asked. "They do a lot. They clean the Havens and the Heart. They cook meals and wash dishes. They wander around doing his will." She shrugged.

He snorted. "One of those 'doing his will' activities is slaughtering every animal they can find."

"What?" she gasped. "Why would they do that?"

He bit his lip as he hesitated to answer. "I'm not sure you really want to know why."

A quiet growl rumbled in her throat.

He sighed. "The City is running out of food faster than we can traditionally grow it. That's not new info. It's why we need to put on a Pageant, so we can grow food fast enough to feed everyone, including the City's animals. If that happens soon, the City will survive. However, Vaylan offers special rewards to his Adopted that bring him meat. Even if it means slaughtering these animals to extinction. The Priests are trying to save enough of each animal so that when the Gifts return, they can start over. But if the Adopted find this place, they'll kill these animals with no thought toward the future."

Rose tried to imagine Hunter or Yasmine or Sister Bria or even Walter coming to this warehouse and slaughtering these animals for Vaylan's table but just couldn't picture it. "That can't be true."

Irritation flashed across his face. "Do you think I'm lying, Rose? I've seen them do it."

"But why would he allow it? He wouldn't take over the entire City, only to have the people starve to death once all the plants and animals are gone."

Wilder shrugged. "I don't know what Vaylan thinks, but it's obvious he doesn't have a plan for how to feed the City. If so, he would have already started."

"I can't believe the Adopted would follow him if he didn't have a plan," she said. "I would've noticed if the Adopted were doing something so reckless."

"Honestly, I'm not sure you would." Wilder's voice was gentle, but she could tell he was trying to make a point.

"What do you mean by that?" she said with clipped words.

"I don't think you've ever had to notice where your food is coming from, so it's not something you think about. You only found out how Priest Mayra paid for your food because she wanted to hurt you with the information. You'd been eating that food for weeks without considering where it came from."

The words stung because they were true. She'd been eating meals at the Heart and in the seized temples for days without any idea of who grew the food or where the meat came from. But she didn't like being reminded of the memory of Mayra or the guilt of eating food purchased by selling Knowledge.

"I guess you always know where your food comes from," she said in a sullen voice.

"Yes, Rose." He spoke gently, trying to lessen the sting. "In the Underneath, all we did was think about where our next meal would come from. Even now that I can grow my own, I still think about it every day."

She looked at the playful goats so she wouldn't have to meet his eyes. "I've had other things on my mind. I'll talk to the Adopted. They'll listen to reason."

"Sure," he said, but his voice was unconvinced.

Their rehearsal room was large but still smelled like livestock. They had turned one side of the room into a makeshift stage area, with a simple backdrop of fake trees and curtains on either side to create the wings. Two Priests added more leaves to the fake plants, while another Priest straightened some costumes on a rack. A small group of Priests sat on the floor in the corner, sketching out what looked like plans for another set piece.

"You've been busy," said Rose.

Wilder smiled proudly as he watched all the activity. "It helps that everyone knows exactly what the Pageant should look like. It's not like it takes much direction other than giving them space to work."

A Priest approached and pulled Wilder aside to ask how they would replicate the fountains for the creation scene. She ignored their conversation and instead considered the number of Priests in the building, all working under Wilder's leadership. She suddenly felt lazy compared to him. What had she accomplished other than begging Vaylan for mercy and eating the remaining animals in the City?

"You made it!" Quinn ran to her side, and her dark thoughts dissipated. He had changed out of Vaylan's white clothing into a simple gray tunic with black pants. Neither fit him very well, but it was good to see him looking more like himself.

He held up a hand and waggled his fingers. "Wilder healed me, then the wolves led me here while he waited for you. There's so much going on!"

"Yes, Wilder's been very busy," she said slowly.

Feather bounded out from behind the curtain and ran to give Rose a hug. "It's so good to see you! I can't wait to show you what we've done so far." She was practically bouncing in delight.

"You're still wearing white," said Rose.

Feather smoothed out the wrinkles on her plain white dress with a little smile. "Well, white is the traditional color of the Goddess, so I thought I'd keep it for rehearsals. To get me in character, you know?"

"That makes sense," said Rose. "So, what are—?"

Feather pulled Rose and Quinn by the hands and sat them down on a sofa directly in front of the stage. "Watch this! It's not perfect, but considering how quickly we pulled it together, I think you'll be so proud!"

Feather ran to Wilder and pulled him out of the conversation with the Priest. He gave Rose an apologetic shrug that said he was indulging Feather and that he would be back soon. Rose sighed and leaned back on the sofa to watch.

They started in the middle of Act One. There was still a lot to work out, but Rose could see the framework was there. They had a couple skilled musicians, and she assumed they would find more when Vaylan kicked the other Priests out of their homes. The set pieces were simple, but with help from Wilder backstage, they came to life. And like always, the singers were excellent, especially Feather.

Rose felt a rush of pride that she was the one who had chosen Feather to play the role of the Goddess. Despite looking like a copper-skinned little doll, her voice rang through the entire room. The other singers' voices complimented hers, but she clearly stood out among them all. Traditionally, none of the singing roles were performed by Priests, but now that no one had Gifts except Wilder, it seemed to be a gray area. But since Priests had been trained on the music their entire lives, it appeared there was very little rehearsal needed.

Feather sang out her line in a sweet, clear voice.

"Who in all creation is mighty enough to be my Companion?"

Wilder appeared from backstage, his voice sending a ripple of desire down Rose's spine.

"My Lady,

My heartbeat pulses with the rhythm of a fiery lute, and I will strum your spirit to life."

It was no secret that the Companion sang to seduce the Goddess. The Pageant never stated it so blatantly, but it was clear from the lyrics and the slow melody how the scene was to be played. The Goddess was powerful and strong, but alone. And only the Companion was cocky enough to woo a goddess.

No one had ever been more suited to the role than Wilder.

"My fingers pluck the strings of a delicate harp, and I am gentle enough to awaken your soul."

He sang each note with deliberate slowness, as if he had all the time in the world to sing for the Goddess. Every word was careful and precise, drawing attention to the way his lips formed each sound.

"My lips curve around tender notes of love, and I will breathe a new fire into your heart."

His melody sang in her bones as it had the first time she had heard him perform. Her heart thrummed with the rhythm of him.

Yet he sang for Feather.

She was the full focus of every note. His eyes locked on Feather's as if she were the only woman who existed. He didn't touch her, yet his nearness threatened to consume her, and she seemed to melt under the weight of his presence. Feather looked up at him with eyes that drank him in, unable to look away. Her thin cotton dress seemed alive because of how she trembled beside him.

Rose watched them without blinking. She crossed her arms over her chest and tapped the pearl dagger in her jacket absently. Her mind was blank, filled only with a sizzling sound that blocked out all thought.

Wilder finished his song, then put his hand on Feather's waist, pulling her into a waltz across the makeshift stage. He held her close, expertly leading her through the steps. Her eyes sparkled with delight. Wilder pulled her to a stop, and they hit their final note with a triumphant pose. Feather giggled, out of breath yet radiant, and Wilder squeezed her shoulder in support.

Rose felt the eyes of everyone in the room on her, waiting for her reaction. Her heart was a violent rush of wind, but her mind was the quiet center of the storm.

"I thought Kieran was playing the Companion," she said calmly.

Wilder shrugged. "Since we aren't sure when he will be released, we started rehearsals without him." He laughed. "Believe me, he knows every line and will catch up quickly."

She merely stared at him.

"Well?" Wilder spread his arms to encompass the stage. "Aren't you going to say anything?"

"Sure. How about this?" She leaned back against the sofa with arms crossed. "I don't think it's appropriate for you to get on stage and literally try to seduce a child."

Wilder's voice was dead calm. "What did you say?"

At this, Quinn stood and took Feather's hand in one smooth movement. Feather's face was a mixture of confusion and hurt, but Rose barely noticed as Quinn pulled the girl out of the room, with everyone else following quickly behind.

She stood and met Wilder face to face at the front of the stage. "She's a child, Wilder. It's inappropriate—"

"First of all, Feather is not a child. She's only two years younger than we are. Second, I was not 'literally' trying to seduce her." He took a step closer, dropping his voice to a low growl. "You, of all people, should know what it is like when I seduce someone." He pointed at the stage. "And that was not it."

Rose raised her chin in challenge. "It sure looked like seduction to me."

Wilder's voice was still a quiet growl. "It's called acting, Rose."

"It didn't look like acting."

Wilder leaned in and whispered, "That's because I'm very good at it."

"Does she know you were acting? She seemed very ... responsive ... to your performance."

Wilder shook his head in disbelief. "I can't believe after everything we've been through, you would suddenly be jealous of Feather. She's part of your crew."

Rose narrowed her eyes. "I didn't say she was the one at fault."

He gave a harsh laugh. "So, you think I got caught up in the role and decided to seduce her?"

"It wouldn't be the first time, would it?"

The words flowed from her mouth as smooth and sharp as a dagger. Rose was looking him in the eyes and saw the words hit their mark. Guilt stirred at the edges of her thoughts, but her blood was still singing with a jealous fire, and it drowned out her remorse. Wilder's jaw tensed, and she felt his furious reply just below the surface. His eyes longed to fight with her, and she basked in the warmth of a battle to come.

But instead of meeting her words with a challenge, he drew in a shaking breath and didn't say a word. His eyes never left her face as he took hold of her wrists with a deliberate motion. She looked down to find flames dripping from her fingers, trailing across the stone floor to bathe the stage curtains in a flickering glow. The fabric curtains remained undamaged, but the bandage on Wilder's hand scorched against her wrist. He didn't flinch, but merely stared at her in accusation. Rose ripped her wrists out of his grasp, suddenly extinguishing every flame in the room.

Her chest constricted at the sudden darkness, yet she was grateful for the chance to hide the blush of shame on her cheeks. As her eyes adjusted to the light coming from the open door, she could see his face held the same silent accusation. She wanted to look at his hands, but her skin tingled with the confusing heat of fire and desire and shame, and she didn't know what another touch from her would do.

She spoke so quietly that she wasn't sure he would hear. "Well, at least that's done."

Accusation turned to confusion, and his voice came out in a ragged whisper. "What's done?"

"The prophecy. I fulfilled it."

He scowled and reached for her hand, but she had already fled, leaving him in the dark.

21

Rose awoke to a Sentinel in her room. She pulled the covers to her neck in the illusion of protection and stared at the armored figure in terror. The Sentinel's head tilted in exasperation, and Rose could practically feel the eye roll beneath the mask.

Rose sat up and crossed her arms over her chest with a huff. "Which one are you?"

The Sentinel peeked out into the hallway before removing her hooded mask. Dany shook out her golden curls and gave Rose an irritated look.

"It's time to wake up."

Dany sounded like Mims, and Rose scowled.

"Don't give me that look," Dany said, further cementing the similarities with Mims. "You've slept later than any reasonable person should."

Rose didn't feel like a reasonable person after her fight with Wilder, which was why she had been avoiding the world by staying in bed. She gave Dany a haughty sniff. "I'm not a reasonable person. I'm the Marked."

Dany rolled her eyes so Rose could see it this time. "That's very clear. However, you only sleep late at the temples. And considering that you always go to bed extremely early, it's … unusual, don't you think?"

Rose slowly narrowed her eyes, calculating how much Dany knew. "What's your point?"

Dany's eyes twinkled, and she chewed on her bottom lip as if containing a smile. "Just a casual observation that I thought would be helpful."

"It's not your job to help me," Rose growled. "Your job is to hold me prisoner."

Dany snorted a laugh. "If that's true, I'm doing a terrible job." She went to the wardrobe and pulled out one of the gray training uniforms. "Put this on. You're obviously in the mood for a fight, so I'm going to find you one."

Rose grumbled but put on the uniform and tied her hair up in a knot. As she followed Dany down to the training room, her muscles prickled in anticipation.

Dany was right. Rose was itching for a fight.

Just entering the training room invigorated her. The familiar sounds and scents reminded her of training as a child. Mims employed the same trick when Rose and her siblings had nervous energy. Go train and fight it out, then come back home and act like reasonable little people.

Rose hoped the same trick still worked on her.

Dany looked around the room, then pointed at a young man, summoning him to their side. He jogged over with an easy smile.

"Good morning, Marked One. Sentinel." He acknowledged them both with a quick bow. "How may I assist?"

Dany patted him firmly on the back. "Jace, the Marked One has some pent-up energy she needs to release. I think you can give her exactly the type of match she needs. Are you up for that?"

He grinned, brushing his soft brown curls off his forehead. "Anytime." He gave Dany a sly smile. "Will you be joining us?"

"Not today," she said with a laugh. "The Marked One needs your full attention. Can you handle her?"

"Oh, I can definitely handle her," he said with a wicked grin.

It was Rose's turn to roll her eyes. How had Dany managed to find someone just as cocky as Wilder? Jace wasn't as stunningly handsome as Wilder, but with his golden skin and playful smile, he was quite attractive. "You remind me of someone, but don't worry. It won't stop me from thrashing you."

"Challenge accepted." He bowed, and they stepped into one of the sparring zones.

She settled into a fighting stance, but he merely looked at her. "Don't you want to take some time to warm up first?"

"Fighting you *is* the warmup," she said with a feral grin.

He laughed and beckoned her forward with a quick flick of his fingers. "Let's dance, sweetheart."

Jace had not attended dance class, but his footwork was good enough that he would probably be a natural. They danced around each other, testing for weaknesses, looking for an opening to attack. Rose determined they had similar height and reach, but Jace was more muscular than her and could probably outlast her, especially considering how lax her training had been lately. If she wanted a chance to beat him, she needed to be quick.

And even though they were just sparring, she still wanted to win.

Rose hit him hard and fast. She used a move that was even more effective when she had the wind at her command, but now all she had was her own momentum. Jace was surprised by the sudden movement, and she bore him down to the mat even quicker than she expected.

She pressed her knee against his chest and smiled with sweet triumph. If she could get a few more quick wins in this morning, perhaps some of her lingering anger would dissipate, and she could think clearly about what she should do about Wilder. She looked down at Jace to savor her victory and realized he didn't appear to be struggling at all.

In fact, he seemed to enjoy her conquest a bit too much.

He chuckled lightly, despite her knee on his chest. "I thought this would be a friendly exercise. I didn't realize your only goal was to get me flat on my back." Her shocked expression made him laugh even harder.

She hopped up and straightened out her gray uniform, pulling herself together. "Funny," she said. "Perhaps it's just that you're a little too comfortable losing."

He made a humming purr of satisfaction as he stepped smoothly to his feet. "I like an aggressive woman. There's no reason you shouldn't get exactly what you want." He grinned as if he knew what that was. "I underestimated you, but it appears you came to play." He stripped off his shirt and rolled his muscular shoulders around in preparation. "I will do my best to exhaust you."

She took a step back. "That's unnecessary—"

"Are you surrendering to me?" His eyes glittered wickedly.

She cleared her throat to calm herself. "Jace, this isn't the training I was expecting today."

He circled her, looking for a weakness. "You usually have boring trainings?"

Rose imagined the times she had *trained* with Wilder. "No, definitely not boring."

Jace's eyes narrowed as if he spotted an advantage. "Then where is he?"

"Who?" She answered too loudly.

He grinned, having won the point. "Whoever it is you

usually train with. Why am I the one dancing with you and not him?"

She spun around, avoiding his grip. "I train with whom I choose."

"Do you fight with him often?"

She snorted. "That's an understatement."

"So, what did you do this time?"

She didn't see the direct attack until she fell into it.

"I accused him of seducing a child."

Jace's eyes widened, and his precise footwork faltered. "He seduced a child?"

She tried to slide out of his grasp, but he caught her. "Well, she's seventeen ..."

Jace laughed and let Rose slip away. "You called a seventeen-year-old a child? I can't imagine either was happy about that."

She ground her teeth in a grumbling reply. "It wasn't the worst thing I said."

"Ah ..." He gave an appreciative nod. "You like to fight dirty."

"I wouldn't say I *like* it. It's not a strategy I'm proud of." She ducked, avoiding a direct hit.

"I think it's good to use whatever tactics works. Don't beat yourself up for it. That's my job." He grinned and threw a punch, which she sidestepped.

"Yes, but sometimes I hurt people when I don't intend to." She let her guard down, and Jace twisted her arm behind her back until she couldn't move.

"You haven't hurt me," he whispered in her ear. "Maybe he's not the right partner for you."

She froze in his arms, suddenly realizing she had not considered her Spark all morning. Despite sparring and a wide variety of emotions, there were no errant flames anywhere in the training room. Jace held her wrists with her twisted hand pressed against his bare chest, and she wasn't burning him at all. And aside from a few small verbal jabs, she had not injured him with her words either.

The only one she hurt was Wilder.

Jace held her firmly, and Rose sensed he was waiting for an answer. She was in a vulnerable position, and she whispered her admission, "I only want to spar with him."

She felt Jace's soft exhale against her neck. He gently uncurled her arm and released her. He bowed to her, but Rose thought it was just an excuse to give her one more thorough look up and down.

"If you change your mind and need a new partner, you know where to find me." He winked, picked up his shirt, and swaggered out of the training room.

Knowledge

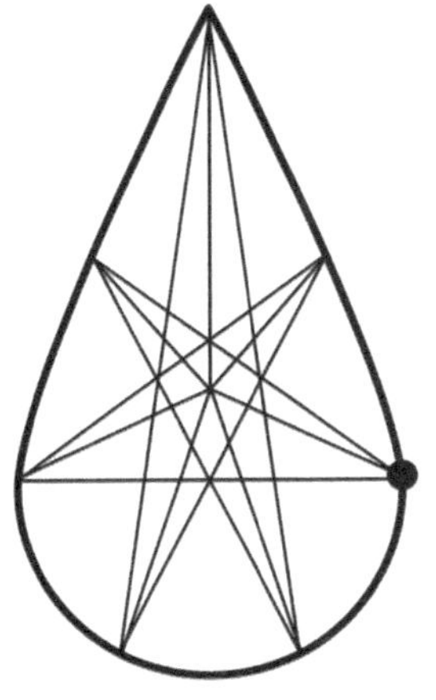

Instinct

22

The sparring session did not scratch Rose's itch for a fight. The Sentinels and Adopted avoided her as she stomped back to the Heart amid their procession. Her body still sizzled with unspent energy, and her mind flitted from one angry thought to the next. She was furious with Wilder, with Vaylan, with the Sentinels and Adopted, with herself. She couldn't pin down a single source, so instead the rage pooled into a bubbling inferno in her mind.

"You seem troubled."

Rose's head spun to find Vaylan suddenly at her side. "That's an understatement," she growled. "You should leave me alone or else have your Sentinels ready to restrain me when I attack."

He chuckled softly. "They're always prepared. And since you can't hide the murderous rage from your face, they know to be watchful."

Rose wished she could hide her emotions, but her scowl deepened. "A conversation with you will not ease that rage, so it's best if you just let me be." She focused again on the road ahead, trying to block out the sight of him.

"It's nice to know that your anger is not always directed at me."

She could tell he was fishing for information, but she ignored him.

"Every time we return to the Heart, you are in a worse mood than when we left. Even though I have released each of the Chosen, you're always more troubled than before." He paused for dramatic effect. "I wonder who causes such unrest in your spirit ..."

She clenched her fists and noticed two Sentinels draw slightly closer. She growled but relaxed her hands. "There is a lot to be angry about in the City, Vaylan."

He nodded his head. "Yes, we still have a lot to do to bring this City under control."

Her angry thoughts sharpened into focus, targeted at him. "Really? Do you actually have plans for this City? Or are you just trying to destroy it?"

"Obviously, I have plans, Rose. You just never ask." He focused his attention forward, as if she was in the wrong for not asking him about his evil plans.

She ground her teeth and masked her anger in a sugary sweet voice. "So, Vaylan, what are your plans for feeding this City? There is no time to harvest enough food to feed everyone, and before long, all the animals will be extinct. If you are to be the Lord Founder of this City, how will you feed it?"

"Of course you would be most worried about food." He smiled as if feeding people was a childish concern. "There is plenty of food for my Adopted and Sentinels until we can harvest a crop naturally. People require more important things than food to survive. That's where I'm focusing my plans."

Her gasp ended in a choking sound. "More important than food?"

He gave her a patronizing smile. "Yes, Rose. Freedom from the Goddess's control."

"But people will starve! Maybe you can hoard enough food for your people to survive, but your Adopted and Sentinels make up a tiny portion of the City. What about everyone else?"

He shrugged. "They aren't my concern."

She stopped walking, unable to process his words.

He sighed patiently and stopped beside her, halting the entire procession without a word. "Rose, I have many plans for this City. I know it's hard for you to understand because you have not seen what I have seen. But I have faith the City will be remade better than before."

She could barely speak with the cold dread shivering through her. "Everyone else will die, Vaylan. That doesn't bother you at all?"

"I am focused on the spiritual heart of this City. I can't spend my time thinking about the individual people or else the new City I'm creating will crumble."

"Then let it crumble!" she roared. "Your vision is not worth it."

His smile was sad, as if he was being misunderstood. "The old ways must die before something new can be born. It will take time, but we will rebuild a new City from the ashes of the old."

She crossed her arms angrily. "And how will you rebuild if you won't allow your Adopted to marry? I think that will hinder your plans to rebuild the population."

He gave a hearty laugh. "They aren't forbidden from having children, Rose. Just getting married." He gave her a knowing look. "Everyone will need to support the repopulation effort, and it's best if they embrace their freedom and don't limit themselves to only one person."

Her mouth fell open. She tried to find words, any words,

but realized nothing she said would change his mind. She closed her mouth, put her head down, and started walking again.

Vaylan joined her, and the rest of the procession followed. He clasped his hands serenely inside his robes, then said, "It will all work out in the end, so there's no need to worry. I have plans for everything."

"Yes, you obviously do." Her energy from earlier had fled, leaving only a bitter resignation.

"You have only briefly glimpsed the prophecies, but to me, they map a clear way ahead. Those who follow me have a future that is certain, and those who choose their own path will have to face the consequences of that decision."

"Even your son?" She had not mentioned Wilder to Vaylan, hoping that if she didn't speak his name, Vaylan might forget about him. However, she knew that was just an illusion.

Vaylan's smile froze on his face, but he answered smoothly. "The prophecy gives Wilder a choice of two paths. It's still unclear which he will choose."

Rose blinked as she tried to process this new information. "The prophecy gives him a choice? I thought everything was predetermined?"

Vaylan's smile remained, but she detected irritation behind his eyes. "Prophecy is complex, Rose. It's difficult to explain to one untrained in its intricacies." He ignored Rose's eye roll. "Besides, Wilder's choice affects no one but himself."

As Rose tried to puzzle this out, Vaylan stopped. They had arrived back inside the Heart, and he stood outside of a large white tent she hadn't seen before.

"Would you like to come inside and share a meal with me? I'm sure the Adopted have prepared something extraordinary." He lifted the tent flap with a wide smile, but she remained outside.

"I'm sure they did," she muttered. She knew that the tent where she usually ate got food from the same source, but she couldn't bring herself to eat at Vaylan's table. "I'll go eat with the rest of the Adopted."

He nodded as if that was an excellent choice. "I'm glad you draw comfort from spending time with them. It's an encouraging sign of the future to come."

She was about to spit out a nasty reply when Walter stepped out of the tent. She gasped and only barely stopped herself from calling out his name.

Vaylan studied her with shrewd eyes. "You remember Walter, don't you? You met him when he was serving as a copyist in the prophecy tent."

She swallowed down her fear and replied calmly, "Ah, yes, he looks familiar. Interesting to find him here inside your tent."

Walter stood between the two, seemingly at peace. His face was relaxed, and he turned his head as they each spoke.

"He's a fascinating man. I enjoy having him entertain me with his stories."

Rose remembered a story Walter had told about a butterfly whispering in his ear and delivering him to the home in Peculiarity. She wondered what Vaylan would make of that story.

"I hadn't pictured you as someone who required bedtime stories, Vaylan."

His grin was entirely too pleased, as if he knew she was deflecting to hide her true feelings.

"I guess you should be off to dinner with the Adopted," he said casually. "Unless you've changed your mind and want to share a meal with me now?"

His eyes were sharp, knowing he had closed the trap.

Her mind screamed to not leave Walter alone with Vaylan, but she couldn't admit how she knew Walter without putting him more at risk. Vaylan knew Walter was important to her, but hopefully he didn't yet know why.

"My feelings remain the same," she said coolly. "I hope you have a pleasant evening."

She walked away, desperately hoping Walter was in better control of his Spark than she was.

23

Rose picked at the food on her plate, unable to eat. She was hungry after the long walk back to the Heart, but with every bite of the simple stew, she wondered if she was eating some animal now extinct. It didn't help that she couldn't identify what kind of meat it was. She had never been a picky eater, but now she was torn between letting the food go to waste or refusing to eat it.

"Good evening, Marked—um ... Rose."

Rose's head popped up at Yasmine's quiet voice. Hunter stood next to her, holding two bowls of stew in his hands.

"May we join you?" Hunter hesitated, studying Rose's face closely. "Unless we are disturbing you?"

She considered telling them just that, except their faces were so hopeful, and she didn't have the heart. She held out her hand to offer them the empty seats across from her. They sat down so quickly that Hunter almost spilled their stew.

"Marked—Rose, we've been reading the prophecies so much since the last time we spoke," said Yasmine breathlessly.

"It's so interesting to actually meet someone discussed in

prophecy," said Hunter. They were both studying her as if she was an unusual specimen. "We have so many questions, but we don't want to be impolite."

Rose shrugged and continued to pick at her food. "I find the whole situation bizarre, but I can't say it's impolite."

They grinned at each other as if this was the permission they sought. Yasmine carefully spread out a rumpled piece of paper onto the table in front of her.

"First question," said Yasmine. "How close are you to Wilder?"

Rose choked on her stew. Even though she was the one who previously mentioned his name, she didn't know if she wanted to discuss him with them. She thought back to the night before when his lips hovered right above her own, waiting for her to be brave enough to kiss him.

"Fairly close," she said slowly.

Hunter and Yasmine looked at each other with concern, as if Rose wasn't there.

"We should tell her," he said. "Maybe she can do something."

"But it's a prophecy," said Yasmine. "That means it can't be changed."

"Maybe it can. Maybe the prophecies are warnings about a possible future, and nothing is predetermined."

Yasmine sighed. "Hunter, we've talked about this for hours. Why even have a prophecy if it won't happen?"

Rose cleared her throat.

"Oh, sorry," said Hunter sheepishly as he brushed his blond hair away from his forehead. "It's an old debate."

Rose arched an eyebrow. "Since I doubt the two of you will solve it at the dinner table, maybe you should just tell me what we are talking about?"

Yasmine took a deep breath and nodded. "Yes, Mark—Rose. We found a prophecy about Wilder."

Rose tried to speak calmly, despite her pounding heart. "Really? What makes you think that?"

"Like all prophecies, it is a little vague," admitted Hunter. "But we feel fairly certain this is about him."

"And have you shared this information with anyone?" She couldn't imagine what would happen if Vaylan realized Wilder was the Chosen, not the crew. Would Vaylan hunt him down? Or use Rose against him?

"We've discussed it with our group of friends that meets to debate the prophecies," said Hunter. "But on this one, we were all in agreement."

"I'm glad you came to me." Rose tried to instill as much authority into her voice as possible. "Tell me what it says, and I will let you know if you are correct." Her brain spun in circles, trying to think of any reasonable argument she could give against Wilder being the Chosen.

Yasmine smoothed her hands carefully over the paper. "We believe Wilder is ... the Scion."

"Uh ..." Rose's brain skidded to a halt. "The Scion?"

Hunter nodded. "Being the Lord Founder's son, we believe the prophecy refers to him as the Scion."

Rose thought back to her conversations with Vaylan and remembered him calling Wilder the Scion.

"The reason I asked if you were close to him is that the prophecies about him are ... grim." She frowned as if in apology.

Rose snorted. "Every prophecy I've read is grim, so I didn't expect otherwise. What does it say?"

Yasmine touched her paper with delicate fingers. "It's part of a long passage, but the important line is this: *The Scion sees death in the eyes of the Goddess's own.*"

A shiver ran down the back of Rose's neck. "That definitely sounds grim," she said. "But what does it mean?"

Hunter and Yasmine looked at each other and shrugged.

"We aren't exactly sure. Our best guess is that the 'Goddess's own' means a Priest. Does he know many Priests?"

She almost laughed when she considered how many Priests Wilder was currently surrounded by. Soon he would know every Priest in the entire City. But before she could laugh, a cold certainty settled over her heart. The knowledge gripped her and wouldn't let go.

She was the Priest.

The title had almost abandoned her, but in this context, she knew she was the Goddess's own. She had so many questions, and these two young Adopted were the only ones she could discuss it with.

"So, he will see death in this Priest's eyes? What does that mean? Surely your group had some ideas."

Hunter leaned forward, a bit of his excitement returning. "We have a lot of ideas. We just aren't sure which theory is correct or if there is anything we can do about it."

"We can't," said Yasmine softly with a flick of her long black braid.

Hunter cleared his throat. "The most straightforward meaning is that there is a Priest who wants to kill him."

Rose turned to Yasmine. "So, you think this prophecy can't be avoided?" She felt her voice rise in panic. "You believe Wilder will be murdered by this Priest?"

Yasmine leaned back with wide eyes. "I didn't say that," she said quickly.

Hunter scooted closer to Yasmine to catch Rose's eyes. "It doesn't say the Priest succeeds. Maybe he sees death in their eyes but stops them."

Yasmine nodded enthusiastically. "Yes, exactly. In that case, Wilder couldn't stop the Priest from looking at him with death in their eyes, but that doesn't mean he dies."

Rose clung to this tiny scrap of hope but continued her interrogation. "But what if this Priest gives up all their murderous thoughts and doesn't get angry anymore? Maybe the Priest can stop this from happening at all."

Yasmine shook her head sadly. "That's not the way prophecy works. Someone is going to look at Wilder with death in their eyes."

Rose's voice came out as a whisper. "What if she promises to never look at him again? Could she save him?"

The two of them exchanged a nervous glance. They sensed she was talking about something more than they understood.

Yasmine stretched out her hand to Rose with a tender look. "We are just guessing at what it means. All we know is that something *will* happen. We won't truly understand the prophecy until after it happens."

Rose slammed her hand on the table, rattling their dishes. "What good does that do? Why study the prophecies at all if we can't do anything about it?"

The two of them didn't answer, but Rose saw them take hold of each other's hand underneath the table. She rubbed her forehead, hiding her face, trying to get her breathing back under control.

"Thank you for telling me," she said with a fake semblance of calm. "I appreciate your concern about Wilder."

Yasmine bit her lip and stared at the hand she had placed protectively over the paper before her. She didn't raise her eyes when she whispered, "There is another prophecy."

Rose's heart hammered in her chest. The two of them appeared nervous to share this prophecy, despite the other prophecy's mention of death.

She spoke in a flat voice. "Tell me."

Hunter fidgeted with the collar of his shirt, plainly embarrassed. "This other prophecy didn't come from the book of prophecies that are regularly shared with the Adopted. There are different levels of knowledge given to those who are most pleasing to the Lord Founder, you understand?"

Rose bit back the hiss of "Heresy!" that threatened to escape her lips. "Of course. That sounds like Vaylan."

Hunter squirmed in his seat. "Well, this other prophecy came from someone at a higher level than us, and they weren't supposed to share it with anyone. They could get in a lot of trouble if anyone finds out."

Her teeth clenched in fury, but she ground out the words, "I don't care if your friend crept into Vaylan's room and ripped the prophecy out of his hand while he slept. Just tell me what it says."

Yasmine gave a small squeak of fear at the ferocity in Rose's voice, but she slid her hand off the paper and read the words that stopped Rose's heart:

"*The Scion will be converted or destroyed.*"

24

———

The next day, Rose arrived in the throne room later than usual, and the procession was almost ready to depart. Vaylan spoke to his Adopted, clasping each of their hands as they waited patiently with bowed heads.

"Disgusting, right?" said Kieran. Two Sentinels stood at his back, but they didn't appear very concerned with guarding him. He rolled his eyes at Vaylan but couldn't flip his blond hair because of the ropes on his wrist. "Some people are just too good at being charming."

She snorted. "You and I have never had that problem."

He smirked and gave her a mock salute.

Vaylan moved to the next Adopted. Rose and Kieran were too far away to hear what the woman said, but Vaylan patted her on the hand and gave her a wide smile.

"Ugh," Kieran groaned. "We're lucky Wilder didn't inherit that dimple. If Wilder wasn't such a goody-goody, he would have formed his own evil empire long before now."

"How dare you say that?" she hissed. "Wilder is nothing like him!"

Kieran raised an eyebrow and as he did, a tear fell off his lashes. He took Rose's hand.

She was suddenly small. Rose/Little Kieran heard a delighted laugh and turned to find a young Wilder, around ten years old, grinning at an older woman. His small brown hand held her wrinkled hand as if they were old friends. She smiled, then handed Wilder a loaf of crusty bread. He gave her a very serious sign of the Goddess, which caused her to sigh with delight. Wilder ran off, but before he turned the corner, Little Kieran watched him break the loaf in half and hand it to an even smaller young Quinn, who pushed his enormous glasses further up his nose and stared at Wilder in awe.

Rose blinked and found herself back in the throne room, looking at Kieran who had a smug look on his face. "See the similarities?"

She crossed her arms over her chest. "Except he shared the bread with Quinn."

"Yeah. He's a goody-goody." He rolled his eyes. "I said that."

Vaylan walked to the tunnel leading out of the Heart, and Kieran and Rose joined the procession.

"I always wondered where he learned it," said Kieran. "From the first moment the headmaster brought him into the school, Wilder knew how to get what he wanted. I thought he was just naturally gifted at manipulating people, but it turns out he was trained by a pro."

Rose growled. "Are you purposefully trying to irritate me?"

He snorted a laugh. "It's not hard. I'm used to the challenge of trying to irritate someone like Quinn. You're so easy to irritate that it's almost accidental."

"I'll pretend that's an apology."

"There's no need to take up an offense for Wilder's sake," he said. "Like everyone else, I have always been in awe of

Wilder's talents. The only difference is that I don't allow him to use those skills on me so easily. Wilder needs people like you and me. We keep him on his toes."

"You're including me in your competition with Wilder?" she said with an arched brow.

"Not in mine. You have your own rivalry with Wilder to deal with. You're able to get under his skin in ways that I've never been able to." He grinned wickedly. "It's quite satisfying to watch him come undone."

Even though their conversation was prickly on the surface, Rose enjoyed talking to Kieran. She was never worried about being too mean to Kieran since he was usually too catty or disinterested to notice. And occasionally she glimpsed a heart beneath the rough exterior that was reminiscent of her own.

"I assume Rev was right," he said. "She almost always is, which is very annoying."

She turned to look at him, confused at the jump in topic. "Yes, it's annoying, but what is she right about this time?"

He held out his bound hands, and Rose hesitantly took them.

Rose/Kieran sat on the floor of the tent with the last remaining members of the crew. She lounged casually on a bedroll but leaned forward to listen.

"Do you think something happened to her?" asked Kai. "She's come to check on us every time she's returned to the Heart. Why hasn't she come yet?"

"I'm sure she's fine," said Fitz. "She probably got distracted by something."

Rev's eye narrowed shrewdly. "No. That's not it. I bet something happened between her and Wilder. She probably said or did something stupid, and now she's too ashamed to come admit it to us." She gave an irritated grunt. "I told her she was being an idiot, and now she's proving it—"

Rose ripped her hand away from Kieran, who couldn't stop laughing.

"Hilarious," she said drily. "That's not why—"

"You don't have to explain to me," he said. "I'm not a fan of Rev's girl talks either."

She sighed and decided to share at least part of the story. "I heard the prophecies the Adopted believe are about Wilder."

"Do you honestly believe the prophecies will come true?" he asked.

"I don't know," she admitted. "But if they are true, I feel like I need to do what I can to stop them."

"That sounds like a sure path to insanity to me. If they are true, there is nothing you can do to stop them. That's what makes them true." He shook his head as if agreeing with Rev's pronouncement that Rose was an idiot.

"Then what do I do? Sit back and wait for the worst?"

"No. If they are true, there is nothing you can do. But if they aren't true, that's where things get interesting." He tapped his lip in thought, despite his bound hands.

"If it's not true, then why would it matter at all?" she asked.

"Because he believes they're true." Kieran nodded to where Vaylan walked with his adoring Adopted. "And that makes him weak."

"Weak?" she asked. "He has access to all the prophecies. He knows them better than anyone and can manipulate their meaning however he wants."

"Yes, but don't you get the sense that he *actually* believes? Sure, he's manipulating everyone around him, but at his core, I think he's a true believer. And because of that, you know how to hurt him." He gave her a catty look. "I've seen you use that trick before."

She frowned at the accusation, mainly because she

knew it was true. Wilder believed in the Goddess, and despite being a Priest, she had used that information to hurt him.

"But how does that apply to Vaylan? He twists every prophecy to mean exactly what he wants. I don't see any weakness to exploit."

She felt dirty discussing someone's faith as a tactical vulnerability, but Kieran seemed unaffected.

"I'm sure as soon as he shows weakness, you'll pounce. Just keep your eyes open to see what he's trying to hide. Especially if it's something he's trying to hide from himself."

They walked in silence for a while as she considered his words. He was right. Rose needed to watch Vaylan for a sign of weakness, and instead of worrying if the prophecies were true, she needed to know what Vaylan believed about them. That way, she could be prepared when Vaylan manipulated them into coming true.

She thought back on her fight with Wilder and wondered if it was possible that Vaylan could have manipulated the prophecy about the Chosen. She had never read it herself and had only taken his word for it. Maybe Vaylan was to blame for her fight with Wilder. Maybe hurting him wasn't her fault.

She glanced at Kieran. "I'm sure the crew will be happy to see you." She dropped her voice to a whisper. "They're working on the Pageant."

"It's unusual that people are actually happy to see me," he said. "How much have they prepared?"

"They've built some props but haven't rehearsed many scenes. I'm sure Feather will be happy that you can take the role back from Wilder."

Kieran tilted his head for a moment in thought. Then he burst into laughter. "Ah ... I see it now. I'm sure that performance was stunning."

Rose answered stiffly. "Of course it was. They are both very skilled performers and—"

"Oh ... no, I meant *your* performance. I bet you were magnificent." He sighed dreamily. "And when you exploded in a jealous rage, I imagine Wilder's answering fury was just delicious." He licked his lips as if savoring a tasty treat. "I can't wait to have the crew back together again."

Rose crossed her arms and ignored him for the rest of their walk.

25

R ose thrust her Spark into the crystal, determined to catch the Goddess. At the last crystal, the Goddess had been unresponsive, barely noticing Rose at all. This time, Rose refused to leave without answers.

White light shimmered around her, settling into the familiar glow of the Goddess's sanctuary. The Goddess sat at the table with a cup of tea untouched before her. She looked as if she hadn't moved at all since the last time Rose had visited.

Before the Goddess could snap her away, Rose sat across the table and grasped the Goddess's hand. The Goddess blinked her sad eyes open.

"Yes, child?" Lady Erenne always spoke with passion and a twinkle of arrogance that proved she knew more than everyone in the room. But now the Goddess's voice was dull and lifeless. It did not inspire confidence in Rose. She was afraid the Goddess would fade away at any moment, so she asked a question she hoped only a goddess could answer.

"Are prophecies real?"

The Goddess's eyes shifted, bringing Rose to the center

of her attention. "Prophecies? I'm dealing with some things here, Rose. I don't have time for theological discussions."

Rose blinked her eyes, unsure if she understood correctly. "You're a goddess but don't have time for theology?"

The Goddess sighed, and a bit of her arrogance returned. "It's a complicated question. We don't have time to discuss the nuances."

"You better talk fast, then." Rose gripped the Goddess's hand tighter, unwilling to let her slip away. "I have heard some disturbing prophecies about your precious Wilder, so tell me what I need to know."

At Wilder's name, the Goddess stirred. "I heard him singing ..." Her eyes shifted to a faraway look. "He's always had such a lovely voice."

"Goddess!" Rose squeezed her hand tightly until her attention returned. "I need an answer. Are these prophecies real? Can I change them?"

The Goddess's haughty look returned. "Rose, it's not a simple answer. Prophets are not known for making their predictions clear. In fact, I think they derive a sick pleasure at watching us try to determine exactly what they're talking about. If they had any intention of making their prophecies useful, they would just come out and say it clearly. Instead, they enjoy watching us act like fools who think they understand."

Rose drew back at the sudden vehemence in the Goddess's voice. It appeared Rose touched on a sensitive subject. She was glad to see some of the Goddess's fire return, so she pressed further.

"Does that mean I should continue down the same path as before I heard the prophecy? Or should I change my decisions to stop it from coming true?"

"Changing your decisions might be the very thing that

causes it to come true." Her eyes took on the faraway look again. "The prophets at the Origin gave me a prophecy that I believed ensured I would have a long and happy life with the Companion. Because of that, I lived with no fear that anything could happen to him. When he died, I believed the prophets were wrong, and I hated them. But when the prophecy finally came true in an unexpected way, over a thousand years later, I realized they were right." Her face hardened. "And I still hate them."

Rose sagged in her chair but refused to loosen her grip on the Goddess's hand. "What should I do? The prophecy says I will deliver Wilder into Vaylan's hands and that he will be converted or destroyed. I can't pretend like I never heard it. I have to do something. I couldn't live with myself if I caused Wilder's destruction."

The Goddess's eyes focused on Rose so intently Rose's spine straightened in salute. The Goddess spoke in a low voice, sharp and deadly calm.

"Here's the answer you came to find, the answer I know from personal experience. Prophecies are real. You are not smart enough to decipher them. And if Wilder is bound for destruction, there is nothing you can do to stop it."

Rose blinked and opened her eyes in the pitch-dark cave, a cold chill wrapped around her heart.

Rose pulled her jacket tighter as she walked toward Temple Knowledge. Four of the seven crystals were now dark, and freezing air from the mountains flowed freely through the streets. Rose had only been outside the City walls to feel the cold air once in her life. When Caed was younger, he snuck outside to test if his Gifts worked outside the City walls. Rose found him and dragged him back before they both got executed. He was willing to die to test a scientific theory.

She wasn't willing to risk Caed's life for science, and she wouldn't risk Wilder's life on a prophecy.

Rose was relieved to see the temple, even though it meant once again convincing the Priests to abandon their home. She ignored Vaylan's usual spiel to the crowd about bringing freedom from the Goddess's control and headed for the temple steps.

She stopped when he delicately cleared his throat. "Rose, you are forgetting something."

"Are you seriously asking me to beg for mercy again? We all know this is the best way to do this. I convince them to leave peacefully, and you are a merciful tyrant."

He clicked his tongue in disappointment. "Rose, you know the prophecies must be fulfilled."

"What if they aren't?" She crossed her arms in defiance. "I could refuse to darken the next crystal. I could refuse to beg you for mercy. I could leave right now. Then where would the prophecies be?"

His eyes bored through her and rifled through her fears and insecurities. His stare never wavered as he said, "You could leave, but you won't."

Of course she wouldn't leave. She had to continue darkening the crystals to save the Companion and stay close to Vaylan to be near the rest of her captured crew. She would never leave the Priests in the temple to be tortured by Vaylan.

The prophecy clinched around her neck so tight she could barely breathe. She sank down into the dirt and begged Vaylan to show mercy to the Priests.

She could feel his smug grin, even though she couldn't see it. She wondered if Kieran was laughing to see her brought so low.

Vaylan touched her hair with a soft hand. "Because of your plea, Marked One, I will show mercy. You may go convince the Priests to leave peacefully."

Rose stood, wiping the dirt off her white pants. She refused to look Vaylan in the eyes.

"Just surrender to the prophecies." His voice was gentle, as if he was trying to be kind. "Use the prophecies to guide you, and you will be like the leaf floating on a stream instead of the rock being crashed by a wave. I want you to find peace, Rose. Rely on the certainty of the prophecies. You will deliver the Chosen into my hands, and all will be well."

Rose lifted her head slowly, scared to see what was written on his face. "You mean, I *did* deliver the Chosen to you. You had them all, and now you are releasing them."

Vaylan's eyes widened a fraction, and he looked at Kieran standing between two Sentinels. "Ah ... yes, of course." He grinned. "That's obviously what I meant." He winked and walked away in dismissal.

Rose stood frozen to the spot. Vaylan knew. He knew Wilder was the Chosen. She mentally kicked herself for not realizing it sooner. Of course he would know. He knew the prophecies inside and out. Of course he would have recognized Wilder in the words, especially after discovering Wilder had all the Gifts.

Vaylan removed Kieran's black robes to reveal the white clothing underneath. The next part of the script was hers, so she walked into the temple to convince the Priests to leave.

At each temple, the Priests seemed easier to convince. It was almost as if they were waiting for permission to leave. She tried to inspire them with the plans for the Pageant and the hope that the Goddess would restore the City, but they all seemed so downcast. She told them to find Wilder and everything would be fine. Find Wilder, and the Goddess would return. Just find Wilder.

After the Priests scattered, she took her usual spot on the temple steps as Kieran waited for sunset to be released.

"So, what are you planning?" asked Kieran.

"What do you mean?" she asked.

"I can tell you are plotting something. From your expression, I can't quite tell if it makes you angry or sad."

She looked the other direction, embarrassed that her emotions were always so clear. "Both," she admitted.

Kieran tapped his lower lip in thought. "The decisions you make while angry are spectacularly bad, but I'm not sure what your sad decisions are like."

She gave him a flat look. "I've thought about this decision for several days, so it's not something I'm doing recklessly."

Kieran raised an eyebrow but didn't respond.

"I won't let Vaylan win," she whispered harshly. "No matter what his Goddess-cursed prophecy says, I will not let him have Wilder."

Kieran gave her a quick nod of approval, then a slow smile curved his lips. "If anyone can fight destiny, it would be you, Rose."

She studied his face to see if he was mocking her, but he merely watched the sunset with a relaxed expression.

Vaylan strode out of the temple with his dark blue robes flowing behind him. He smiled serenely as Rose and Kieran stood to meet him at the bottom of the steps.

"Time to fulfill another prophecy, Rose. Cause the Chosen to suffer, then send him off into the dark."

She pulled the pearl-handled dagger out of her sheath with a resigned sigh.

Vaylan made a thoughtful sound. "Unless there is some reason you think this isn't necessary."

She wanted to hiss that none of his prophecies were necessary, but she knew what he implied. Why would she need to cause Kieran or the others any suffering if they weren't the Chosen?

Kieran looked at her with an eyebrow raised, curious what she would do. She closed her mouth on her angry retort and sliced quickly across Kieran's hand.

Vaylan chuckled quietly as he walked back up the stairs.

She quietly wrapped a bandage around Kieran's wound. When she finished, she pulled a letter out of her jacket. "Give this to Wilder."

He held the letter carefully with his uninjured hand. "What does it say?"

"It's for Wilder!" she said in a too loud voice. She cleared her throat and replied more calmly, "He will understand when he reads it."

Kieran raised the letter to his lips and inhaled. "He's going to be furious."

She punched him in the arm. "Stop that. Just give the letter to him and walk away."

"Of course I will, Rose." The anticipation in his eyes said he definitely would not.

She narrowed her eyes at him. "Leave now before I get the dagger back out."

He gave her a pleased smile and headed out into the dark.

26

Rose lay in bed, wondering how Wilder reacted to her letter. Did he get angry and crumple it up? Did he shed a tear onto the page? Or did he read it stoically, unaffected? She rolled over, ashamed of herself for imagining a passionate response.

After Kieran walked away with her letter in his pocket, Rose ate a small meal but barely tasted it. Adopted had bowed to her in deference, but she ignored them. When she went to her room early and said good night to her Sentinels, one of them snorted a laugh.

The Sentinels would be surprised to learn she didn't plan to leave her room tonight.

She sighed and shoved off the covers. Despite only wearing a short white slip, she was sweating. Her small room felt stifling hot, even though the City's air was colder than ever. The hot air threatened to suffocate her, but it didn't compare to the fire still raging in her chest.

She was thankful the only light came from a thin stream of crystalline on her lamp. If it had been a candle, it would've flickered as wildly as her thoughts. She closed her eyes, trying to smother the flame of her anxious mind.

Then suddenly, a cool breeze sprang goose bumps to life across her legs.

"You like to act tough, but inside, you are just a coward."

Rose's eyes shot open at Wilder's scathing words. He stood in the corner of her room, barely visible in the thin crack of light. He wore black leather pants and a tight black shirt with sheaths crisscrossing his chest. His face was completely neutral, but she sensed the fury pouring off him.

She wished her thin nightgown had a sheath for her dagger, because she suddenly felt very vulnerable.

"How did you get in here?" she whispered.

"You aren't the only one with experience sneaking in and out of temples." He didn't move from his position. He just stared at her with hard eyes that shook her confidence.

"You shouldn't be here!" she whispered sharply, glancing at the door as she stood. "There are Sentinels right outside my door."

"I'm not afraid of Sentinels." He refused to whisper, and his arrogance infuriated her.

"This is exactly what I hoped to avoid! Don't you see? Because of me, you entered a temple with Vaylan inside. This is how the prophecy will come true!" Her voice rose in desperation, but he remained unmoved.

"I'm not afraid of prophecies."

"Well, maybe you should be!" she hissed. "The Goddess said prophecies are real."

He narrowed his eyes at her. "Did she say you could prevent a prophecy from coming true?"

Rose ground her teeth, angry that he could see through her. "I will stop him, Wilder. He will not get what he wants. I won't let him have you."

"You say that like I belong to you," he said with a chilly calm. "Yet you walked away from me very easily."

"This was not easy!" she snapped, all pretense of whispering gone. "I agonized over this decision."

"Instead of saying this to my face, you wrote a letter and handed it to Kieran, of all people. He watched me read the whole thing, salivating like a dog waiting for scraps to fall from the table." Wilder growled softly. "He's lucky I healed his hand before he gave me the letter."

She crossed her arms defiantly. "So, you read the letter, got angry, stormed over here, and broke into the temple? If I did something like that, you would be furious. And if Vaylan finds you, it will be because of me. It means I'm a danger to you. My decision to avoid you was right."

Wilder crossed the room in three brisk strides until they stood face to face. "You think it's right to abandon me without a word? To leave and never see me again? Honestly, you are even more like my father than I realized."

She drew back at the harsh words. "I am not like Vaylan," she whispered.

"Besides the ease with which you abandoned me, you also place these prophecies above your relationship with me or anyone else. You've wrapped all your decisions around prophecy instead of what's best for the people you care about."

"Of course I was thinking of you! That's why I have to avoid you. To keep you safe."

"Can't you understand how insane that sounds?" His voice was a low roar, and his body practically vibrated with the force of his restrained anger.

Her fury burned in response, and she rose on her toes as if prepping for a fight. "Is prophecy any more insane than someone who can manipulate crystalline? Someone who can cause a fire that won't burn? Someone that can heal or grow food or any of the other miraculous things we do in this City? I believe Brother Owyn had a Spark, and I believe in his words."

His voice finally dropped to the low rumble of a whisper. "Do you have more faith in a dead man than you do in me?"

The question caught her off guard. Did she have faith in Wilder? Did she trust him with her life and his own? She couldn't bring herself to say the truth, so she let Brother Owyn do it for her. She dug through the wardrobe until she found Yasmine's paper with prophecies, then moved closer to the thin strip of crystalline to read.

"Listen to this: *The Scion sees death in the eyes of the Goddess's own.* The Goddess's own, that's a Priest, me. And the Scion is you, the Lord Founder's heir."

He laughed. "Rose, those words mean nothing! Or rather, they could mean anything! I can't believe you are making decisions based on this!"

"You aren't listening!" she said sharply. "These words *mean* something. Can't you feel it? Listen to the whole passage:

"*The Scion is beloved by many yet is still lonely, still set apart.*

Guilt rips at the soul until all the Scion sees is death.

The one who could heal instead brings torment.

The Scion sees death in the eyes of the Goddess's own."

As Rose read, the fury dissipated from Wilder like steam, and he plopped onto the bed, staring ahead sightlessly. Rose knew he would feel the truth of the words, but she didn't realize how hard it would hit him. She sat down gently beside him.

"That's why I have to avoid you, Wilder. I can't stand the thought of you seeing death in my eyes."

"It's not you," he whispered faintly.

"I'm sure it's me—"

His quiet voice was firm. "It's not you."

"Then who—"

He refused to look at her, only staring blindly ahead. "I always meant to confess to you. I just—"

"Confess?" She was completely confused. "Confess what?"

"The 'Goddess's own' isn't you or anyone else trying to kill me." His voice was so quiet, Rose had to lean closer to hear. "The prophecy means I see death in her eyes because I killed her."

Rose's mind was screaming, but she whispered, "You killed ..."

"I killed a Priest."

His confession was a soft sigh of breath that slammed into her with the force of a hurricane. She couldn't speak while her mind tried to comprehend the words.

"And when you learn why ..." He scrubbed his hands roughly across his eyes, and Rose saw tears glittering on his palms. He drew in a shaking breath, then his shoulders sagged in resignation. "The Priest healed Ylena and would have discovered her secret. So, I killed her."

Rose gasped at his matter-of-fact tone. "How can you say it so calmly?"

His voice rose in pitch. "What do you want me to do? Cry my eyes out? I've done that countless times, and yet I still see Alys's eyes when I fall asleep. Beg for forgiveness? I've done that at her grave so many times, but it hasn't helped. Confess it over and over? Rev has taken my confession so often she stopped accepting payment. But none of it can change what I did."

"Rev knows?" Rose asked in shock.

"Of course she knows. I would have died if I didn't confess it." He sighed. "I was planning to tell you too, I just was—"

"Waiting for a good time?" She stood, unable to sit so

close to him. "When exactly do you think would be a 'good time' to tell me this?"

He closed his eyes and sat unmoving before her. "I knew it would be hard for you to hear. Especially knowing why."

Rose felt her blood boiling and was surprised the room hadn't burst into flame yet. Her voice dropped to a rough whisper. "Because that's how much you loved Ylena ... You killed a Priest for her."

Wilder reached up, grasped her by the arms, and whispered fiercely, "I would destroy the entire City for you, Rose!" His dark eyes were so intense, she couldn't look away. "I know I shouldn't, but I would do it if you asked." He drew in another shaking breath. "But please, for the sake of my soul, don't ask it of me."

Rose blinked down at him, unsure of what to say.

"That's how I'm broken, Rose. No matter how much you hurt me, I will still love you. No matter what you ask ... I would give it." He looked down, embarrassed by the confession. "I showed you the memory of my childhood. My mother abused me, and I couldn't stop myself from loving her. I know Vaylan will ruin this City and kill everyone inside, but even if I had the chance to kill him, I couldn't do it."

He let go of her arms and stood. She couldn't turn to face him.

"Maybe you are right to avoid me," he said. "My devotion only brings destruction."

Her mind was a flood of emotions, anger and jealousy and sadness and pain. She couldn't open her mouth for fear of the wrong words slipping out. She had no idea what the right words were, but she knew plenty of the wrong ones.

She stood unmoving even when she felt another cold blast of wind flow over her. When she finally turned around, he was gone.

27

Rose awoke to a Sentinel in her room again, but at least this time, Dany had already removed the mask. She stood silently above Rose, watching her with wary eyes.

"What are you doing?" asked Rose.

"Trying to determine your mood. At the last temple, you woke up itching for a fight. I wondered if today would be any different."

"Why would today be different?" Rose asked with what she hoped look like a casual shrug.

Dany just looked at her like she was an idiot.

Rose had gotten enough of that look last night from Wilder, so she huffed and rolled back over.

"That's what I thought." Dany threw the covers back and tossed the training clothes onto the bed. "You're in luck. Jace is here. He can assist."

Rose huffed again but slipped out of her nightgown into the training clothes. "Assist with what?"

"You seem to be itching for a fight, along with other ... physical diversions. Jace appeared to be more than willing to accommodate last time." She raised her eyebrows suggestively.

Rose opened her mouth to explain that she told Jace she wasn't interested in the diversions he was offering. But Dany was standing next to her bed in the same place Wilder had stood, and her black Sentinel clothes reminded Rose of Wilder's black Priest clothes, and that reminded her he had killed a Priest for Ylena ...

Her fingertips felt like she had dipped them in scalding hot water. She scrubbed them against her training clothes before any flames could appear. It wasn't safe to think about Wilder right now. She definitely needed a diversion.

She turned to Dany and said calmly, "Yes, let's find Jace."

Jace was unbearably pleased that Rose had come back for another match. His smug attitude was almost enough for her to call it off, except that she really needed some activity to take her mind off Wilder. And if she was going to beat up someone, it was best if it was a willing participant who happened to be as flirty as Wilder.

Not that she planned on thinking about Wilder during this match.

Not at all.

Jace entered the sparring area and promptly removed his shirt. Rose noted each of his muscles as he stretched his arms overhead. She studied him from his soft brown curls to his tanned arms to his muscular legs.

A purely tactical study, of course.

Jace grinned, appreciating the attention. "Imagining what you're going to do to me?"

"I need a good fight," she said. "I'm just wondering if you are strong enough to be a challenge."

He smirked. "Sweetheart, I won't stop until you're so spent you can't even walk out of here."

Yes, that's exactly what she was itching for.

She bowed to him, and the match began.

He was slightly better than her, and Rose had to push herself to keep up. Even though she liked to win, she was relieved that he was more than her match, since she didn't have the energy to pull her punches today. She needed to hit hard and fast and not be worried about injuring a weaker opponent. She wanted to feel the rush of the fight and let it wash away her other concerns.

Jace won several rounds, and Rose was sore from the countless times he flipped her onto her back. As he bore her onto the mat yet again, she remembered training with Wilder and how he had flipped her on her back, then pinned her in place with the slightest touch. The thought gave her such a rush of energy that she twisted to the side and used her hip to tip Jace off his feet and onto the ground.

His breath escaped in a whoosh, and she ended up straddling him, one arm twisted at his side and the other hand pressed firmly against his chest. She held him in place as she tried to catch her breath until she felt the soft rumble of his laugh under her palm.

"I don't know what your other sparring partner did to upset you, but I'm so glad you found me instead." He tilted his head to look at her hand, still pressed against his bare chest, then followed her arm until he looked her in the eyes. "If you aren't exhausted yet, I have a few more techniques I can show you."

His warm brown eyes promised a lot more distraction. But even without diving into the mass of roiling emotions in her chest, she knew the diversion he offered wouldn't fix anything.

She lifted her hand and stood swiftly. She offered a hand

to help him to his feet, and when he used it to pull her close, she took a step backward and shook his hand awkwardly. "Um ... thanks for the fight."

He chuckled softly and gave a brief nod of understanding. "I'm happy to spar with you anytime your other partner isn't available. You can always come find me and let me know what you need."

Rose watched him leave, knowing she had made the right decision, but when he turned around and playfully bit his lip, she almost second-guessed herself.

Dany appeared at Rose's side and startled her out of viewing his exit.

"That's it?" Dany sighed. "I was pretty sure I figured out your type, but I guess I'll have to try again," she said with a shrug.

"My type?" asked Rose.

"Yeah, I thought his flirty playfulness would be a good match for you." Dany tapped the hooded mask in her hands as she thought. "Were you worried that he was too young?"

"Too young?" Rose hadn't even thought about his age.

"If it helps, he's probably almost eighteen." Dany shrugged.

"Probably?" she squeaked. Considering her accusation of Wilder seducing a child of seventeen, Rose's cheeks reddened at her hypocrisy.

"We were in the first group of Gifted children stolen by the Wardens. They weren't sure if the tea would suppress our Gifts enough to keep us all alive, so they didn't bother keeping detailed records on us. None of us know our actual birthday, but I know Jace is close to my age."

Rose felt a slight relief that she hadn't quite fallen from her moral high ground, but it was soon followed by sadness. "Most Priests don't know our true birthdays either. We celebrated birthdays based on the Pageant when we were sworn to the City.”

Dany’s eyes took on a faraway look. “Sometimes I wonder what my life would have been like if the Wardens had never discovered that tea. I would have grown up in a temple, learning the same things you did … We might have been part of the same family.”

Rose’s eyes widened as she considered the possibility. Based on Dany’s age, she would have been their younger sister. Caed would have loved not being the baby.

Dany sighed. “But without us, the Wardens wouldn’t have defeated the High Priests. They might still be in power, even now. Things might have stayed the same for another two hundred years.”

This wasn’t the sort of conversation Rose ever imagined having with a Sentinel. But Rose felt a connection to her, almost as if she were a sister Priest. “I hated the High Priests. I dreamed of the day they would be overthrown. But the City I imagined was the same as before, just without High Priests.” She pointed to the world outside the training room. “This isn’t what I imagined at all.”

“I didn’t know what to imagine,” said Dany. “I spent my entire childhood locked inside the Warden’s Den, only to be released for a battle we ultimately lost. Everything here feels so strange and complicated. Most days, I’m grateful to just have a place to hide.” She tapped the mask in her hands with a rueful smile.

“But why do you follow him?” Rose felt like this was a dangerous conversation, but she had to know the answer. “Vaylan isn’t a good person. Why follow him?”

Dany looked at her with piercing eyes. “Why do *you* follow him?”

“Um …” All of Rose’s explanations were too complex or too dangerous. “I have my own reasons.”

"So do I. So does everyone here." Dany shrugged. "When the Wardens fell and we lost our Gifts, we had nowhere to go. Training to fight their battles was the only thing we knew. Vaylan offered us food and a place to stay, and beyond that, he offered us a purpose: to fight in defense of him and the Adopted. And in defense of you. That's enough for most of us."

Rose turned her head slowly, barely catching Dany's last two words.

"For now."

PURITY

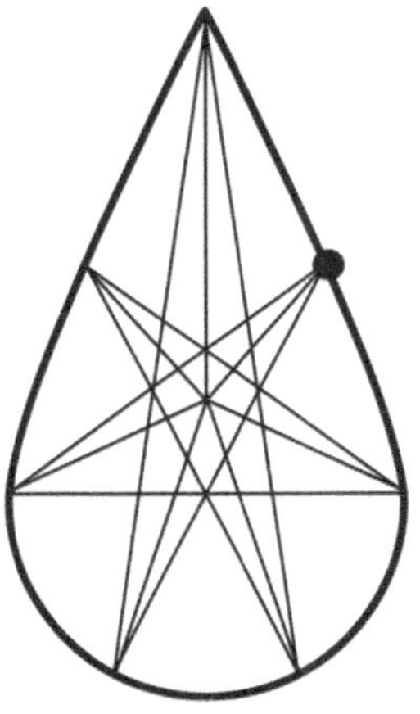

DESIRE

28

Rose entered the shadowy black tent, and Rev, Kai, and Fitz immediately stopped talking. They studied her face just a little too long before Kai jumped up to give Rose a hug.

"We worried about you when you didn't stop by," he said. "We thought something might have happened to you."

Rose gave Rev a pointed glare. "Not all of you were worried. I saw that some of you assumed I was hiding after acting like an idiot."

Rev mumbled, "Leave it to Kieran to use the Goddess's Gift to gossip."

"He just as easily could have told me as showed me. If you didn't want me to find out, maybe you shouldn't have said anything."

Kai lowered his voice as if Rev and Fitz couldn't hear. "Ah ... so I take it she was right?"

Fitz bit his lips to hide his grin, and Rev leaned back on her palms with a smug expression.

Rose sniffed haughtily. "I've had a lot to handle out there. I haven't just been sitting around chatting like the rest of you."

Kai crossed his arms and gave her a hard look. "We're being held prisoner, Rose. It's not a vacation."

Fitz snorted. "I see how our lavish accommodations might confuse you. Why, just look at our spacious bathroom!" He pointed to a chamber pot that was off in a corner but still open to the rest of the tent.

Rose's eyebrows scrunched in irritation. She was still fuming and didn't like it when other people tried to be grumpier than she was.

"It's just a few more days," she said. "I'm shutting down the crystals as fast as I can, then you can join Wilder and the others for the Pageant."

Rev narrowed her eye, but Kai took Rose's arm with an excited grin on his face. "You saw them? They're already rehearsing?"

"Yes, and Kieran should have taken over by now. I'm sure everything is going great." She tried to inject her voice with cheeriness to avoid Rev's suspicious glare but was unsuccessful.

"Wilder was playing the role of the Companion with Feather?" Rev's question was casual, but Rose knew she was poking for information. And Rose was not in the mood for a girl talk.

"Yes, but Kieran returned, so I'm sure that's fine now." She said the words quickly, hoping to move on to something else. "Anyway, I just wanted to stop by to check on you. I should probably go—"

Rev stood up slowly and walked directly in front of Rose. She was at least a foot shorter, but she didn't need height to be intimidating.

"It's good you stopped by, Rose. You're our only link with the outside world, and without you, we wouldn't have a clue what's going on." She narrowed her eye, looking closely at

Rose's face. "And even when you do stop by, it's still hard to tell."

Her searching gaze irritated Rose. She deserved to have some secrets, and since she hadn't sorted out her feelings yet, she didn't want to discuss it right now. Especially not with Rev. She made her voice as sincere as possible. "Since it's so difficult being a prisoner, perhaps it's best if you just focus on yourself for now. No need to waste time being nosy about anyone else."

Kai's eyes widened, and he took a small step away from Rose, leaving her alone in Rev's line of sight. Rev's lips curled in the smallest of smiles.

"It's my job to be nosy. Secrets aren't healthy. It's best to get them out in the open."

"Out in the open?" Rose clenched her fists, nails biting into her palms, but she kept her voice calm. "You just want to keep all the secrets for yourself."

"That's my job," Rev said smoothly. "People need to talk about their secrets so they don't erupt suddenly and do something stupid."

Rose felt the words pointed at her, but she refused to flinch. "Perhaps if you had done your job better, you would have sat Wilder down for a girl talk before he killed a Priest," she hissed.

Rev's eye widened. "Ah ... well, that explains it."

"That explains what?" Rose asked with an angry huff.

"It was just a matter of time before he told you. If we hadn't been stuck in such strange circumstances, I'm sure he would have already told you by now."

Rose could barely keep her voice from raising to a shout that the Sentinels outside could hear. "Who cares *when* he told me? He murdered a Priest out of some bizarre infatuation he had for Ylena. Then he confessed it to you, who covered up his secret."

Rev crossed her arms over her chest. "It's my job to hear confessions, ranging from silly to despicable, but no matter what I hear, I do not speak of it. If the High Priest of Purpose himself had come to me and confessed that he was abusing children, I would have listened to his confession in a professional manner. After he finished, I would have immediately killed him, but I would never speak of what he confessed to me."

"And that was your plan with Wilder? To cover up his sin indefinitely?"

"I do not feel one scrap of guilt for listening to Wilder confess," said Rev calmly. "I'm honored that he reveals his burdens, hoping I can carry part of the load. Once you get yourself back under control, you will realize the trust he placed in you by confessing to you, too. Hopefully, you haven't mucked that up beyond repair." She patted Rose on the arm. "No matter what you said, I'm sure Wilder will forgive you."

"Forgive me?" Her voice was a barely contained shout. "You think I'm the one who needs forgiveness here? He's the murderer." She lowered her voice to an angry hiss. "He's lucky the High Priests never found out. His execution would have been one of the few that was justified."

Rose initially thought Rev was moving to hug her. It wasn't until Rev pulled the dagger from inside Rose's jacket and held it to her throat that she realized she was in trouble. Rev's other hand clutched Rose's jacket collar, and she pulled Rose's face closer to her own, with the dagger poised at her throat.

"It's time for a little girl talk, okay, Rose?" Rev's voice was deadly calm, and she stood with the confidence of one who would be listened to. Judging by Kai and Fitz's surprised expressions, they would not attempt to stop her.

Rev took a deep breath, and the cold dagger shifted

against Rose's skin. "I accept you as the leader of this crew. Even if you occasionally muck it up, you make a good Alpha Wolf. However, I am the Mama Bear. I will gladly let you lead, but if you threaten any of my cubs, I will take you out. Wilder is my cub, and if I ever hear you say anything even as remotely threatening as what you just said, you will not live to regret it." She dropped her voice to a throaty whisper. "Do you understand?"

"I understand." Rose spit out the words between her clenched teeth.

Rev's smile held an edge as sharp as the knife. "The good news is that you are also my cub, so I'll pretend the threat you just made was a slip of the tongue. I'll give you one more chance to be a good baby cub."

Rose ground her teeth but didn't respond.

Rev tilted her head and stared up at Rose with a steady blue eye. "You and Wilder have a fun combative relationship, which I hope never changes, but Vaylan has you all twisted up inside. You have to get that poison out of your system if your relationship with Wilder is going to progress. I'm willing to hear your confession or you can try to figure it out on your own, but you must ask yourself the hard questions before you ruin everything."

Rose's emotions swirled with anger at being condescended to, fear of the cold metal at her throat, and surprisingly, a faint sense of guilt below the surface. She bit her lips to hold it all inside.

Rev lowered the dagger, then slid it back into Rose's sheath. "So ... anything you want to confess?" she asked in a business-like manner.

Rose didn't answer. She straightened her jacket, then walked out of the tent without looking back.

29

Rose was still fuming as she sat down to eat. Most days, she found Rev to be fun yet wise, but this time, she had gone too far. Rev had turned the situation back on Rose when Wilder was the one who had committed murder, and it infuriated her. She already knew Wilder's smile let him get away with a lot, and now she realized that included murdering a Priest.

She had hoped her expression would be enough to make people leave her alone, but apparently, the Adopted weren't the best at picking up on her mood. They still bowed and waved and greeted her with blessings despite her continued glare.

Hunter and Yasmine were just as oblivious to her mood. They sat down across from her with delighted smiles.

"It's so good to see you ... Rose," said Yasmine.

Rose wondered how often they spoke about her using the title Marked One if they still stumbled over her name when they saw her. They both stared at her so earnestly that she tried to put on a kind expression before getting rid of them.

"Good evening to you both. I'm too busy—"

Hunter spoke over her escape. "We hoped you would be here tonight." He stood up and waved across the room before sitting back down with a big smile. "We invited our friends."

Rose groaned as three girls and one guy sat down on the benches surrounding her. When she had been a Priest eating in the dining room, the other Priests knew when to avoid her based on the look on her face. What was wrong with the Adopted that they couldn't pick up on that?

Yasmine pointed to the two girls who sat next to Rose. "That's Darby and Farrow." She pointed at the guy next to her. "This is Athary, and beside Hunter is Sian. The group of us get together to talk about the prophecies. They were all so jealous to know how often we've talked to you, so we said they should join us for dinner since you are always so nice to talk to us."

Nice? Rose didn't have a reputation for being nice. She rubbed her forehead, trying to decide if she could contain her simmering rage long enough to escape politely or if she should just yell at them to set an example for anyone else who wanted to disturb her at dinner.

Hunter leaned across the table to look at her with wide eyes. "We read some more prophecies that don't make sense, and we want to ask you about them."

Rose gave a harsh laugh. "A prophecy that doesn't make sense? Well, that's new."

Athary didn't seem to pick up on her sarcasm, because he nodded eagerly. "Yes, we thought so, too, Marked One."

She sighed. "It's just Rose."

The group turned to one another and sighed as if she had just bestowed on them the greatest honor.

"Thank you ... Rose." Farrow said her name as if it were a treasure.

"This has been fun, but—" Rose tried to grab her bowl

to leave, but Darby pushed it out of the way to spread some papers on the table in front of them.

"Here are the prophecies we've been reading," said Darby. "We'd love it if you could explain them to us."

"Me?" Rose barked out a laugh. "What makes you think I can explain prophecies?"

Athary looked at her as if he wasn't sure she was serious. "Because a prophecy said you could."

"Of course it did," she said dully.

They all smiled, happy they knew the right answer.

Darby reached for a paper that Farrow had laid out. "Here is one that we don't understand."

When the blacksmith leaves a sword on the anvil
The one with eyes to see will pick it up and wield it
A discarded weapon can be dangerous
Even to the one who crafted it

They all turned eager eyes to her.

"You think I understand that?" she asked.

Yasmine nodded. "Of course. *The one marked by pain can see where others cannot.*"

"Well, that's encouraging." She lifted the paper to take another look. "Why do you care about this specific prophecy?"

"We care about all the prophecies." Sian slipped into the enthusiastic lecture of an intellectual. "This specific prophecy is only shared with Adopted who've reached a certain status. Because there are so few people at this level, there is not much discussion about it."

"Why don't you ask Vaylan?" asked Rose.

They all stared at her like she was crazy.

She spoke hesitantly, wondering if maybe she *was* crazy. "Um ... aren't you his followers?"

Sian looked at her like she was explaining something to a child. "We follow the prophecies. Just like the Lord Founder follows them."

Rose wondered if Vaylan truly knew the theology of his Adopted.

"That's good to know." She looked at the prophecy again. "So, you're interested in this prophecy about weapons? This feels ominous."

"Yes, the words are ominous," said Yasmine. "That's why we want to understand it. Each of us has our own reason to be concerned about dangerous weapons lying about."

"What's your reason?" she asked.

"My parents were killed by the High Priests," said Yasmine.

She inhaled sharply. "I'm ... sorry."

"They were just two of the many people the High Priests murdered. It's why I felt so connected to Brother Owyn. I understood the loss he felt ... the rage ... But he remained strong while in prison and became a conduit for all this wisdom." She touched the papers spread before them with a loving hand. "If there is someone out there forming new weapons, then we want to know about it."

"But it doesn't say new weapons," said Rose. "It says *discarded weapons*. Maybe the Wardens had a stockpile of weapons? I don't think the High Priests had anything like that." She looked up, contemplating her escape route through the full dining hall, when her mouth dropped open.

"It's the Sentinels," she whispered.

Sentinels stood at every entrance, keeping quiet watch. Vaylan had not only picked up the discarded uniforms, but he also picked up the discarded child Champions, plus any other discarded soldier he could find. Even though the High Priests were gone when he came to power, he definitely used the Sentinels to harm the remaining Priests. She turned her focus back to the group to find them staring at her with rapt attention.

Farrow spoke in a breathless voice. "We knew you would explain it."

Darby turned to face Farrow. "I don't recall what the rest of the passage says about the one wielding the weapon. Does it say they *should* wield it?"

Farrow said, "I'm sure it must. The Lord Founder knows the prophecy better than anyone. Why would he choose to go against it?"

"Why indeed ..." muttered Rose.

"About the other prophecy we mentioned ..." Yasmine looked at Rose with concern. "Do you think Wilder is in danger?"

Rose felt a ripple of conflicting emotions at his name. "He might still be in danger." Possibly from her. "But the prophecy about seeing death in the eyes of the Goddess's own ... that one already came true, and he survived."

Yasmine sighed in relief, and Rose was surprised to see Darby, Farrow, and Sian all give the sign of the Goddess.

"Thank you for telling us, Rose," said Hunter. "Obviously, we are pleased Wilder is okay, but every time a prophecy comes true, it strengthens our community."

"I'm sure Vaylan will be grateful for my contribution," she said drily.

"We aren't sure how he will feel," said Sian as she rapped a finger anxiously against the table. "He appears to keep most of the prophecies about the Scion to himself."

Rose raised an eyebrow. "That's interesting. How did you find the ones you shared with me?"

Hunter and Yasmine exchanged an anxious look, but Sian spoke with no reservation. "I discovered them."

Rose gave the young woman an appraising look. "Am I to

understand you gained this knowledge in ways that are not sanctioned by Vaylan?"

Her response was immediate. "Knowledge is available to all."

Rose's face lit up with surprise. "And how do you come by that theology?"

"I was formerly a Priest in Knowledge."

"Formerly?" Rose said hesitantly.

Sian fixed her with a knowing look. "Being a Priest right now is complicated." Rose snorted at the understatement. Sian continued, "When I discovered a whole new form of Knowledge in these prophecies, I took this on as my personal service to the Goddess. I will discover everything about the prophecies I can and share it with as many people as possible. Even if the means of acquiring that Knowledge is somewhat questionable."

Rose was shocked at the amount of devotion required to become one of the Adopted in order to gather Knowledge. She looked at the other members of the group.

"And you're okay having a Priest among you?" she asked.

Hunter shrugged. "Some of the Adopted worship the Goddess, and some don't. The prophecies don't speak out against the Goddess, even though Brother Owyn himself wasn't a believer."

Rose stared at them in shock. This was clearly not what Vaylan was saying at the temples when he commanded the Priests to renounce the Goddess. She had no way to figure out the disconnect other than to ask a blatant question.

"Do all the Adopted think like you?" She kept the rest unsaid—because Vaylan does not.

Darby laughed. "I've never met a group of people that all think the same. But most of the Adopted we've spoken to are united by our belief in the prophecies. We might disagree on a lot, but prophecy is what holds us all together."

"Fascinating ..." breathed Rose. They were tied together by the prophecies. Not Vaylan.

"I have enjoyed talking to you," said Rose truthfully. The group grinned as one. She tapped her lip as if she just remembered something. "Oh, I talked to Vaylan recently about his plans for the City, and I thought I'd share with you, to ease your mind about the future."

They looked at her as if she was giving them a great gift. She felt a little guilty about setting them up, but she liked them and wanted them out of Vaylan's control.

"He said not to worry about food. There is plenty of food for the Adopted and Sentinels. Obviously, everyone else in the City will eventually starve, but you have nothing to worry about for yourselves." She smiled sweetly, hoping she had judged them correctly.

"Everyone?" asked Athary. "What about my parents? They didn't join the Adopted, but they've been fighting for freedom from the High Priests and Wardens for decades."

Rose frowned. "It's unfortunate they aren't Adopted. Vaylan has nothing for them."

Farrow whispered to Darby something about her younger sisters, and Darby squeezed her hand with a worried frown.

"And Yasmine and Hunter, I know you mentioned Vaylan said you shouldn't get married. Luckily, he told me you can still have children together, just not get married. With the smaller population, it's going to be up to all of you to repopulate the City. However, you shouldn't expect that 'repopulating' will be with only one person, if you understand what I mean."

She knew it was a cheap shot revealing it that way, but by their shocked faces, she knew her aim had hit the mark.

Rose tapped her lips thoughtfully as she prepped them for the task she had for them. "Both ideas are pretty extreme. If only the prophecies said something to contradict his plans. I'm sure if prophecy spoke of a better way, Vaylan would listen." She shrugged as if it were obvious. "Someone who truly believed in the prophecies would definitely listen."

She knew she had them when Yasmine reached across the table and grabbed her hand. "Rose, you truly can see where others cannot. We will devote ourselves to figuring out what the prophecies say about this."

"Good," said Rose. "And remember, Knowledge is available to all, so please share whatever you learn with as many of the Adopted as you can."

Sian gave her the sign of the Goddess, and the rest of them nodded eagerly. She wished them a good night and left them at the table, discussing the best way to sort through all the prophecies to find the answers they needed.

She let go of her guilt as they went about happily seeking Knowledge together. They might be a sword crafted by Vaylan, but she was ready to wield them.

30

Rose woke up early to do some training but ended up teaching dance class instead. She never knew which of her Sentinels was which, so she didn't realize Latham had been guarding her, waiting for her to teach another class. When she walked onto the abandoned stage where they had danced before, she noticed one of her Sentinels leave the room. He returned a few minutes later with nineteen other Sentinels behind him.

She stared at them in shock. Before she had time to panic, Latham removed his mask.

"I found a few more people this time!" he said cheerfully. "I'm so glad you are teaching another class. We know you're busy, and we've tried to be patient, but we've been looking forward to this for so long!"

She wasn't in the mood to teach a class, but his enthusiasm was endearing, so she sighed in acceptance. "Okay, but just a quick class." She considered her lesson plan. "It's a shame we don't have any musicians. Music makes everything feel like dance."

Latham's eyes lit up, and he put his mask back on and ran out of the room. Rose had just finished leading the remaining Sentinels through a warmup when two Sentinels arrived, one with a guitar in tow.

Latham removed his mask and said, "This is Thaen. He's agreed to play for our class."

Thaen sat down on the floor near the front of the class and removed his gloves but not his mask.

Rose stared at him, waiting to see his face, but Latham whispered in her ear. "He likes to keep the mask on. He's shy."

A shy Sentinel? Rose opened her mouth to respond but then closed it and began the class.

Rose taught them a simple combination they could repeat over and over. As she counted out the rhythm of the steps, Thaen experimented with a melody until he'd put together something Rose thought was quite lovely.

A shy, musical Sentinel ... Apparently, that was normal.

She divided them into groups and let them take turns doing the combination. She was surprised at how much they got into it. They each picked up the simple footwork quickly enough, but their grace and musicality ranged from slightly awkward to extremely awkward. But despite the fumbling and flailing arms and faces scrunched in concentration, they seemed to enjoy themselves. They waited patiently for their turn on the floor, then cheered as they watched each other.

By the end of class, Rose was pleased with their progress. "You are excellent students. You took this class seriously but also enjoyed yourselves. I would be happy to teach you again when I return to the Heart."

The Sentinels bowed low in respect, then dressed back in their uniforms. She noticed a few with tears in their eyes. She hadn't realized how meaningful the class was to them. Dance was something she had taken for granted her whole life. She never considered what it would be like to only train to fight and not also train for art's sake.

She changed out of her dance clothes and back into her white leather jacket and pants. When she made it to the throne room, she found the Adopted and Sentinels waiting for Vaylan to arrive. And in their midst ... Rev.

Rose sighed and joined her.

"Good morning, Rose! I hope you aren't still upset with me for being so firm with you yesterday."

"Firm?" Rose asked incredulously. "You had a knife to my throat."

Rev gave her a stern look. "Despite your name, we both know you aren't some delicate flower. You don't respond to sweet suggestions, so I had to make sure you knew I was serious."

"I picked up on that," she said flatly.

"Good," said Rev cheerfully. "Because it's upsetting to me when one of my cubs threatens to kill the other."

Rose didn't comment on the hypocrisy of Rev threatening one of her *cubs* for the same offense. She straightened her leather jacket calmly and refused to meet Rev's eye. "Despite the words I spoke in anger, I do *not* want Wilder killed."

"Of course you don't. But because of this prophecy nonsense, combined with your own fears, you aren't admitting what it is you truly desire."

Before Rose could respond, Yasmine ran up and grasped her by the hand.

"Thank you so much for sharing your wisdom with us last night, Rose!" She was breathless with excitement and held Rose's hand as if offering her tribute.

"It was nothing." Rose tried to pull her hand away, but Yasmine held tight. Rev cocked her head to the side, watching the interaction with curiosity.

"We stayed up late reading the prophecies and making notes," said Yasmine. "We've found several things Brother Owyn said that contradict the plans Vaylan mentioned. You are close to him ... Would you be willing to share with him what we found?" She handed Rose a paper with prophecies listed out neatly with notes annotated in the margins.

Rose was amazed at their resourcefulness and depth of sincerity. She read the beautiful words on the page and nodded soberly. "I will share with Vaylan anything he is willing to hear."

Yasmine's face lit up, apparently assuming Vaylan would listen at all.

Rose offered to hand her back the page, but Yasmine shook her head. "You can keep that copy. We made plenty. You said Knowledge should be available to all, right?"

Rose's lips curved into a grin. "Yes, I did say that."

Yasmine bowed reverently and said, "May the light shine upon you, Marked One."

As Yasmine hurried off, Rose mumbled automatically, "And also on you." She read through the prophecies with a smile, then looked up to find Rev watching her curiously.

"What is it?" Rose asked.

Rev looked around the throne room as several Adopted caught Rose's eye and smiled shyly. Two Sentinels bowed low to Rose before moving into their formation.

Rev whispered in amazement. "What have you been doing out here?"

"What do you mean?"

Rev continued to study the room, and when Vaylan walked in, her eye darted between groups of Adopted and Sentinels, studying their reactions.

"Haven't you noticed?" whispered Rev. "The dynamics are completely different from the last time I was in this throne room. What have you been saying to the Adopted and Sentinels?"

Rose shrugged. "I had a few meals discussing prophecy with the Adopted, and I've taught the Sentinels a couple dance classes."

Rev used her bound hands to cover her laugh. "Well, keep doing it, honey. Keep doing it."

Despite Rev pretending that everything was fine between them, Rose spoke little on their walk to the crystal. Rev tried to start a few conversations, but Rose just mumbled agreement and didn't engage.

She didn't want Wilder dead, but she couldn't just forget what he had done. It infuriated her that Rev could act like it wasn't a big deal. He had been keeping this secret the whole time Rose knew him. How could he let her fall in love with him without mentioning it?

When they arrived at the crystal, Vaylan turned to summon her with his usual pageantry, but she moved past him without a word and smacked her hands against the crystal.

She blinked in the sudden white light. The Goddess sat in her usual position, unmoving.

Rose crossed her arms over her chest. "It must be nice to be a goddess and just sit around all day."

The Goddess slowly turned her head to look at Rose. "Aren't you in a pleasant mood?" Irritation flickered behind her eyes. Rose preferred that over the sightless stare.

"I'm dealing with a lot, including your precious Chosen One, so I could really use your help."

The Goddess sat up straighter in her high-backed chair

and stared at Rose. "You're asking me for help? You had the help of my so-called *Chosen One,* but you abandoned him."

Rose's mouth opened in surprise. "How do you—?"

"I'm a goddess, Rose." Her voice was full of haughty disdain. "I can see beyond these walls when I choose."

Rose snorted. "So, you only paid attention since it was your special Wilder? Did you keep listening? Do you know what he did?" Rose smacked her hands down on the table and leaned closer to whisper. "He killed a Priest. One of *your* Priests."

The Goddess steepled her fingers on the table in front of her and gave Rose a cool stare. "I didn't expect you to be a tattletale, Rose. It's quite unbecoming."

Rose stood up with a sharp inhale. "You're turning this around on me, too?" she hissed. "A Priest is dead. And no one in this whole Goddess-cursed City cares but me."

The Goddess raised her eyebrow. "It's ironic how you are so pious, considering you recently tried to strangle me with your bare hands."

Rose's lips tightened at the accusation. "Everyone is happy to point out my mistakes, but you and Rev and everyone in the City act like Wilder can do no wrong. Well, he did. And if you knew and still gave him all your Gifts, then I don't understand you at all."

The Goddess stood smoothly from her chair and moved directly in front of Rose. Her voice was a low threat. "You are right, Rose. You don't understand me at all."

She leaned so close that Rose could pick out gold flecks in her eyes that looked like individual shining suns. Rose couldn't breathe while pinned by the Goddess's stare.

"And if you don't understand why I chose Wilder, then you don't deserve him."

The Goddess tapped Rose on the forehead, and she opened her eyes back in the Underneath.

31

Rose fumed silently as they walked toward Temple Purity. Was Rose truly the only person who cared that Wilder killed a Priest? The High Priests got away with killing people for years while the Goddess did nothing. Apparently, she didn't care who you killed as long as you didn't say anything bad about Wilder.

The Goddess really got on her nerves.

Rose glanced at Rev and found her watching with a strange expression. Rev would often size her up, judging her with that cold blue eye and reading Rose in a way that felt very intrusive. But this time, Rev's curiosity seemed almost tentative.

There was nothing tentative about Rev.

"What is it?" asked Rose.

"You really see her?" she whispered.

Rev's expression turned almost shy. She scooted closer to Rose as they walked and asked, "Do you see her each time? The Goddess." She spoke in gentle awe but seemed almost embarrassed, as if asking a very personal question.

Rose had spoken to the Goddess so many times now she had forgotten how miraculous it was. The Goddess didn't exist in physical form anymore, so when Rose touched the crystal, she traveled to another dimension and had whole conversations in the blink of an eye. It was a miracle beyond Rose's understanding, which she took for granted.

But to be fair, the Goddess was really irritating.

"Yes. I see her," said Rose. When Rev's expression kept searching, Rose continued, "I have conversations with her, which are less productive than you might imagine, before she sends me back into my body ... however that happens." She shrugged. "I'm not exactly sure how it works."

"What is she like?"

Rose let her interactions with the Goddess cycle through her head. "Beautiful and demanding. Infuriatingly arrogant. She has a strange sense of humor, but as time passes, she just seems more and more sad." Rose chewed on her lip. "I don't think she is well."

"It must be hard to be a goddess." She squeezed Rose's arm. "I'm glad she has you."

Rose turned to her with surprise. "You're glad she has *me*?"

Rev's expression turned thoughtful. "I discovered a group of the Goddess's followers when I was young. The way they spoke about hope and liberation resonated with me. I believed there was more to life than what we experienced in the Underneath. There was something more, and the Goddess held the key."

Rev sighed, lost in the memory of the past. "But to us, the Goddess was more of an ideal, a symbol of deliverance. She was an icon to cling to when all seemed lost. But through everything, I never truly imagined her in human form until she appeared as a shining beacon atop the amphitheater during the Uprising. And she still lives." She turned to Rose with a small smile. "But she's alone now. Separated from her people in a different way from before.

And if the Companion is fading ... I'm sure she needs someone to talk to. I'm glad she has you."

Rev had a very optimistic view of what Rose's interactions with the Goddess were like. She continued walking in silence, unable to admit that she hadn't been a very good confidante of the grieving Goddess.

Vaylan's performance at the temple was as dramatic as usual, but when Rose followed Rev's roving eye, she noticed something different. Rose usually spent her time rolling her eyes at Vaylan, then groveling for mercy, but this time, she studied the crowd as Rev did. The Adopted at his side watched him with reverent faces, and there were people in the crowd that nodded along to his sermon about being set free from the Goddess's control. But beyond those few adoring fans, the crowd was unconvinced.

Unconvinced and cold.

Despite the previously warm weather, the people of the City had always worn jackets and boots and scarves for the sake of fashion, but now they piled on mismatched layers and still shivered. The Underneath was still relatively the same temperature as it had always been, but despite the sunshine, the City above was getting colder every day.

The people did not appear to enjoy this freedom as much as Vaylan believed.

When Rose played her expected role and begged Vaylan to show mercy to the Priests, Rose peeked out from her bowed head and followed Rev's eye to the crowd. The ones surrounding Vaylan still looked at him in adoration, but behind them, several people gave the sign of the Goddess.

Rose stumbled over her litany of pleas in surprise. She thought this crowd was the faction of people who had been following Brother Owyn, calling for the overthrow of the Priests, but it appeared the dynamics of the City were shifting once again.

After she convinced the Priests to abandon the temple, she sat with Rev on the temple steps.

"What's the plan?" asked Rev. "When the sun goes down, you slice me up, I head into the City, and you sneak out later to find us?"

"No," Rose said firmly. "It's not safe for me to be with Wilder. Vaylan will use me to get to him. Even though I'm angry, I refuse to be the cause of his destruction."

"You're being ridiculous." Rev tossed her blond ponytail. "You are pushing away the one person most *gifted* to help you defeat Vaylan because you're afraid."

Rose clenched her jaw and refused to respond.

Vaylan glided down the steps with his Sentinels in tow. He merely stared as the last sliver of sunlight disappeared, then turned to Rose without a word.

Rose knew he was once again testing her to see if she would admit that Wilder was the Chosen, not Rev. She wouldn't let him win. She pulled out her dagger and gestured for Rev's hand.

Rev held out her hand calmly and clenched her teeth without a sound when Rose cut her.

As Rose bandaged her hand, Rev hissed quietly. "I can't wait to get out of here and find Wilder. I can read him like an open book, so the second I see him, I will know if he has any part to play in this nonsense."

Rose grumbled, "I'm sure you'll decide it's only my fault."

Rev huffed in exasperation, then disappeared into the dark City.

"Are you worried about sending another pretty girl off to find Wilder?" Vaylan asked.

Rose had assumed he went back inside the temple, so the sound of his voice surprised her. When she realized what he said, she turned around slowly to face him, a cold fury raging in her gut.

"What are you implying?" she asked slowly.

"Oh, nothing." His dimple proved it was definitely something. "I know they were once your friends, so it's probably strange knowing they are all out there without you."

"Yes," she said flatly. "Strange."

"Ah well, I'm sure you've assisted with many Pageants in the past. You can leave it to others this time."

"Pageant?" She said the word even though she couldn't breathe.

He chuckled. "I know they're planning a Pageant."

"And just how do you know that?" Rose often spilled secrets when she got angry, but she was sure she had never breathed a word about the Pageant around him or any of his people.

"It's how I know everything, Rose."

She wanted to punch the smug look off his face. "Don't you even say—"

"*The Bard's music must be sung again before the final crystal goes dark.*"

She stared at him in astonishment. "If you know that, why would you allow it?"

"It's not about me allowing it, Rose. It's prophecy. It will happen."

"But it's a production honoring the Goddess. Why would you want that?"

He laughed. "It's not about what I want. It's about what the prophecy says will happen. I'm just prophecy's faithful servant, as are you. We do what is foretold."

Rose couldn't believe he would just let the Priests hold the Pageant with no consequences. He had to have some end game in mind. He had to be planning something for the Pageant.

She gasped. "That's when you think I ..." She shut her mouth before she could finish the words ... *will deliver the Chosen into your hands.*

His lips curled in a grin as if he had heard the unspoken words. He shifted into his usual condescending tone. "Rose, most of the prophecies are fixed, with no hint of ambiguity, but there are some that speak of two paths."

The Scion will be converted or destroyed. She refused to speak that prophecy aloud.

"I find it fascinating," he said. "Two paths ... Did Brother Owyn know which path would be chosen? Or does it mean those two paths haven't been laid yet?" He shrugged. "I'm not sure. All I know is that it *will* be one of those two paths. There are no others."

She saw it in his eyes. Wilder would be converted or destroyed, and he honestly didn't care which. Each would be beneficial to him in some way. He truly seemed interested in discovering which it would be. His face was serene, as if he was the enlightened one.

"You don't care," she whispered. "No matter who you hurt along the way, you don't care at all."

He smiled in the approximation of compassion. "I was once like you, Rose. I cared. A lot. I burned with rage and passion and fury." He sighed, as if in nostalgia for his foolish past. "I loved and hated, sometimes unsure which was which. But during my time imprisoned with Brother Owyn, I learned a better way. And I moved beyond those simple emotions into peace."

He held out a raised palm, and the crystalline lamps flickered gently. "My rage is still there, Rose. Bubbling like a pool of crystalline inside. But I've learned to use it to give me power. To give me strength. You have the potential to harness that same power. Take your fury and compress it into a core that can ignite you." He clenched his fist so tightly his hand trembled. The crystalline pulsed in a steady rhythm. "If you can control your rage, squeezing it into the smallest pinprick of energy, you will discover your true power."

His words chilled her. She wanted to deny that she was like him, deny that she was filled with rage and passion and fury, but he was right. She burned day and night with passion she sometimes wasn't sure was love or hate, and the realization made her sick.

"But what about love, Vaylan?" she whispered. "Without the passion, what happened to the love you used to feel?"

He lifted his still clenched fist, and with a serene face, he raised a shaking pinkie finger. Crystalline lanterns along the street pulsed wildly. The crystalline glow coming from inside the temple flared in a bright flash. Vaylan used his other hand to gently lower his finger, and all the lights resumed their steady glow.

"Love is too dangerous, Rose. It has taken a long time to gain this control, and I won't let anything disturb my peace." He stared at his clenched fist and laid his other hand atop it as extra protection. "Because if I relax even for a moment, I might burn this whole City to the ground."

32

R ose had already crawled into bed when a Sentinel entered her room. The Sentinel threw a pile of clothes at her, then cocked their head as if commanding her to dress. Rose would have flat-out refused, except the hand on the Sentinel's hip made her believe it was Dany, and Rose was intrigued.

But just in case it wasn't Dany, she went into the bathroom to get dressed. When she came back out, the Sentinel was gone, so Rose opened her window and climbed down the tree to the courtyard. Even though she hadn't planned on sneaking out since she was avoiding Wilder, she had still picked a room with a sturdy tree outside her window.

Just in case.

Rose ducked into shadows in the courtyard, passing two Sentinels that didn't feel quite like Dany. She jogged down the steps and into the City.

She found Dany leaning against a lamppost.

"Finally!" Dany was dressed in similar clothing to Rose with mismatched pants, cloak, and scarf.

"There were a lot of layers to put on!" said Rose. "Where are we going?"

"You'll see." Dany winked and started walking.

Rose fell into step beside her. "Why are you helping me sneak out? I thought you were supposed to be guarding me?"

"I choose to translate 'guarding' you as 'protecting' you. And I think you and everyone else around you will be safer if you find an outlet for your excess energy."

After Rose's conversations with the Goddess and Rev and Vaylan, her fingertips tingled with the thought of flames. That's why she had tried to go straight to bed, but maybe Dany was right.

Dany gave a tentative smile. "Besides, I thought this was what people our age were supposed to do. I grew up locked inside the Warden's Den, and I kind of wanted to try sneaking out for myself."

Rose gave a sly grin. "I never sneak out, so I might not be very good at it."

Dany snorted a laugh, then ushered her inside their destination.

Rose recognized the location as a former water shrine. The last time she had been in the shrine, Purity Priests had shaped water sculptures in the middle of the shallow pools of water inside the courtyard open to the bright sunshine. People had walked along the gently curving sidewalks looping around the pools or would lounge in the sunshine as they contemplated the water sculptures. It had been bright and pristine and lovely.

That was not the case tonight.

Instead of sunshine, the City was so dark that a sky full of stars bloomed overhead. The shallow pools held no water sculptures, but they weren't still. Dozens of people danced and splashed in the central pool, and the loud music pulsing through the shrine caused a slight tremor in the calmer pools along the edges. Along the outer perimeter of the shrine were relaxation rooms. A couple rooms had been converted to bars with bartenders selling drinks, but a few were being used for activities that appeared the opposite of relaxing.

The sacrilege was shocking, but the thing that froze her in place was the fire.

The shrine had only been occupied during the day, so the Priests had never formed crystalline lamps inside. Candles lit the interior of the relaxation rooms and lined the bars, but the biggest concern for Rose were the giant bonfires spaced throughout the pools. The City was too cold at night for splashing around in water, especially considering the tiny swimsuits everyone wore, but they compensated for the cold air with bonfires heating giant cauldrons of water that were regularly poured into the pools. People stood around the fire, drinking and warming up, then returned to the water to dance.

"I didn't expect you to be shy," said Dany.

"I'm not shy," said Rose quickly.

"Great." Dany led Rose to a curtained off changing room. "Then let's strip down to the bottom layer and go dance!"

Rose had assumed that swimming might be involved because they were in Purity and because Dany had included a hot pink bikini in the pile of clothes. But Rose hadn't planned on the place being filled with bonfires. She didn't trust herself around that much open flame. But that wasn't something she could tell Dany. She needed a more believable excuse.

"It's sacrilege, Dany. I can't take part in this." She raised her nose in a haughty look, hoping to avoid Dany's eyes.

Dany snorted. "It's not sacrilege, Rose. This isn't that different from what you did here before. That little swimsuit is from a vintage shop here in Purity Diocese. And those relaxation rooms ... let's be honest. They weren't always used for relaxing." She leaned closer to Rose and whispered loudly, "I don't think the people in Purity were as pure as you remember."

Rose wanted to disagree but couldn't. She huffed, "Fine. It's true. Like most of the City, it wasn't real." She sank into a chair with a sigh. "But sometimes I miss the illusion."

Dany stripped down to her plum-colored bikini. "I'm going to find drinks. I'll meet you in the center pool so we can dance!"

Rose reluctantly removed her outer layers and piled them next to Dany's clothes. Even though the color proclaimed her as an Adopted, she couldn't bring herself to remove the long white blouse she wore over her bikini. Her skin tingled with the proximity of the giant bonfires, and the soft cotton felt like a thin layer of protection.

She stepped out of the changing room to look for Dany but was distracted by the sound of a dozen giggling girls. She turned around to discover the obvious source.

Wilder.

She ducked behind a column lining the courtyard and peeked around carefully to avoid catching his eye. He wore short black swim trunks and nothing else but his smile. The girls surrounding him stared with rapturous eyes, and he basked in their attention. Nearby, Rev, Quinn, and Feather danced and splashed in the center pool while Kieran and Tayeh lounged in a calmer pool next to the steady stream of hot water. None of them had noticed Rose, so she hurried back inside the changing room to grab her clothes and escape.

The wolves stared at her with cold blue eyes.

She pointed an angry finger at them. "Don't you look at me that way! I'm avoiding him so I can keep him safe. What about the two of you? How are you protecting him? He's out there in the middle of a crowd of strangers, with no weapons and practically naked!"

Pickles ducked her head in shame, but Storm Fang still glared at Rose.

"I thought you'd be happy," said Rose. "Now that I'm out of the picture, you can finally have your boyfriend to yourself."

"They don't like to see me upset."

Rose spun around to find Wilder lounging against the door frame with crossed arms. He had thankfully put on a black shirt but hadn't gone to the trouble of buttoning it. He stared, his dark eyes silently considering her.

Warring emotions flared to life in her chest. She wanted to kiss him. She wanted to run away from him. The painfulness of her conflicting desires reminded her of her conversation with Vaylan, so she said the only thing that would be helpful.

"Vaylan knows you are rehearsing a Pageant. You have to be careful."

His only reaction was the slight lift of an eyebrow. "I'll let them know. Since Kieran was released, he's resumed his role of the Companion. It's unfortunate for me. You know how I enjoy seducing children with the Goddess's music."

She ground her teeth but didn't respond to his sarcasm. "I'm serious, Wilder. There's a prophecy about the Bard's music being sung before the final crystal goes dark. Vaylan is planning something."

He stood from his relaxed position against the door frame, taking a step further inside. "Why do you care? Maybe Vaylan's plans will be retribution for what I've done." He took another slow step toward her, his voice a low rumble. "This is your opportunity to see me rightfully punished. Maybe you should deliver me to Vaylan yourself."

Her heart fluttered to a stop at his words. He had spoken

aloud her greatest fear. What if she got so angry that she did just that? She had done stupid things in anger before, but the thought that she might betray him terrified her. And with the fury still simmering in her chest that he killed a Priest, she felt more dangerous to him than ever.

"I have to go," she said.

She tried to sneak past him, but he pulled her back into the small room. His hand on her arm was cool through her cotton sleeve, and she wondered if his burns had healed. He studied her face with his sparkling dark eyes, and despite the cold night air, Rose felt flushed.

She wanted to run but couldn't bring herself to move. His eyes trailed across her face and lingered on her lips. She held perfectly still, refusing the urge to wet her lips in response. A warm wind blew in from the courtyard and tickled the fine hairs along her neck. Her logical mind screamed that this was exactly what she should avoid, but Wilder was in front of her, full of power and vitality, and any threat from Vaylan seemed so far away.

Her body melted a fraction closer to him, and at the sign of her yielding, he pulled her into an embrace. His lips felt cool against hers, but only compared to the fire that roared beneath her skin. Wilder's hands clung to her back, holding her up when she thought she would dissolve at his feet.

She was only partially aware of the startled gasps outside as the flames under the giant cauldrons of water surged, causing the water to bubble in a super-heated frenzy. Steam poured out of the cauldrons, covering the entire shrine in a thick fog.

Wilder appeared unconcerned as he kissed her, running fingers up her back into her now damp hair. Her thin cotton shirt clung to her, but the droplets of water on her skin sizzled on impact.

"Rose? Are you still in there?"

At Dany's concerned voice, Wilder took a step backward. Before the dense mist hid him from view, a teardrop fell on his cheek, and he swirled his hands as if washing them. The steam turned into a gentle rain, returning everyone to visibility. The crowd clapped their hands as if the entertainment had been intentional, then resumed their dancing even more fervently than before.

Dany stumbled into the room, blinking mist out of her eyes. "That was strange. The cold weather must make everything act weird." Then her eyes widened in surprise to see they weren't alone.

Wilder had returned to his casual stance, leaning against the door frame. He appeared cheerfully smug after knowing how much Rose enjoyed kissing him. "Who's your friend?" he asked playfully.

Dany's mouth dropped open in surprise.

Then she giggled.

Rose felt her usual heated flash of jealousy, but it was immediately smothered by cold fear.

Rose had delivered Wilder to a Sentinel.

Purpose

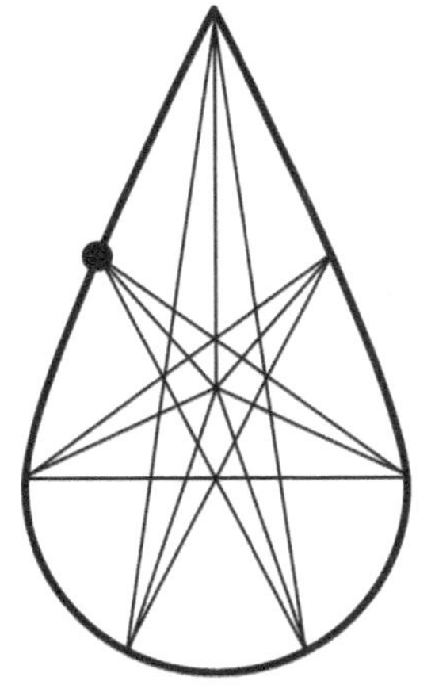

Delirium

33

Rose woke up to the sound of Dany snoring softly. After Rose had kicked Wilder out of the shrine last night, she had forced Dany to get dressed and return with her to the temple. Dany had been confused and a little pouty, but she smiled when Rose suggested Dany have a sleepover in her room. Dany said she was excited to have another adventure she never had growing up as the Warden's prisoner.

Rose knew it was the only way to make sure Dany didn't sneak out to find Wilder and hand him over to Vaylan.

She rubbed her forehead, irritated at her own stupidity. She had led a Sentinel right to Wilder. It had been so simple, and she hadn't thought twice about it. The ease with which Vaylan could get to Wilder terrified her. Rose kept allowing herself to get pulled into Wilder's arms, and it was only a matter of time before Vaylan followed Rose right to him.

"Now can we talk?" Dany propped herself up on her elbows and stared at Rose. "You're clearly awake. You can't pretend otherwise."

Last night, Dany had jumped into bed, ready to gossip

about what she had seen, but Rose had rolled over and pretended to sleep. It was terrible behavior for a slumber party host, but Rose couldn't be tricked into revealing information about Wilder if she pretended to be asleep. It appeared she couldn't pull the same stunt again, so she needed other distractions.

Rose hopped out of bed. "Yes, I'm awake. Now that you're up, let's go work out." She pulled on her gray training clothes.

Dany sat up, a big pout on her lips. "This is not what I heard slumber parties were like."

"No, it's not," said Rose. "But the two of us aren't normal girls, are we?"

Dany's pout turned into a thoughtful expression, tinged with sadness. "I guess you're right. It's just one of those illusions that is nice to enjoy for a time." She changed into her training clothes in silence.

The training room was emptier than usual, which left Rose to spar with Dany. As they stretched to warm up, Dany grinned at Rose.

"I see why you weren't that interested in any of Jace's 'alternative' training sessions. If Wilder's the one you've been sneaking out to see, then it makes complete sense."

"I'm not sneaking out to see Wilder," Rose said firmly.

Dany gave her an innocent look. "True. Sometimes he sneaks inside instead."

Rose grumbled quietly, unsure how to shut down the conversation.

"However, I am proud about reading you correctly," said Dany with a smug grin. "I definitely guessed your type, didn't I?" She laughed as she did a few deep lunges. "I knew you would be a sucker for a confident man, someone who could really challenge you. Plus, it helps that he's sweet to go with your ... um ... spice."

Rose narrowed her eyes at Dany. "You sure know a lot about Wilder."

Dany rolled her eyes. "Everyone knows about Wilder, Rose. I just hadn't met him before now. And I had no idea that the two of you are ... whatever you are. That information isn't common knowledge."

Rose gave a grunting laugh as she sat down and stretched over her legs. "I guess Wilder doesn't share that information with all the giggling girls who fawn over him."

Dany nodded in agreement. "Exactly. That intel could make its way back to Vaylan. It's better to keep that secret."

Rose sat up quickly. "You think we could keep this secret from him?" she asked incredulously.

Dany sighed. "Probably not. He knows a lot and rarely shares the information needed beyond what it takes to do the job. I knew it was my job to watch for Wilder, but I only found out recently that Wilder was Vaylan's son."

Rose studied Dany closely, trying to determine if her words were just an elaborate trick or not. "He told you?"

"No," said Dany. "The Adopted told me."

Because Rose had told them.

"Really?" said Rose. "The Adopted share information with Sentinels?"

"Not all of them. The Adopted have a wide variety of reasons they choose to follow Vaylan. But some see it as their job to look after us Sentinels." Dany's lips curved into a soft smile. "It's really quite sweet."

Adopted who looked after Sentinels sounded crazy, not sweet, but since Rose just had a sleepover with one, she couldn't really judge.

"Do you think Vaylan knows?" asked Dany. "Does he know what Wilder is up to?"

"And just what do you think Wilder is up to?" asked Rose slowly.

"I don't know. Whatever you saw him doing last night. Dancing in a nightclub, I guess?"

"If he doesn't know yet, you can tell him," said Rose.

"Me?" said Dany. "Why would I tell him?"

"Because you belong to Vaylan."

Dany's face hardened. "I belong to no one."

"I didn't mean—"

"Rose, the Champions didn't just belong to the Wardens—we were owned by them. We serve Vaylan, but we are not his."

Rose raised her eyebrows and leaned back as she studied Dany's face. She wondered if Vaylan knew his Sentinels interpreted their service as loosely as the Adopted did.

"So, you won't tell him?" asked Rose.

"Telling him would mean admitting that I snuck out of the temple. Even though I haven't been expressly forbidden from doing so, I don't want to cause a new rule to be enforced."

They stopped their conversation to spar a few matches. Rose lost most of their bouts because she felt herself pulling her punches in ways she never did with Kai or Caed. She wondered again if this was what it would have been like to have a younger sister.

After Rose tapped out for the last time, they both dressed in their normal clothes. As Rose looked at Dany in the Sentinels' armor, she wondered if she would pull her punches any less if they fought now. Or maybe the old fear would kick in, and she would freeze.

Before Dany put her hooded mask back on, she said, "Are you really not going to tell me *anything* about you and Wilder? Nothing at all?"

Rose looked at her suspiciously. Dany waited until Rose was tired and would now get secret information from her that Vaylan could use. Rose wondered if she could concoct a lie to throw him off track.

"What do you want to know?" Rose asked calmly.

"Is he a good kisser?" Dany's eyes took on a dreamy expression. "I feel like he would be a really good kisser."

The question caught her off guard, and a blush formed on her cheeks. She hated it when Wilder caused her to blush, even when he wasn't in the room. She wanted to lie just to spite him but felt the truthful answer tingling on her lips.

"Oh yes," she whispered.

Dany's eyes widened in delight. "I knew it! I can't wait to share this intel."

Rose nearly choked. "You want to tell Vaylan *that*?"

Dany laughed. "Not Vaylan! There is a bit of a Wilder fan club among the Sentinels and Adopted. They will be so excited to hear that he's a great kisser. I'm sure they will have a lot more questions for you."

Rose's cheeks burned even hotter. "What? No!" She gave Dany a stern look. "You absolutely cannot tell anyone. Do you hear me? Tell no one."

Dany gave her an innocent look. "Of course, Rose. This is our secret."

By the end of the day, every Sentinel and Adopted knew Rose's opinion of Wilder's kisses.

34

Despite the Sentinels' notorious silence, they were remarkable gossips. Every Sentinel she passed turned their head to watch her pass. She couldn't determine their facial expressions beneath the masks, but a few nodded slowly at her as if in admiration.

Admiration for kissing Wilder? He had made it very clear she was not the only girl he had kissed. Not by a long shot. Yet somehow, the rumor about her kissing Wilder brought a new level of reverence that her status as the Marked One had never given her.

She buzzed with irritation at the extra attention, so instead of eating dinner in the main dining hall, she took her food to her room to eat in peace. However, Yasmine bowed her way inside, then kneeled on the floor near the desk where Rose sat.

"I'm sorry for disturbing you, Mar—Rose. I have a question to ask you."

Rose sighed. "Yes, Yasmine. Wilder's a good kisser. I won't reveal any details beyond that."

"Oh …" Yasmine drew out the sound as if unsure how to

respond. "Thank you for the information, but that isn't what I came to discuss."

Rose rubbed her forehead, mostly to hide her embarrassment. "Of course not. What's the question?"

"Have you seen Sian anywhere?"

Rose thought back to the last time she had seen the former Knowledge Priest. "The last time I saw her was with all of you. Why do you ask?"

A shadow passed across Yasmine's face, but she bowed to hide it. "She took a risk, and I'm not sure it paid off."

Rose turned away from her food to focus on Yasmine. "Tell me what she did."

Yasmine fidgeted with her hands in her lap and refused to meet Rose's eye. "Sian believes it is her mission to gather Knowledge at all costs. She heard about some secret prophecies and wanted to read them for herself."

"Okay ..." Rose shook her head in confusion. "So, what's the—"

"They were in Vaylan's tent."

Rose tried to contain her frustration at someone who was currently missing. "She snuck into his private tent?"

"You once said that you didn't care if someone snuck into his room and stole it out of his hand while he slept. Sian took that as your blessing."

Rose barely kept herself from yelling. "My blessing?"

"He wasn't there," Yasmine said quickly, as if that helped. "It was last night while he was still Upstairs like you. But we haven't seen her since then. And ... we're afraid."

Rose covered her mouth with her hand, trying to hide the worried expression that she knew was there. If Sian told them she was sneaking into Vaylan's tent and never returned, they were right to be afraid.

"Is there anything you can do, Marked One?" Yasmine

asked. "Please. Vaylan listens to you. Will you ask about her?"

She huffed a rueful laugh. "Vaylan doesn't listen to me."

Yasmine looked up. "Of course he does. He listens to you at every temple and spares the lives of the Priests."

"It's not that he listens to me. It's that he enjoys watching me beg for their lives."

"Then beg for her life, too!" Yasmine's voice caught in her throat before she said calmly, "Please, Rose. Please beg for her life, too."

Rose took a deep breath and considered telling Yasmine that it was probably too late to make a difference, but the hopeful look on the young woman's face changed her mind.

"I will beg him," she said.

Rose wished Yasmine good night, then went to find Vaylan. Two Sentinels followed her out of her tent, but she couldn't tell if she knew them or not. They silently walked behind her and didn't stop her as she approached Vaylan's tent. The two Sentinels guarding his tent opened the flaps and ushered her inside.

"Rose! How nice of you to come! Have a seat and join me for dinner."

The long wooden table seemed way too elaborate to be inside a tent. Vaylan sat at the head of the table in a wooden chair carved like a throne and gestured for her to take the smaller chair at the other end. She wanted to march up to him and demand he tell her what he did to Sian, but she knew better by now. She had to play the game if she had any chance of getting what she wanted.

She took a seat.

Vaylan gave her a warm smile as an Adopted placed a

platter before her and removed the lid with a flourish. Rose almost swooned at the smell alone. Thick steak medallions rested alongside potatoes topped with a rich gravy and two slices of dark brown bread with butter slowly melting on top. This was not the same food that was growing cold in her tent.

"You eat well," she said simply.

He smiled. "Yes, I do. My Adopted like to please me, and I allow it."

"How generous of you."

He failed to notice the sarcasm in her voice. "I care for my Adopted above all others. They have been rejected by everyone, but I've adopted them. They are more loyal than you understand."

She cleared her throat nervously. "I wanted to speak to you about one of your Adopted. Her name is Sian."

He made a show of considering the name, then smiled. "There are so many Adopted. I don't know everyone by name."

"She was looking for secret prophecies last night, and she came here."

He laughed. "Here? You and I were up in the City last night, so it appears she stopped by at the wrong time. If I would have been here, I would have told her what anyone could have told her: you can find the prophecies in the prophecy tent."

"All the prophecies?" she asked. "I heard you hand out different prophecies to each person, depending on how they serve you." She looked down at her meal. "Depending on how many steaks they bring you."

He smirked. "Are you jealous that I hand out Brother Owyn's words to my devoted followers? You could read all those prophecies and more if you simply bring me what I desire."

He didn't even need to say Wilder's name to fill her with terror.

"I don't need to read them. But Sian did. And I'm asking you: Please tell me where she is."

"Now, Rose—"

She cut off his patronizing tone by dropping to the floor beside the table. She bowed her head low against the beautiful woven rug that took up the entire floor.

"Please, Vaylan, spare her. I beg you. Save her, as you have been so merciful before." She repeated the words over and over, hoping that Sian was still alive somewhere, hoping he would relent.

"Rose." He said her name in a warning tone of irritation. "Your begging isn't useful here. There is no prophecy regarding this."

"But please," she begged, sitting up to look into his dark eyes. "Just tell me if she is still alive."

He steepled his fingers in front of his mouth. "Rose, very few people are allowed inside this tent. In fact, only two people get welcomed into my tent the way you did tonight. The rest only pass the Sentinels by my word alone. She did not have my word, so it appears she did not enter my tent at all."

Rose's lips hardened into a scowl. "It does appear that way, doesn't it?"

He smiled, then his eyes lit up as he looked past her to the tent entrance. "Walter! The other person who is always welcome in my tent. Join us for dinner." Vaylan glanced down at Rose, still on the floor. "Rose was just begging me for someone's life, but I've never heard the name Sian, so I'm afraid I can't be much help."

Rose picked herself off the floor and found Walter settling into the seat with her untouched food. He started eating it without a word.

Vaylan laughed. "Isn't he delightful, Rose? So innocent and almost childlike; however, I've found records that say he is over five hundred years old. Can you believe that?"

Her thoughts slowed to a crawl. Vaylan knew about Walter. Had he already convinced Walter to use his Spark to grant him long life? She watched Walter calmly eating mashed potatoes. He was still alive. Would Vaylan keep him alive afterwards? She didn't think so.

"Did you hear me, Rose?" Vaylan seemed impatient for her to speak. As if he was waiting to hear what she had to say.

Waiting, as if he didn't have all the answers yet and was hoping she did.

She brought her awareness into sharp focus. "What did you say?"

He flexed his jaw but smiled anyway. "Walter is over five hundred years old."

Walter looked up at the sound of his name. "Really?" he appeared confused. "I feel much older than that."

Rose wanted to smack her forehead, but she kept her concentration and laughed instead. "How charming! You did say you enjoyed his stories."

Walter finished the last bite of potatoes, then pushed the plate out of the way as he took out a little notebook from his pocket. Rose peeked and saw him draw a rose with a stem full of thorns.

Vaylan's eyes were hungry with curiosity as he walked to Walter's side to watch him sketch. When he finished the drawing, Walter moved to hand it to Rose, but Vaylan pulled it out of his hand. Vaylan studied it, then laughed.

"It looks like he knows you well," said Vaylan. "Not only is the rose covered in thorns, but he also drew it growing in a field full of daggers. When have you met him before?"

She didn't fall for his quickly sprung question. "Your

tent and the prophecy tent. You were there both times. Don't you remember?" She laughed haughtily. "Maybe Walter's confusion is rubbing off on you."

Fury blazed behind his eyes, then was immediately smothered. "You should probably go. Walter and I have things to discuss." He handed her Walter's drawing. "You can keep this as a souvenir. In case this is the last time you see him."

His eyes stared at her in challenge, so she took the paper as casually as she could. She headed back to her tent, counting the moments until she could find Quinn and have him translate the old language Walter had hidden in the drawing.

35

———————

After a morning teaching dance class to Sentinels, Rose walked quietly at Fitz's side on the way to the next crystal. Over thirty Sentinels had shown up to class. If more showed up, they would have to find a bigger rehearsal space. But how much longer could she really hope to teach them? What was the point?

During their final stretches, she had looked at their joyful, exhausted faces and wondered if one of them had been guarding Vaylan's tent when Sian arrived. Did one of them capture her until Vaylan returned? Or did they kill her on Vaylan's standing order? Her class was mainly young former Champions, but a couple older Sentinels had joined them, too. She didn't know what their story was, but she wondered if they were there simply to spy on her.

Fitz noticed her frustrated sigh and gave her a kind smile. "It's going to be okay, Rose. I truly believe this will all work out."

She grumbled, "Once again, you have more faith than I do, Fitz. You will make a much better Priest than I ever was."

He ducked his head as his pale cheeks grew pink. "Thanks, Rose."

Vaylan had made sure that Fitz was dressed in the symbolic black robes as all the Chosen had been, and Fitz held his bound hands inside the sleeves of the robes, giving him a serene bearing as they walked.

She smiled as she remembered the quirky, mismatched clothing he usually wore. "And you look good in black. It suits you."

His blush grew, but his words were hesitant. "I'm not sure if it's right for people like me to wear black. Maybe that should be something only for those the Goddess chose to be Priests."

She gave him a reproving look. "The Goddess literally chose you above all her Priests. You are what she dreams her Priests would be like. You can wear black if you choose."

His smile lit up his face. "Your support means a lot. Thanks, Rose." He bit his lip, an expression she had learned meant he was unsure if his next statement would lead to an attack. "You didn't have the same response to Wilder wearing black."

She sighed in resignation. "With Wilder, it's ... complicated."

He snorted loudly.

She turned to glare at him, but he stared ahead with an innocent expression.

"But Wilder wearing black is growing on me." Her thoughts flashed to Wilder in the little black swim trunks, and a smile curved her lips. "It suits him, too."

"When this is over, will you wear black again?"

He didn't ask the implied question: will you return to life as a Priest?

"I don't know." Besides asking how she could defeat Vaylan, it was the question that kept her up at night.

Fitz's thoughtful eyes pierced her to the core. "The Goddess would be lucky to have you again as one of her

Priests. But I think there might be something else for you. A calling beyond that of her Priest."

His words were kind, but the implied challenge intimidated her. She didn't know what to say, so she gave him the sign of the Goddess and continued their walk in silence.

When they arrived at the crystal, Vaylan spoke to his adoring fans, but Rose noticed the people gathered around the perimeter. They didn't look as cold as the people Upstairs, but their faces were wary. Some carried lanterns, having heard what happened in the other Grottos when Vaylan arrived. He had always forced the crystalline to flow again after she stopped it, but apparently these people didn't trust him.

Rose grinned at the sign of Vaylan's waning influence, then placed her hands on the crystal.

The Goddess's cave was dark and cold. Rose and Wilder had seen this version of the Goddess's sanctuary when she first set them on their task. The cave appeared carved out of the mountain, roughhewn and silent in a way the glittering cave was not. The Goddess sat at a rickety wooden table with a cup of tea in her hand.

"Goddess?" Rose flinched at her own echoing voice, but the Goddess stared down at her tea with unblinking eyes.

Rose took a step closer, and the entire cave *rippled*. Nausea turned her stomach, and she placed a steadying hand on the table, which suddenly flickered into the shape of a bed. The Goddess sat in the same position, except her hand clasped the hand of the Companion, who lay in the bed with his eyes closed.

Rose had seen him in a previous vision with the Goddess, but then he had been full of life with a constant twinkle in his eye. Now his face appeared carved in stone, completely still. Rose had steadied herself by holding the table, but she realized with a start that her hand now rested on the blanket covering his shins. She pulled her hand away quickly, shocked at how cold he was.

She dropped her voice to a gentle whisper. "Goddess? Can you hear me?"

The Goddess didn't look up. "Wilder stopped singing," she said sadly.

Rose tried to soften her voice, as if speaking to a scared child. "Kieran is the one playing the Companion now. He's very good. I picked him myself."

The Goddess stroked the Companion's hand, and Rose thought it must be like touching a statue.

"Wilder has always had a lovely voice. Even when he was little." The Goddess spoke in a wistful tone, never taking her eyes off the Companion.

Rose wondered if the Goddess was speaking to her at all.

"Did I tell you how we met?" Rose opened her mouth to answer, but the Goddess smoothed back a lock of the Companion's hair and continued speaking to him. "I don't think I did. When you wake up, I'll tell you all about it."

The room shifted, and Rose steadied herself again, this time on the smooth surface of the long mahogany table inside the glittering cave. The Goddess lifted her eyes from her cup of tea and stared at Rose with listless eyes.

"Why did Wilder stop singing?"

Rose explained again. "Kieran is—"

"Tell him to sing for me." The Goddess turned to look back at her cup of tea. "You may go."

Rose blinked her eyes and was back in the Grotto.

It wasn't as dark this time, thanks to the lanterns around the perimeter of the crowd. Vaylan raised his hands overhead, and the crystalline flowed again.

After their procession made it to the top of the looping bridge, Fitz looked at Rose with concern.

"Are you all right?"

She shook herself out of her thoughts. "Yeah, I think so." Her mind curled back on what she had seen. "But I don't think the Goddess is."

He looked at her shyly with the same look of awe that Rev had. "What's wrong with her?"

"Some days, she's better than others. Today was a bad day." She sighed. "They have to hurry up and perform the Pageant. The Goddess says it's the only way her power can return."

He nodded in understanding. "She needs the people of the City to believe. That's where her power comes from. It's why the Goddess's followers in the Underneath always performed their own Pageant each year."

"You did what?" Rose stopped walking and the Adopted and Sentinels walking nearby slowed down in confusion.

Fitz grabbed her arm and pulled her along. "We held our own Pageant," he whispered, trying to avoid the eyes of the others watching them.

"But you didn't have any Priests." She couldn't wrap her mind around the idea.

Fitz laughed. "Rose, the acolyte performers are traditionally not Priests. You never performed onstage, did you?"

She practically choked. "No, of course not!" The idea was disturbing in many ways.

He shrugged. "We lacked the Priests backstage to make the flowers grow and the living water fountains, but we found other ways to make the performance special."

"But the Pageant is about pouring the Priests' tears into the basin to bond them to the City for another year."

"Yes, that is one function of the Pageant. But the other purpose is to reestablish the Goddess's power."

"How do you know that?"

He bit his lip and appeared unsure if he should respond. "It says so in the liturgies, Rose."

"Oh," she said simply. Once again, he had proven to know the liturgies better than her.

He spoke as if trying to fill her embarrassed silence. "It's a shame the Pageant has to be performed in secret. I'm worried that the fewer people that take part, the less powerful it will be."

She was grateful for the shift in conversation. "Wilder has collected a lot of people by now. We just have to find a secret warehouse big enough."

He looked thoughtful and a little sad. "There are several underground bunkers tunneled into the stone between the Upstairs and Underneath. I used to have a vague sense of them before they started giving me the tea and before ..." He looked at the dull gray crystal of the temple as they approached.

Rose frowned, angry at forgetting that when she darkened the crystal, she ripped away his Gift. "I'm sorry, Fitz."

He dropped his voice even lower than they had before. "But Wilder still can sense them. He can shape them into a space big enough to fit everyone we can find." His eyes shot to Vaylan at the front of the procession, then he whispered even quieter. "Some of the underground bunkers were formerly prisons."

They could perform the Pageant in the same underground prison that Vaylan and Brother Owyn had been trapped in.

36

——————

A crowd had already gathered at Temple Purpose by the time they arrived. Rose frowned to see them all bundled up and shivering in the cold. Luckily, she had finally found clothes that were warm enough. Her white leather boots and pants were thick enough to keep her legs warm; plus, her white jacket had a fitted waist and was so long that it flared behind her when she walked. She was pleased to finally be stylish *and* warm.

There were so many people in the crowd that Vaylan walked brazenly to the top of the temple steps to address them. The Priests huddled inside, obviously waiting until the last moment before they had to flee their home. Rose sighed and sank to the ground near the bottom step, preparing to beg Vaylan to let them go.

Vaylan halted his sermon at the gasps from the crowd. Rose raised her head to see Vaylan's face lit up in ecstasy. Whatever pleased him that much was likely terrible news. She turned around to discover she was right.

Wilder strode down the center of the street, two white wolves by his side, and his eyes firmly locked on Vaylan. He was dressed in his now normal uniform of tight black leather with sheaths crossing his muscular chest. He walked with such purpose that the crowd parted to let him pass.

Rose couldn't move from her kneeling position on the ground. Terror and fury crushed her, holding her in place. She heard whispers from the crowd speculating on what would happen next. Vaylan had made no move to order his Sentinels to attack, and she feared if she stood, she would disrupt the moment's tenuous equilibrium.

"Hello, Vaylan." Wilder's voice stilled the crowd. "I've come to propose a deal."

"I'm listening," said Vaylan, dark eyes glittering.

"You know we are rehearsing for a Pageant."

"I do." His lips curled in a smirk.

"We need a location to perform it. And right now, you are in control of the best venue."

Wilder stood just a few feet away from her, and Rose tried to communicate with her eyes that she and Fitz had already made a plan, so Wilder could just turn around right now, but he wasn't watching her. His eyes were still fixed on Vaylan at the top of the steps.

"It's true. The amphitheater is mine." His voice was so smug it made Rose ill. "What do you offer to make it worthwhile for me to let you use it?"

"If you allow everyone in the City to attend the Pageant and leave safely at the end of the performance, I will surrender myself to you."

"No!" Rose leaped to her feet. "Are you crazy?"

He didn't look at her, but just continued staring at Vaylan.

Rose thought Vaylan would command his Sentinels to attack Wilder where he stood, but he merely stared at his son with calculating eyes. She wished he would give the order, if only so Wilder could escape and make Vaylan look weak in front of the crowd.

But Wilder was offering to surrender himself to Vaylan without a fight—the only cost, a Pageant that Vaylan believed was foretold. And prophecy said Wilder's surrender would end in one of two ways. She watched Vaylan's slow grin, helpless to stop the horrifying bargain.

"It's a deal," Vaylan said smoothly. "I will tell my Sentinels to allow you into the amphitheater tonight, if you wish. I'm sure you want to rehearse."

Wilder nodded once, then turned and walked away.

Rose stared at him for several moments before realizing he actually was leaving without saying another word. She ran forward and caught him by the arm, spinning him around to face her.

He stared at her calmly, waiting for her to speak. She opened her mouth to let out a long string of curses when Vaylan gently cleared his throat.

"Rose? Aren't you forgetting something?"

She turned to find Vaylan looking at Fitz who seemed small standing between two tall Sentinels.

"There is still a prophecy to be fulfilled." He smiled, and his dimple mocked her. "Unless there is some reason you can leave without fulfilling it?"

Wilder's eyes never left her face. He was completely relaxed, as if he hadn't just offered himself up as a sacrifice. Leaving with him would be to admit that he was the Chosen. She wasn't sure how that could be any worse, but she feared it might be. His arm was still gripped in her hand, and she squeezed it until her arm shook with the pressure.

Then she let him go.

Wilder gave her a smug look as if he had won an argument, then walked off.

Rose sat on the temple step with Fitz, her leg bouncing in a nervous rhythm. Her eyes hurt from staring at the sun and waiting for it to set. She had no idea what to do. Go see Wilder and convince him to change his mind? Or avoid Wilder so that she didn't cause something worse to happen?

Fitz smacked his hand against her leg. "Stop fidgeting. You are driving me crazy."

"Sorry. I just can't decide what I should do."

"Really?" He looked shocked. "You seem to always know exactly what you want to do, then rush into it without thinking."

She wanted to be upset at his statement, but it was true. Which made her current indecision unusual.

Vaylan walked down the steps, and Rose jumped up. The sun had finally set, and she could move on. Although, move on to what, she didn't know.

Vaylan watched as she pulled the pearl knife from her jacket sheath, then he said casually, "You know, Rose, I was thinking... Maybe it's best if you head off with Fitz tonight. You could check in on the performers as they start rehearsals at the amphitheater. Be my representative there."

Her hand stilled, fingers numb on the blade. "Your representative?"

He beamed as if it was a brilliant idea. "You can make sure they have everything they need to make the show successful. Enjoy your time together."

The idea sounded wonderful, but she narrowed her eyes at him, waiting for the hidden catch.

"You can just meet us at the next crystal. There's only one left, and since it was formerly your own, you should be able to find your way there easy enough."

"Yes ..." she said hesitantly. "I could do that."

If she went to the amphitheater tonight, she could

convince Wilder to change his mind, then go to Mims's house and sleep there. The thought was wonderful …

Except that Vaylan suggested it. Whatever he wanted, it was best for Rose to choose the exact opposite.

"And if you head off to the amphitheater, don't worry about your brother. I will make sure he arrives safely at the next temple. I can't have anything happen to the Chosen, so obviously, that means your brother will be safe."

Ah … the catch. "Kai needs to be safe for the prophecy to be fulfilled *correctly*," she said.

"Of course," said Vaylan with a twinkle in his eye.

She turned to Fitz, who held out his hand as an offering. She cut a quick slice on his palm, and as she wrapped the bandage, she hid a small slip of paper in his hand.

"Give that to Quinn," she whispered. "And convince Wilder to change his mind. Please."

Fitz gave her a look that said he was pretty sure that would be impossible, but he was polite enough not to say it out loud.

Rose watched Fitz head out into the City, then turned to go hide in her room alone all night. She found Yasmine waiting outside her door.

"Did you find Sian?" she asked hopefully.

Rose wanted to offer her hope, but she knew it would be false. "Vaylan says he knows nothing about her."

Yasmine gave the sign of the Goddess, then nodded bravely. "We suspected that. Thank you for asking."

"I wish I had better news." Rose sighed. "You deserve better news."

Yasmine's lips turned up in a small smile. "There was one bright spot to the day."

"There was?" Rose tried to think of anything good that happened, and except for teaching dance class, everything else had been awful.

Yasmine's eyes turned dreamy. "We got to see you and Wilder together. All of us were swooning."

Rose snorted. "Wilder didn't say a word to me, and all I asked is if he was crazy. That made you swoon?"

She giggled. "Haven't you ever really liked two people and realized they belong together? Everyone likes Wilder, and all the Adopted and Sentinels like you. Even though you barely spoke, we all felt the connection." She closed her eyes as if replaying the scene and savoring it. "It was very powerful." She took a deep breath and opened her eyes. "A love like that should not be denied."

Rose gave her the sign of the Goddess in farewell, nodded to the Sentinels as she closed her door, then snuck out the window to find Wilder.

37

———

Wilder found Rose sitting on a bench inside the stone garden. The last time she had been in the garden, the white stone landscape had been brightly lit by the crystals, but now it was dull and life-less. Wilder walked quietly down the stone path until he stopped a few feet away, watching her warily.

"How did you find me?" she asked.

He glanced into the branches of the stone trees arching over the bench where she sat. "Spies." An owl hooted, and his lip curved in a small grin. He looked at her bright white leather pants and long white jacket. "Besides, you are hard to miss."

"I wanted to be found," she said quietly.

He crossed his arms over his chest and gave her a gently smug look. "You aren't very good at avoiding me."

She couldn't speak above a whisper. "I came to beg you not to do this."

He sighed and sat down beside her. "I have to do it, Rose. For the Goddess's power to return, we need everyone to watch. The amphitheater is the only place big enough."

"But Fitz and I had an idea—"

"I can't tunnel out a location as big as the amphitheater. Plus, there's no way we can keep it secret from Vaylan. This is the only way I can assure the safety of everyone involved."

"Everyone but you!"

He gave her a tender look. "I still have all the Gifts, and when the crystals relight, I believe the Goddess will return her Gifts to all the Priests. Vaylan will be met with an entire amphitheater of Gifted Priests, and the prophecies will be proved false. He will have to admit he was wrong."

She stared at him in shock. "You actually believe that?"

"Yes. I believe the Goddess—"

"Not that." She cut him off. "You believe Vaylan will admit he was wrong? I promise you that will not happen."

"He won't have a choice—"

"Yes, he will!" Her voice raised to a shrill cry. "He will do whatever it takes to make it appear that the prophecy has come true. If he can't convert you, he will kill you, no matter what else occurs outside his plans. Promise me that if he captures you, you'll pretend he's converted you. That's the only way he'll keep you alive."

Wilder gave her a hard look. "I can't do that."

"You must! Vaylan will not suddenly realize he was wrong. The prophecies are everything to him. He's a true believer."

"So am I, Rose." His eyes were unflinching. "So am I."

She stood up with a roar. "You are just as stubborn as him, but you're the one who will be dead in the end."

He stood and took hold of her hand. She wanted to shake him off in anger but couldn't bear to let him go.

"I don't know why she chose me." His voice was soft and thoughtful. "I'm not perfect, which you enjoy pointing out. I've made a lot of mistakes, some that still distress me deeply. The only thing I have to offer her, the only thing I ever had, was my devotion."

A tear landed on his cheek, and Rose was no longer herself.

Rose was young Wilder, singing on a busy street in the Underneath. Young Wilder instinctively knew which person required what song to provide him with the greatest tip. That woman wanted a love song that would make her swoon. She placed two small coins into young Wilder's hands. That man wanted a funny song, one so dirty that young Wilder didn't even understand the lyrics he sang. That man gave him three coins.

Young Wilder spotted another woman, and his eyes trailed over her jewelry and clothes, noting the quality. But even more promising was the bag of food she carried. Young Wilder's stomach rumbled. If he picked the right song, perhaps she would pay him with something to eat. As he considered which song the woman would like best, his eyes landed on a different woman. The part of Rose that was still herself recognized her.

The Goddess.

Young Wilder didn't recognize her at all.

The woman leaned against the side of a building, staring with unseeing eyes at the glowing amber crystal overhead. Her long brown hair was coiled in a sloppy knot, and she wore a ripped sweater hanging loosely around her shoulders. Young Wilder tried to catch her eye and smile, knowing instinctively that a smile usually caused others to smile in return. But the trick didn't work this time. The woman didn't break eye contact with the crystal, and her green eyes were unbearably sad.

All thoughts of the rich woman's food forgotten, young Wilder's new goal was to cause the sad woman to smile. He sang one of the dirty songs, hoping to shock her into laughing, but she didn't move. He tried the sweetest love song he knew, drawing out each note with as much passion as his eight-year-old heart could hold. She still didn't move. He ignored every other passerby as he considered what might cause someone that sad to smile.

He decided to sing for her the saddest song he knew.

The song was the Goddess's Aria, sometimes known as the Goddess's Lament. He had heard the song a few times when he snuck into a building with the Goddess's followers. They had a painting of the Goddess kneeling beside the fallen Companion, one hand caressing his cheek, the other hand wiping her own tear in the sign of the Goddess. The Goddess in the painting was beautiful and sad, and he felt that this woman looked like she had lost someone she loved, too. He wanted her to know that she wasn't alone.

Young Wilder began the song, weaving as much of his own feelings into the words as he could. Into each note, he poured his sadness for being abandoned by his father. He added his heartbreak at loving a mother who hurt him. He combined his pain from hunger and his sorrow from loneliness, and he twisted them into the notes so that she knew he understood her.

But deep inside every note and in-between each breath, he wound hope.

Hope that one day he would grow big and strong and would defeat the Wardens. Hope that one day, the Underneath would be free to live Upstairs, whatever that was. Hope that one day, he would have a family of his own that he would love in a way that he never was.

And hope that the woman would live to see it all and smile.

He was almost finished with the song before he realized that her previously lifeless eyes, now pooled with tears. With his final note, she closed her eyes on a sigh, and the tears spilled down her cheeks. He felt a moment's disappointment that he hadn't brought a smile to her face when suddenly she turned and walked toward him.

She towered above him, limned in the golden light of the crystal at her back. Her green eyes were bright with tears and so compelling he could hardly move.

He could hardly breathe.

Her voice was scratchy, as if she hadn't spoken for some time. "You are blessed with eyes to see what others do not, little one."

He whispered breathlessly, "Thank you, Goddess."

A few people nearby laughed at the idea of calling this ragged looking woman "Goddess," but young Wilder barely noticed. His eyes were fixed on hers.

Waiting.

She stared at him a few moments longer, an eternity passing behind her eyes. But eventually, she did as young Wilder wished.

She smiled.

"Come, little one." She held out her hand.

Young Wilder put his hand in hers and answered her smile with one of his own.

Rose jolted back into her own mind. A sob escaped her lips.

"Oh, Wilder ..." Her legs gave out, and she fell back onto the bench.

He waited for her to recover, sitting by her side and holding her hand.

She swallowed another sob threatening to escape. "I had no idea," she whispered.

"I've never told anyone that story," he said seriously. "Not even Rev."

She tried to put words to what she had seen, what she had *lived*, but couldn't. "You met her that long ago?"

He nodded. "I took her hand that day, and she led me to a corner near the performing arts school. She told me to sing, then watched me from afar. Eventually, the head-master walked by and convinced me to come live at the school. When I turned around to look for her, she was gone." He stared off into the distance as if sorting through his memories. "I saw her a few times since then. I even saw her the night of the Pageant when she became the High Priest of Purpose."

"And you said nothing?" she asked incredulously.

He smiled. "I don't poke around in a woman's private affairs, especially when that woman is a goddess."

She looked into his eyes, seeing him in a way she never had before. "The Goddess said you were a good singer, even as a child. She wants you to keep singing to her. She can hear you."

He gave her a soft smile and nodded in acceptance.

"Why are you showing me this now?" she asked.

His eyes were solemn as he squeezed her hand. "Because I want you to know if the prophecy really is true, and if there are only two options for me, there is just one path I can take."

"Wilder—"

His words were a solemn vow. "He will not convert me. Not even as a ruse."

She wanted to pound her fist against his chest until he relented, but she had seen his memory. Had lived it. She knew what he would choose.

As she left the stone garden, she heard him begin the Goddess's Aria, this time in the voice of a man instead of a child. The two melodies, an octave apart, blended together in her mind until the night rang with his song.

She hoped the Goddess roused enough to listen, because soon enough, the Scion would be destroyed.

DISCIPLINE

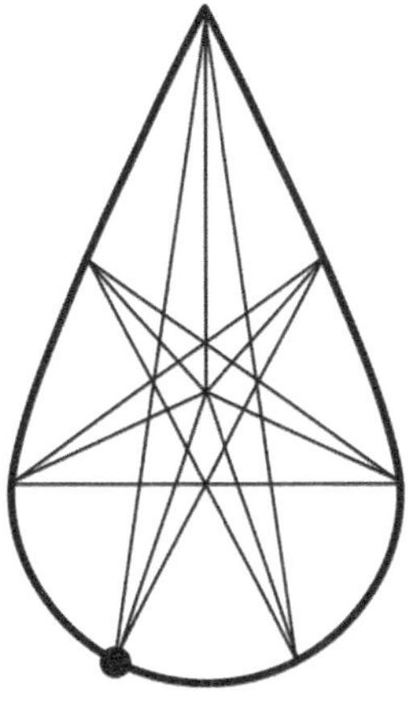

INDULGENCE

38

———

When they returned to the Heart the following day, she went immediately to find Kai. Since Vaylan's veiled threat, Rose had been terrified he would hurt her brother, but she returned to find him practicing katas alone in the black tent.

She showed him the translated note Wilder had given her from Quinn.

She was right but failed.

I will continue.

"It's about Sian," she whispered. "I know it is."

Kai's face fell. "You think Vaylan had her killed?"

"I'm sure of it," she hissed angrily. "But what does Walter think he is doing? He's going to get himself killed, too!"

He studied her with eyes that knew her too well. "There are some things worth dying for."

She smacked him hard on the arm. "You sound like Wilder. His idiotic plan is going to get him killed."

His voice was gentle, but she didn't like it. "I wasn't talking about Wilder."

Their siblings.

She crossed her arms over her chest and grumbled,

"Their plan got them killed, too. And with nothing to show for it."

"They thought it was important to resist. To fight. You, of all people, should understand."

After her two older brothers and sister were killed, she refused to speak to anyone, even Kai and Caed. She spent months training in silence, afraid the fury and grief within would consume her. There was a day she saw Kai and their older brother Spencer sharing stories about their siblings, tears freely running down their faces. She had run in the other direction, afraid that if she let her tears fall like that, they would never stop.

"I do understand," she whispered. "But why didn't they take me with them?"

Kai took gentle hold of her arm. "Rosie, we were just kids. There was nothing we could do."

That feeling of helplessness drove her to train. It's what shaped her into the person she was today. She refused to ever be that weak again.

"I won't let Wilder surrender himself," she whispered harshly. "I will not let Vaylan have him."

Kai raised an eyebrow. "A few days ago, Rev had a knife to your throat because you threatened Wilder, and now you're back to being overprotective of him?"

She opened her mouth to give a perfectly reasonable explanation when two Sentinels stepped inside and held the tent flap open for her. She grumbled at the silent summons, hugged Kai, then followed them to Vaylan's tent.

Vaylan sat at the head of his long table, staring into a glass of wine, lost in thought. Walter sat next to him, a stack of notebooks piled around him, his eyes completely focused on writing neat little lines of what appeared to be gibberish. Vaylan looked up and appeared startled to find her but recovered enough to wave her into the seat at the far end.

She sat down slowly, wondering if Vaylan was preparing to do something awful to get Walter to talk.

"Who are Sian's friends?" he asked suddenly.

She was completely shocked at his line of questioning and blurted out, "Why do you want to know?"

He smiled, but there was something forced about it. "You mentioned she was missing. I'd like to help."

She narrowed her eyes. "You didn't seem interested in helping before. What happened?"

Walter lifted his head from his notebook. "Someone broke into Vaylan's room last night." He patted Vaylan on the hand as if comforting a child.

Vaylan's lip twitched in irritation, and it took all of Rose's strength not to stare at Walter in shock. Instead, she kept her eyes on Vaylan and noticed something interesting. Besides being irritated that Walter had ruined his plan to get information out of Rose, he didn't appear to suspect Walter at all. His eyes watched Rose, seeing what she would reveal.

"You think Sian's friends broke in?" she asked.

"Possibly." His voice was calm, but she detected a faint ripple of tension behind it.

"Did they take something?" She tried to restrain her excitement at the thought that Walter found the prophecies Sian had been seeking.

"No." He seemed confused, so Rose thought he was telling the truth.

She tried to contain her frustration. "Then what's the problem?"

Anger flashed behind his eyes before it was quickly smothered. "The problem is that someone violated my privacy. I'd like to find out who."

"I only met Sian once. I'm afraid I don't know her friends." She tried to keep her voice as casual as possible.

Vaylan steepled his fingers in front of his face, and Rose detected something strange in his eyes but couldn't identify it yet.

"I know about Walter," Vaylan blurted out unexpectedly.

Walter didn't look up but continued writing in his notebook.

"What do you know about him?" she asked slowly.

Vaylan pursed his lips. "I know he can grant long life."

She laughed in what she hoped was a convincing manner. "Is this another of your prophecies?"

His twinkling eyes hardened. "I know you know something, Rose."

"So, you think he has some Gift from the Goddess? I'm surprised you'd be interested in that."

"It's not from the Goddess. It's something else." His voice was brittle and less confident than she had ever heard.

"Something like your ability to manipulate crystalline?" It was risky to antagonize him but she couldn't help herself.

"It's nothing like that," he spat.

Walter raised his head. "I remember having this conversation once ..."

Vaylan and Rose both turned to look at him. Rose was terrified at what he might reveal, but Vaylan was practically salivating at the promised information.

Walter flipped through the pages of one of his notebooks. "I can't remember who I was talking to ..." He tapped his finger on the table as he thought. "Was it the calico or the tabby?"

Vaylan hung on his every word and repeated, "The calico or the—cats ... Walter, are you talking about cats?"

Walter ignored him and continued flipping through the pages. "I'm sure I wrote it down somewhere."

Rose put her hand to her mouth to cover a laugh, but

Vaylan's face went slack as he stared at Walter. She had never seen his face so expressionless.

Then Vaylan straightened his shoulders, took a deep breath, and smiled at Rose with his dimple on display. "Walter is such a delight, isn't he? I always enjoy my time with him."

That's when Rose heard it. What Kieran had told her to watch for.

Just keep your eyes open to see what he is trying to hide. Especially if it is something he is trying to hide from himself.

Vaylan needed Walter, and not just because he was power hungry.

He was desperate.

And now was the time for her to attack.

"Why are you so interested in this rumor about long life, Vaylan? Don't the prophecies already tell you how long you will live?"

Suddenly, all the crystalline throughout the Heart flared. Even though Vaylan's cheerful expression never shifted, the light coming through the fabric of the tent let her see deep into his eyes. She finally found what she was looking for.

Doubt.

"Do not mock the prophecies." His lips still curled in a frozen smile, but his voice was deadly calm. "Their complexity is above you, Marked One."

All thoughts of a precise attack flew away, and Rose opened her mouth for an unfiltered rant when Walter raised his head again.

"Marked One ..." he said thoughtfully. He tilted his head and recited:

> *A flower contained will not grow.*
> *She must be replanted in an open space.*
> *Her heart has been broken and marked by pain,*

But the shattered pieces let the fire shine through.

"Thank you, Walter," said Vaylan, his serene voice restored. "Yes, Rose is the one I marked by pain."

Rose continued staring at Walter, all thoughts of attacking Vaylan forgotten. She raised a hand to Vaylan's fingerprint on her collarbone. It still stung as on the first day she got it. But that pain was nothing compared to the other pain she had lived through. The pain of losing her siblings and being powerless to stop the High Priests. That heartbreak was greater than anything Vaylan could do to her.

The shattered pieces let the fire shine through …

She absently touched the fingerprint and whispered, "You aren't the one who marked me …"

"Of course, I—"

Her voice grew louder. "You aren't the one—"

Walter reached across the table to grab another notebook and knocked over Vaylan's wine, spilling it down the table and onto Rose.

As she stared at the red stain on her white jacket, she realized that arguing about her Spark with Vaylan was a terrible idea. She looked at Walter, appreciative for the accident, but he ignored her as he flipped through the notebook in his hand.

"I think that conversation with the calico is on page fifty-seven." He opened to a page where he had drawn a cat tiptoeing across letters written in the strange language. He tapped his finger on his lips thoughtfully. "Yes, page fifty-seven … Fascinating …"

Vaylan smiled patiently, but she heard the shaking sigh he tried to hide.

As she left his tent, she bowed, hoping he wouldn't see the grin spreading across her face.

39

Rose tried to guess the identities of the two Sentinels that followed her to the laundry. She was sure one of them was Dany, although she couldn't say exactly why. Dany hadn't laughed or rolled her head in annoyance or any of the more obvious things she did that identified her. But somehow, Rose had an odd feeling of comfort with the two Sentinels walking quietly behind her, and she could only attribute that to one of them being Dany.

They took up positions outside the entrance to the laundry and allowed Rose to enter alone. Rose always made it a priority to know the people who cared for her clothes, so she received several smiles and waves, but it was Luca who ran up to her first.

"Rose! What did you do?" He gently touched her stained jacket and clicked his tongue. "I've come to expect dirt and bloodstains, but wine?"

She held up her hands in mock surrender. "It wasn't my fault, Luca! I'm the victim here."

He patted her on the back comfortingly. "Come with me, dear. I will find you another jacket to wear while I work on this one." She took off the long, sleek jacket, and Luca handed her a puffy coat.

The coat made her look frumpy, and she frowned. "Are you punishing me?"

He gave her a sly look out of the corner of his eye that said perhaps he was. "I've heard it's cold Upstairs, dear. I'm trying to keep you warm."

"I'd rather be cold," she grumbled but obediently took the ugly coat. "I promise I'll be careful. Your job is much harder than the people who cared for the Priests' black clothing."

He brushed his fingers against the stain, but his expression softened. "I'm sure I'll be able to fix this for you, dear. You'll be back to your fashionable self in no time."

"Thanks, Luca." She bowed respectfully, then turned to go, but he pulled her back.

"Wait! I've got something for you." He rummaged through a stack of white clothes and pulled out a small notebook. "That nice older gentleman dropped this off for you this morning."

She took the notebook and held it with careful fingers. "Walter left this for me?"

"He said you would stop by." Luca gave her a catty look. "Apparently, he guessed you'd be sloppy with your wine today."

"Yes," she said slowly. "He *guessed*."

She tucked the notebook inside her lumpy coat and tried to walk calmly back to her tent. Even though she felt safe in her assumption that it was Dany at her back, she didn't want to reveal the notebook to anyone. She knew it must contain what Walter had discovered in Vaylan's tent. Vaylan was hiding something, and she prayed Walter had discovered it.

She threw back the flap of her tent, ready to pick through Walter's writing, but froze in the doorway.

"Who did this?" whispered Dany as she removed her mask.

The room was in shambles. Rose only had the few possessions the Adopted had brought her, but they were scattered throughout the tent. Her bed had been torn apart, pillows and blankets tossed carelessly on the floor. Her small desk had been emptied of all its papers, and the stack of books had been knocked to the ground with the pages crumpled as if someone had rifled through them with a rough hand.

Dany picked up the fallen rack of clothes and looked at a pair of pants that had the pockets turned out. "What were they looking for?"

Rose clenched her hands into fists to keep them from floating to the notebook tucked inside her coat.

"I can't stay here." Rose fled the tent, Dany hurriedly putting her mask on to follow.

Rose found her way to the black tent and stopped outside. "Dany, can you bring me a candle? It's dark in there."

It was just as dark as it had always been, but Dany jerked her head, and the other Sentinel nodded in compliance before walking away. Dany then moved to stand in front of the tent flap despite the other Sentinels already stationed there. Rose touched her on the arm, then ducked inside.

Kai stopped in the middle of a kata at the look on her face. He rushed to her side and whispered, "What happened?"

"Someone searched my tent."

"Do you know what they were looking for?" he asked in a low voice.

She nodded and touched the front of her coat.

His eyes widened, but he didn't speak.

A Sentinel opened the flap of the tent, holding a lantern with a burning candle. She bowed gratefully and took it to the center of the tent, as far away from any listening ears as possible. Kai sat close to her as she pulled the notebook out of her coat with shaking hands.

"It's from Walter," she breathed. "It's what Vaylan has been hiding and what Sian died trying to discover."

They both bowed their heads in reverence before she opened the notebook to the first page.

It was a recipe for cranberry muffins.

The next two pages were written in the old language, and the following page was a drawing of a curvy woman bending over to knead a loaf of bread. Rose flipped through several more pages of recipes before she groaned.

"This is what he left for me? Why did I expect something from him to make sense?"

Kai studied the pages, trying to understand. "Did he say anything else? Any other clues?"

The next page had a small cat curled up on a recipe for an omelet. She tilted her head as she thought back to what Walter had said about the calico cat. Then she flipped ahead to page fifty-seven.

A vine of roses wound around the neat letters.

The City cannot be ruled by one alone.

Even seven, when standing together, control as a single body.

Give others a voice, those who do not believe as you, and the City will prosper.

"Why would Vaylan be so desperate to keep that a secret?" asked Kai.

Rose's voice hardened. "He plans to rule alone. He's never been afraid to admit that. I guess he doesn't want his followers knowing Brother Owyn said ruling alone was no better than the High Priests in charge."

"So, he doesn't believe everything Brother Owyn taught?"

Rose tapped her lips in thought. "I'm sure he's rationalized this and believes it means the complete opposite for him."

Rose skimmed through the next several pages, which all appeared to be Brother Owyn's teaching. Once again, she was struck with the beauty of his words. The ideas he proposed were revolutionary for a City that had been ruled by High Priests, but these passages were all about the danger of power and the illusion of control.

"Vaylan's hiding this from the Adopted," she said. "Yasmine and her friends will pour over these passages, examining each word for hidden meaning. He might have some explanation that makes sense in his brain, but he knows he wouldn't be able to convince anyone else." She grinned wickedly. "I can't wait to share this with them."

She flipped to the next page, which only held a single sentence.

The Founder's life will be cut short.

She slammed the book on the ground and jumped to her feet. "This is it!" She pressed her hands against her mouth to keep her voice down. "This is what I've been looking for. Everything is going to be okay!"

Kai had picked up the book and studied it with a curious expression. "Does this mean Vaylan will die soon?"

"This is why he's so desperate to get Walter to use his Spark. He's hoping to find a loophole to keep this prophecy from coming true."

"Why wouldn't he just rewrite the words to say what he wants?"

"Because he's a true believer, Kai. He wrote down everything Brother Owyn said in painstaking detail and believes it so much he had to hide the passages that scared him." She laughed viciously. "But he has doubts ... I bet it's eating him up inside."

"Um ... Rosie?" Kai's voice was tentative. "Can you take a few deep breaths for me?"

She spun around to look at him and noticed the shadows flickering oddly on the wall. Her eyes dropped to the dark lantern on the floor.

The shadows danced from the flames simmering on her fingers.

She looked at her hands, amazed at the warm energy prickling against her skin. "Sorry, Kai. I guess—"

The room brightened as the tent flap opened suddenly. "Someone was in your tent, Marked ..." Yasmine's voice trailed off as she stared at Rose standing with burning hands outstretched.

Rose closed her hands into fists, plunging the tent into the usual shadowed interior.

"Yasmine ..." Rose cleared her throat, trying to find the right words. "That was—"

"*The one who grants freedom is the one who controls the light*," she breathed. She looked Rose in the eyes. "It's not him. It's you."

"Um ... It's just a little fire—"

"We should have seen this earlier ..." Yasmine stared off into the distance, lost in thought. "We thought the one who controlled the light was Vaylan ... It seemed so obvious."

Rose took a tentative step closer. "Yasmine, I don't know what you are talking about, but I need you—"

"But you've been the one controlling the light of each crystal. It's been you all along." A smile spread across her face, and she bounced eagerly on her toes. "I can't wait to tell the others!"

"No!" Both Rose and Kai rushed to her side.

"Yasmine, you can't tell anyone what you saw," said Rose. "I need you to promise me."

"But this changes everything! We have to discuss this and figure out what it means."

Rose rubbed her fingers through her hair in frustration. "This isn't just theology, Yasmine. If Vaylan finds out, it will ruin everything."

"But …" Yasmine looked torn between following the orders of the Marked One and spreading a juicy bit of gossip to her prophecy small group.

Rose grabbed Walter's notebook off the ground and held it before her reverently. "Do you know what this is?"

Yasmine's eyes lit up even as she shook her head no.

"It's what Sian died trying to find. It's the prophecies Vaylan has kept secret."

Yasmine appeared to stop breathing for a moment, looking even more surprised than when she saw Rose with flames on her fingers.

"I will make you a deal," said Rose. "I will give you this book to share and discuss with your friends, but you have to promise me you will tell no one what you saw."

Yasmine bit her lip, torn at the difficult choice, but in the end, the book full of prophecies won out. She nodded and held out her hands.

40

Rose didn't want to go back to her wrecked tent, so she stayed the night with Kai. It had been a long time since they had shared a room, and she remembered getting in trouble with Mims for talking too much and sleeping too little. This time was no different, as they spent most of the night discussing prophecies and boys. When the Sentinels arrived in the morning, it felt like she had hardly slept at all.

When they entered the throne room, Rose looked around for Yasmine but didn't see her. Rose hoped she was off with her friends, pouring over the prophecies Walter had discovered. She hoped the prophecies were so distracting she forgot all about seeing Rose's Spark.

Rose was so busy looking around she was surprised to see Kai staring at Vaylan with wide eyes.

"He's dangerous, Rosie," he breathed out in warning.

She coughed a laugh. "He's held you prisoner for days, has tortured people with crystalline, and had his own followers killed, and you just now realize he is dangerous?"

He disregarded her sarcasm and continued watching Vaylan. "His smile seems more brittle than the last time I saw him, but the difference is in the people around him. Look at their eyes. Does it remind you of anything?"

The Adopted closest to Vaylan stood with bowed heads and a woman hurried forward to place something in his hand before backing out of the room with a bow.

Rose shrugged. "They seem just as subservient as always."

"Look harder, Rosie." Kai's gaze followed a man in white as he rubbed his hands together nervously. The man's eyes were firmly planted on the ground in front of him, but Rose sensed that he desperately wanted to look up to see if he was in danger so he could flee.

"Look familiar?" asked Kai.

Rose's breath escaped in a rush when she noticed it. Her whisper was as quiet and small as she suddenly felt. "It's the way we acted around the High Priests."

Kai nodded slowly. "He's changed. Or maybe it's only that they recognize it now. I'm glad they finally see who he truly is."

Rose watched a woman exhale in relief after Vaylan passed her by. Rose's whisper was bitter. "What does it matter? We knew exactly how evil the High Priests were and still couldn't stop them."

He didn't have a good answer, but he took her hand as they walked out of the Heart.

When they arrived at the final crystal spire, the gathered people watched her with wide eyes. Vaylan summoned her forward with his usual cheerfulness, but Rose felt the dread rippling through the crowd. She wanted to give them hope by saying this was the final crystal, that now the Companion would recover and all would be made well soon.

She just didn't think she could say the hopeful words as honestly as she wished.

She placed her hands on the crystal and pressed her heart inside.

The Goddess sat with her eyes closed in the dark cave at the old wooden table. She looked just like the woman from Wilder's vision. Messy hair, ripped sweater, and unspeakably sad. Rose took the seat across from her, waiting for the Goddess to speak first.

The Goddess's red-rimmed eyes opened. "Thank you for asking Wilder to sing."

She looked so fragile, yet after seeing Wilder's vision, Rose's heart clenched with the same feeling of reverence young Wilder had felt. She held her breath, unable to respond.

The Goddess stared off into the distance. "I hear the others rehearsing ... That's good. You must hurry."

Rose's lips opened, but she couldn't form the question. She was too afraid to know the answer.

The Goddess answered her anyway. "He's not gone yet." She closed her eyes, and Rose had the feeling she was sensing something Rose could not. "A fragment of him remains." She opened her eyes with a piercing stare. "I believe you will take away even that fragment before the end."

Rose whispered, "I'm so—"

The Goddess waved her apology away. "Don't apologize for something I told you to do," she snapped. "I'm gambling with his life that this will work. I'd prefer I was betting on my own skill instead of relying on yours, but I'm desperate, so ..." She shrugged.

Rose's eyebrow twitched in irritation. "It's unfortunate that you have to rely on a mere mortal."

The Goddess rolled her eyes. "That's how this whole thing works, Rose. Do you think a yearly Pageant is really what I would choose if I had my way?"

Rose leaned back in her chair and crossed her arms over her chest. "I'm not sure which version of you I prefer: catatonic or combative."

A flicker of pain flashed behind the Goddess's eyes, and Rose realized that wasn't honest. She knew which version she preferred.

Rose looked away from the Goddess's pained look and said loftily, "No need to worry. I will make sure the other mortals sing your silly songs. The City will be saved, and Vaylan will be defeated. Then you can roll your eyes next year as we do it all again."

Rose found it amazing how a woman in ripped clothes and wrecked hair could glare at her with such regal condescension. The Goddess tapped her nail on the table as she stared at Rose with piercing green eyes until Rose was so uncomfortable, she had to look away.

"Poor Wilder," said the Goddess. "That he should be cursed to fall in love with someone as willful as you. He has a hard road before him."

Rose's eyes snapped up. Her heart stirred at the mention of Wilder's name, then immediately flared into anger.

"He has no road ahead of him, thanks to you, Goddess," she spat the name. "Because of his devotion to you, he will choose to let Vaylan destroy him. If you would just release him—"

The Goddess grabbed Rose's hand in a grip hard as stone and spoke in a voice just as cold. "I surrender nothing that belongs to me. If you or Vaylan believe otherwise, you are mistaken."

Rose blinked and was suddenly back in the Grotto.

After they arrived at the final temple, Rose kneeled for her usual plea to save the Priests. But before she could walk inside to convince them to leave, Vaylan stepped in front of her.

"There is no need for you to convince them to leave, Rose. I've decided to let them remain here until the Pageant."

She narrowed her eyes at him. "You've decided to *let them remain* ... Do you mean they are your prisoners?"

He gave her a look that said she had poor manners to call it such. "The Pageant must be performed again, as the prophecy says, but I need a guarantee to make sure Wilder keeps his end of the bargain."

She crossed her arms. "You don't think he can be trusted?"

Vaylan's eyes twinkled. "Oh, I trust him to do what he says. However, his good intentions would be in vain if you knock him unconscious and drag him off somewhere I can't find him."

She ground her teeth in irritation that he had figured out one of her plans.

He chuckled. "You are just too obvious, Marked One. But don't worry, I have other ways to make sure the prophecy is fulfilled." He held out his hands and drew his fingers together, interlocking them in a slow pattern. A fine crystalline mesh formed across each of the arches leading inside the temple, leaving only one arch guarded by Sentinels.

He smiled at Rose, but his eyes were sharp. "This was your home, so I'm sure you know almost everyone inside. You will want to keep them safe."

She felt the familiar helplessness settle over her. There was a part of her that wanted to strangle him with no regard for the consequences. And yet, there was still a part of her just as frozen in fear as when the High Priests ruled.

He lowered his voice, as if to comfort her. "As an act of good faith, I will release your brother now." He nodded his head, and the two Sentinels to either side of Kai removed his ropes and his black robe and left him standing in simple white linen trousers and shirt.

Kai shivered in the cold air and looked around, unsure what to do next.

Vaylan shooed him as if waving off an annoying fly. "Go on now. Tell them the Pageant must be ready by tomorrow night. After the Pageant, I expect Wilder to meet me inside the amphitheater, as promised."

Kai looked between Rose and Vaylan with a confused expression. Kai shrugged and turned to head into the City, when Rose called out, "Wait! Aren't you forgetting something, Vaylan?"

Vaylan gave her an innocent look.

She growled, "I'm supposed to cause the Chosen to suffer before sending him into the dark. It's still daylight, and I haven't hurt him yet."

Vaylan chuckled. "I think we can dispose of that little illusion now, can't we? At the Pageant, you will do what the prophecy says. You will deliver Wilder into my hands. You will cause him to suffer, then he will disappear into the dark. Thanks to you darkening all the crystals, that last part should be easy, but I'm sure you will figure out how to do the rest as needed."

Vaylan had already hinted that he knew Wilder was the Chosen, but to hear him say it out loud shocked her. She wanted to deny it, to say she would never hand Wilder over to him, but there was still a deep fear in her heart that she might.

She watched Kai melt into the crowd of people under a bright, cold sky. When she could no longer see his white clothing, she walked inside the temple, locking herself safely away behind Vaylan's crystalline.

41

Rose sat atop Temple Discipline, her back pressed against the cold crystal. She had often climbed to the top of the temple when she was younger, but she'd never had to wear a bulky jacket before. The wind was biting cold against her cheeks, which did a good job of quickly drying any rogue tears. She wasn't sure how long she could last in the cold, but she couldn't bring herself to go inside at the risk of seeing any familiar faces.

Instead, a familiar face joined her.

Mims pulled herself onto the ledge, then plopped down next to Rose with a sigh. "It was much easier for me to find you up here when you were little. I'm not as young as I used to be."

Rose snorted a laugh. Mims had raised Priests in the temple for decades and had to be over sixty, though Rose knew better than to ask. Despite her age, Mims was still agile enough to train with the other Discipline Priests. She was a lot more winded than Rose from the climb but not struggling.

"I don't think I'm good company right now, Mims. I'm in a bad mood."

"If I avoided you every time you were in a bad mood, I would never see you, dear." She patted Rose's hand sweetly to remove any sting.

Rose found the words too true to be offensive.

"I first looked for you in the training room," said Mims. "That's where you usually go to wrestle with your thoughts. Then I went to your old room to see if you were hiding in there, but they told me you chose another bedroom. Escaping to the roof only happened when you were avoiding something ... or someone."

Rose sighed. "I'm trying to do the right thing, Mims. I'm hiding to keep someone safe, but he's unwilling to listen when I tell him how dangerous this situation is. Vaylan is going to use me to get to him, and even though I know that, it's so hard to stay away."

Mims leaned her head back against the crystal, and her lips curved in a small smile. "I prayed to the Goddess that someday you would fall in love with someone who drove you crazy."

Rose gaped at her. "Why would you do that?"

Mims turned to her with a serious expression. "Rose, dear, if you fell in love with a weak man who always let you have your way, you would walk all over him, leaving you both miserable. I prayed you would find someone strong willed enough to be your match. I knew it would be such a surprising experience for you that it would drive you crazy."

Rose grumbled, "It appears your prayers were answered."

Mims squeezed her arm warmly. "Wilder is a very attractive young man."

Rose rolled her eyes. "He will be glad to know that you agree with everyone else in the City in that regard."

"He helped us that night with the young Priests." Mims

looked away with an innocent expression on her face. "He's very good with babies."

"Mims ..." said Rose warningly.

"A couple former Priests are now pregnant," she continued in her innocent tone. "I just want you to keep that in mind."

Rose's mouth dropped open.

Mims face took on a dreamy expression. "I've been a mother to over a dozen children, but I've never considered being a grandmother."

Rose sat forward abruptly to look Mims in the eyes. "You are getting ahead of yourself here. There is no guarantee that Wilder and I will make it through this together. I've hurt him so many times I'm surprised he hasn't given up on me entirely." She sighed dramatically. "It's probably best for the both of us if we just figure everything out on our own."

Mims raised an eyebrow, and her sharp look told Rose to prepare for a lesson.

"You've always wanted to do things on your own, Rose. The hardest part about being your mother was trying to convince you to let me help. You never wanted to show weakness, even as a child."

Mims smiled as she sank into the memory. "When you were three years old, you toddled past me with a determined look on your face. A few minutes later, you walked by with a screwdriver in your hand. Naturally, I followed you to see what you were up to. In the nursery you shared with Caed and Kai, you had pushed a chair up to the dresser and were climbing up. The shade on the crystalline lamp had come loose and was hanging crookedly. I have no idea how you planned to fix it, but one thing was clear. You had no intention of asking me for help."

She chuckled softly. "I took the screwdriver from you and explained you were not allowed to touch crystalline lamps or to use screwdrivers or any other tools *because you were a baby.* You weren't old enough to articulate your defense or to call my pronouncement unfair, because again, *you were a baby.* That is just one example of what you've always believed: You can and should do everything alone."

She placed her hand on Rose's arm. "You have grown into a young woman with a strong body and an even stronger will, and there is no doubt in my mind that you could be happy living your life alone. But if you want a partner for your journey, it will require a level of strength you have not needed until now ... The strength to trust in someone else."

Rose leaned her head back against the crystal and closed her eyes. She couldn't look at Mims when her words felt so weak. "But I'm afraid. What if something happens to him? I can't bear losing him, Mims. I just can't."

"The pain won't be less if you give him up now and live a lifetime without him, dear. But it's up to you to decide if he is worth your trust. Standing toe to toe with you will require a formidable young man. Is he that?"

Rose pictured Wilder full of passion and energy and magic and strength and sighed, "He's quite impressive."

She patted Rose on the leg. "Well then, dear, you must decide if you are brave enough to trust him."

Mims pulled herself to her feet, then offered Rose a hand. "If you aren't in your old room, where are you staying?"

Rose brushed off her white pants and said, "I took one of the acolytes' rooms."

Mims grinned knowingly. "It's obvious Vaylan never had to raise teenagers. Otherwise, he would have known to block off the second-story windows as well." She winked and climbed down as Rose just stared in surprise.

42

Rose heard the music coming from the amphitheater before she made it inside. A pair of Priests at the backstage door bowed to her before letting her in. Even though Vaylan had given them permission to use the amphitheater, Rose thought they were wise to keep a lookout.

Rose hid in the wings as best she could for someone wearing all white. Feather and Kieran stood center stage, singing the newest song of the Pageant, the Wedding of the Goddess and Companion.

Before she left, Ylena had transcribed the entire score with the help of some musicians, so as a result, the song was as beautiful as the day it had first been written. Rose found the Goddess to be quite irritating sometimes, but she still hoped the Goddess perked up at hearing something so lovely.

Rose took satisfaction in Feather's skill, considering Rose had picked her for the role. Though she still felt a little guilty for overreacting while watching Feather perform with Wilder. She sang the love song with Kieran, who Rose had also picked, despite Wilder's initial objections. She watched them both with pride and smiled. The Pageant would be beautiful, the Goddess would return her Gifts, and Rose would have plenty of time to save Mims and the other Priests at Temple Disciple after she kidnapped Wilder to stop him from his insane plan.

Simple.

As they finished the last note, the cast cheered. When the backstage lights brightened, Rose looked out from behind the curtain to see Wilder standing in the orchestra pit. He raised his fingers in an intricate pattern, moving the stone to adjust the flow of the crystalline lights. She wasn't sure what Vaylan would think about that, but it comforted Rose to see crystalline once again flowing upward around stone pipes as it should.

Wilder finished with the lights and talked to the orchestra leader. The man had short silver hair and wore a gray fur coat with a purple scarf. He appeared to be the warmest person in the cold amphitheater.

Wilder looked stunning, as usual, with his tight black pants and a sleek leather jacket. But in his eyes, Rose saw a deep exhaustion. He was working too hard and not sleeping enough. She needed to force him to lie down and take a nap.

She imagined curling up beside him as he slept. His broad chest rising and falling with each breath. Her head resting on his shoulder with his arm wrapped around her, hand resting casually on her hip. Before she could sigh at such a pleasant thought, Wilder's eyes snapped up and caught hers.

His lips curved into a smug grin, and she swore he had plucked the thoughts out of her mind. Her cheeks reddened, but she tried to pretend it was from the cold wind.

Goddess-damn that smug grin.

And Goddess-damn Mims's prayers.

She straightened her back to regain her dignity and walked onstage. Feather took one look at her, then ducked her head and hurried away. Kieran smirked and gave her an ironic salute before heading backstage. Rose walked to the front of the stage and kneeled by the basin.

It still glowed with a faint white light. The Goddess said a fragment of the Companion remained. Rose would need to darken this crystal as well.

"I think you should wait until tomorrow during the Pageant," said Wilder quietly. "Hold off until the moment before the Gifts return."

Even kneeling, she was taller than him from her position on the stage. She tried to use that sense of authority to her advantage. "Neither of us will be here tomorrow night. There is no way I am giving you to Vaylan, either accidentally or on purpose."

Wilder hopped nimbly onto the stage and stood over her. "I will be here, Rose. You can't stop me."

She scrambled to her feet angrily, prepared to launch into an argument, when Rev dashed on stage.

"I brought food!" Rev crooned. "Let's eat!"

Wilder spun on his heel and helped Rev spread blankets over the stage with a big smile. "Good timing, Rev."

The rest of the cast had already been dismissed for the night, so it was only their crew that gathered on stage to eat. Kai and Quinn both smiled at her before they sat down on a blanket together, eating and totally ignoring the rest of them. Fitz waved at her while Tayeh punched her on the arm warmly. Rev smiled but never stopped watching her with her sharp blue eye. Feather sat as far away as possible, apparently finding Kieran safer company than Rose.

Rev picked up an apple with a shaking hand. "It's so cold I can barely eat," she whined.

Rose looked at the stack of bright red apples next to a

platter of some other fresh fruits and vegetables. Wilder had also found time to grow food for everyone? How was he not falling over from exhaustion?

Wilder sat down on the blanket next to her, and she was startled when she caught him staring. "What?"

"The crew is cold," he said casually. "Surely you have the means to help?"

"Oh ... I hadn't considered that." Most of her experience using her Spark was accidental, and she hadn't found time to experiment. "I'm not exactly sure what to do." She looked around at the wooden stage and flammable curtains. "I can burn this whole place down or do this ..." A small flame appeared to hover above her palm. "I don't know how to do much in between."

Wilder leaned over and blew gently on the flame. She felt his warm breath not only on her palm, but on the imaginary nerve endings of the flame itself. It pulled an embarrassing gasp from her lungs, but thankfully, the others were distracted by Wilder's arm movements. He grabbed hold of the warm wind he had stoked and swirled it into a slow whirlwind surrounding them.

He looked at Rose with a steady gaze and blew one more slow, sultry breath across her palm. She bit her lip to keep from gasping again. He held her stare as he gathered up all the warmth and wrapped it around the crew, pressing the cold air away.

Rev sighed. "Wilder, you are a blessed genius." She took off her heavy coat and stretched out on it like a cat.

Wilder's eyes hadn't left Rose's face, and it infuriated her to know he could read every sensation written there.

"You've been practicing." She tried to sound nonchalant, but her voice came out squeakier than she hoped.

"I like to do things well," he said with a knowing grin.

Rose bit into an apple, determined to not let him distract

her from her actual goal. She swallowed the bite, then took a deep breath, turning away from him and facing the crew. "Vaylan knows Wilder is the Chosen and is determined to get him tomorrow night."

Wilder shook his head. "Rose, it doesn't matter. I've already said I'm handing myself over to him. The Goddess's Gifts will return by the end, so it will be fine."

She intentionally didn't look at him, determined to win over the rest of the crew. "Here's the plan: Rev, Quinn, and Fitz will stay here at the amphitheater, watching over Feather and Kieran as they perform. Tayeh will go with Kai to Temple Discipline and free the Priests there before Vaylan can harm them. The wolves and I will take Wilder somewhere safe and hide him. It's a good plan." She clapped her hands together. "Questions?"

The only one willing to look at her was Wilder, who simply stared at her with a hard expression. The others looked in every other direction except at her.

She crossed her arms over her chest. "Why aren't you saying anything?"

Kieran rolled his eyes, then finally looked at her. "I think we all have a good idea what the plan should actually be, but no one wants to speak up and become the first one you murder."

Her voice was cold and tight. "If everyone would just follow my orders, no one will be murdered at all."

Tayeh looked up with hard eyes. "We follow you by choice, Rose. We aren't mindless soldiers obeying commands."

Tayeh's words made Rose sound too much like Vaylan, so she stifled her wish they would just obey her. Instead, she ground out the words between clenched teeth, "Fine. What do you think we should do?"

Kai looked at her with an unflinching stare. "We think Wilder should play the role of the Companion."

Her eyes flared. "Do you think I won't stab you just because you're my brother?"

Fitz bravely spoke up. "It's our best chance, Rose. We need the performance to be as powerful as possible to return the Goddess's Gifts. You said yourself that the Goddess loved hearing Wilder sing."

"You made this plan without me?" Rose snapped. "You've all just been sitting around, figuring out a way to get Wilder killed the fastest?"

Rev rolled her eye at Rose. "No, honey, we haven't discussed it at all. It's just obvious to everyone what needs to happen. The Pageant is about stirring the hearts of the people." She waved her hand in a circling pattern to encompass all of Wilder. "Let's give the people what they want."

Rose's head snapped to Feather, who was still quietly hiding behind Kieran. "And I suppose you agree with this brilliant strategy?"

Feather gulped, then straightened her shoulders, bravely facing Rose. "Actually, my plan goes a step further ... I believe you should play the role of the Goddess alongside him."

Rose's mouth dropped open in shock.

Kai gave a barking laugh. "Rosie? Play the Goddess?" He fell over from laughing so hard.

Rose shot him an angry look. "Shut your mouth, Kai." She reared back and threw her apple at him, aiming for his head.

Quinn plucked the apple swiftly out of the air. His eyes were fiercer than Rose had ever seen. "You are being irrational, Rose. Don't blame us because you don't like the plan."

She wanted to scream that she was *not* being irrational

but was afraid that if she opened her mouth, flames would spill out. The entire crew stared at her with a mixture of determination and pity, and it enraged her. She jumped to her feet, hoping to find cooler air when standing.

She looked at the crew, still avoiding Wilder. "You don't know Vaylan like I do. He will twist these prophecies to mean what he wants, and he won't stop until Wilder is dead and the City is under his control. I won't let that happen. Wilder will be nowhere near the Pageant tomorrow."

She felt Wilder's looming presence behind her as he stood. His low voice was calm, yet cold. "I will be on this stage, Rose. I will sing, and the Goddess's Gifts will return. I don't care what the prophecies say. Vaylan will be defeated."

She turned to face him, and her voice was a low growl in her throat. "I'm serious, Wilder."

"So am I, Rose. I will be on this stage. You can join me or not. That's your choice."

"Um ... Wilder ..." Kai's voice was hesitant to draw attention to himself. "Rosie really shouldn't play the Goddess."

She hissed at him without losing her focus, but Wilder broke his stare to look at her brother.

Kai looked at Rose apologetically and said quietly, "She's a brilliant dancer but a terrible singer."

Rose's shield of anger dropped slightly as a wave of embarrassment flooded in. Wilder's head turned slowly back to meet her.

"You aren't a good singer ..." he said slowly, comprehension dawning on his face. "You sat through audition after audition, cutting each person down to their core, and you aren't a good singer?" His voice rose in anger. "You made those girls *cry*, and you aren't even a good singer?"

Rose shoved down her embarrassment and growled, "I will deal with you later, Kai. All of that is irrelevant, Wilder. The only thing that matters is that you will not be on this stage. I will knock you unconscious and drag you out of here myself before I let that happen."

A feral grin slowly curled on his lips. "That's your plan? To fight me to keep me away?" His voice dropped to a low rumble as he stepped closer. "Fine. I will fight you, Rose. And I'll make you a deal. If I tap out first, I will do as you want and run away." He stalked a step closer. "But if I win ... if you surrender to me ... you will watch me perform on this stage. And no matter what Vaylan does, no matter how close he gets, you won't say a single word."

She felt the fire coursing through her blood, the same inner fire she had felt for years. Only now she knew what to do with it. This was a fight she would win.

"Deal," she breathed.

"That's our cue," said Rev, and the crew grabbed their things and scattered.

Rose and Wilder barely noticed them leave.

43

———

Rose stripped off her bulky clothing until she was only in her sleeveless tank and white pants. She made mental note of her hidden blades, including the sharp pins holding her hair in place, then took the two blades from her jacket in each hand. Wilder hadn't moved from his place center stage, watching her with solemn eyes.

"Are you keeping that on?" She pointed at his leather jacket. "You look hot."

"Thanks for admitting it." His normally playful tone was pure intensity. "I considered removing my shirt, but I won't make this any harder on you than necessary."

She had sparred with him several times without his shirt on and found it extremely distracting. But she stoked her anger further and didn't allow him to fluster her.

"Are you hoping the leather will repel the flames? Because I'm telling you, it won't." She gave him a lofty look. "I'd rather explain burned skin than singed leather to my tailor any day."

From the uneasy look in his eye, she thought he might

273

have a tailor as particular as hers. He frowned and cast off his jacket, throwing it backstage.

She grinned savagely, counting it as her first battle won.

"You will surrender to me, Wilder. You know it's the right decision."

"Not this time." He bowed in the traditional manner. "Tonight, you will surrender willingly."

She growled and leaped at him.

He slid easily out of her grasp and circled her warily. He wasn't wearing his usual sheath crossing his chest, and he hadn't pulled any blades out from a hidden sheath, either. Maybe she could end this quickly.

She struck at him in a rapid succession of jabs, thrusts, slices, and kicks, and he blocked each one smoothly. Until her elbow connected squarely with his jaw, and he staggered back a step. He looked at her in surprise and gave her a grudging bow of respect before falling back into his defensive stance.

She had come a long way from the first time she had sparred with him. Back then, she had been almost paralyzed by the shock of losing her Gift and couldn't figure out how to fight at all. But he had coached and trained her, first how to fight without the wind and then how to fight someone like him who had a Gift. And lately, she had been training with Sentinels every day. Sentinels who previously had a Gift and then had it taken away. They taught her to fight in ways she hadn't expected.

And Wilder wouldn't expect it either.

He blocked several more of her shots, then ducked away from her faked punch, which threw him off balance, and she rammed a knee into his ribcage. He stumbled back with a gasp.

She lunged toward him, hoping to carry him down to the ground to get him to surrender quickly, but he straightened faster than she expected. He twisted her arm behind her back, forcing her to the back of the stage and pressing her against the floral backdrop.

His body was warm against her back, and the scent of honeysuckle filled her nose. Her shoulder screamed in protest as he twisted it behind her.

She was impressed at how calm her voice sounded despite the pain. "I don't care how bad you hurt me. I will not cry out." A drop of cool sweat landed on her shoulder, and she savored the tiny bit of relief.

"You won't surrender because of pain." Wilder's whisper was tender and tickled against her ear. "But you will surrender." He pressed his lips against her shoulder, and only then did she realize it hadn't been sweat, but a tear.

A cold blast of healing shot through her as Wilder stepped back, throwing her off balance. She grabbed hold of the floral wall and stared at him in shock.

"Why would you heal me? Don't you want to win?"

"I think we have different definitions of winning," he said softly.

She growled at him. "The deal was whichever one of us cries out first in surrender loses. And I intend to win."

He took a step backward and beckoned to her with a quick flick of his fingers. "Then try again, dear."

His cocky smile was too much for her to bear, so she spread her arms wide and summoned the flames. She had said earlier that she could burn down the amphitheater, which wasn't far from the truth.

Flames lit the perimeter of the stage and began a slow crawl inward, toward Wilder. The wooden stage floor wasn't burning, but she could feel the heat radiating from the flames. This time, it was actual sweat that poured down Wilder's neck, and despite the flames moving away from her and closer to him, sweat trickled down the back of her own neck as well.

Wilder stood in the midst of the flames as if he didn't have a care in the world. He raised his hand and curled his finger in a sultry invitation. At first, she thought he was beckoning her forward again, until she felt the wind.

A thin stream of cool air blew past her. It twirled around her once, lingering on the back of her neck, until she shivered from the sweat, now cold, on her skin. Wilder's finger curled again, and the wind left her to swirl around him.

She watched the breeze playfully tease him, blowing his hair gently in the middle of the firestorm. She was reminded again that the wind was a woman, and her anger caused the fire to burn brighter.

Wilder held out his hand, and Rose saw the cool breeze slide out of his hair. His fingers were spread as if he gently contained the wind inside. He lifted his hand to his mouth and blew.

The cool breeze shot from his hand and landed atop the flames. Rose felt the wind land as if the fire was her own skin, and it sent a shiver down her spine until she had to grip the floral wall for support. The wind sped along the perimeter of the encroaching flames and, instead of blowing them out, stoked them even higher. Wilder sent the wind racing around the circle of flame until the fire almost reached the rafters above the stage. Rose watched the rippling flames in fascination and terror, wondering if she really would burn the whole place down.

Before she could try to contain it, Wilder raised both arms overhead, palms outstretched to gather the wind. Then he slammed his hands down to his sides, bringing a sharp snap of wind crashing down onto the stage.

All the flames were suddenly snuffed out, and Rose staggered once again. She grasped hold of the honeysuckle vines for support, but she didn't notice until Wilder walked her way that the vines grasped her back.

A vine curled itself around her wrist, pulling her against the floral wall. Another vine snaked its way across her boots, while another began looping itself across her shoulder. Wilder came close enough to watch her struggle against the vines, but he didn't touch her.

Rose looked at her wrist and imagined her skin as the flame. The vines charred against her skin and fell away. Her hand shot forward and grabbed Wilder by the front of his shirt, pulling him closer. Another vine grew until it twisted around her wrist again, forcing her hand to release him. She burned away the vines as fast as he could wrap her in them.

He stepped closer, his voice curling around her as smoothly as the honeysuckle. "When you first knew I had all the Gifts, you were intimidated by me. Then, when you realized Vaylan had wicked plans, you were terrified for me. So, which is it, Rose? Am I too much for you? Or too little?"

The vine on her other hand burned away, only to be replaced by another, quicker than she could reach for him. She grumbled in concentration but didn't answer him.

"I'm not either, Rose. I'm your match. Your equal." He spoke with a fervent voice, urging her to respond. "You won't surrender because you're in pain or because you're weak. I'm asking you to surrender because you trust me." He leaned so close she saw the tear fluttering on his lashes. "Trust me like I trust you."

He brushed his lips across hers with such delicate sweetness that she stopped struggling beneath the vines.

She looked at herself but was not herself.

The sensation was even more disorienting than most experiences with the Gift of Knowledge. Her mind settled and placed the moment. She was standing in the dark amphitheater, shortly after speaking to the Goddess and discovering she had a Spark.

*She saw herself in her white showgirl outfit from the perfor-
mance, as her mind currently resided in Wilder's form.*

*She saw her own face as she said, "I love you, Wilder. I will
save the Companion, rescue the crew, then come find you. I
swear it."*

*She felt herself as Wilder smile as he said, "I believe you,
Rose. I'll be waiting."*

*Then she watched herself head into the Heart of the Grottos,
Vaylan's lair, all alone.*

*She felt a dizzying mix of Wilder's emotions. Sad, watching
her go. Lonely, not knowing how long until he would see her
again. But in the midst of it all, she felt his resolute faith in her.*

He believed she would do all she promised and more.

He was not diminished by her strength.

He was enraptured by it.

She returned to herself with a gasp, only to find herself
covered in vines, with Wilder a single step away. She took a
deep breath and burned all the vines away in one quick puff
of ash.

Wilder hadn't moved, so she spun him around and
pressed him against the floral wall, a flaming dagger held
against his throat. She still felt disoriented by the vision, but
the fire in her blood was pounding hard enough that she
knew she had to win.

She had to win to keep him safe.

She had to …

Wilder didn't struggle against her. She pressed him into
the floral wall, honeysuckle clinging to his hair and petals
falling on his shoulders. He looked at her with such intensity she could barely meet his eyes.

"You have the power to make me cry out and end the
fight, you know." He shifted slightly so her blade moved
closer to his throat. "You could cut me, then immediately

cauterize the wound. I'm strong but not strong enough to stay silent through that."

Rose's heart was pounding in her chest, but his voice remained calm. "You could do so many things to hurt me enough to win … And if that's what you want, then do it. I'll surrender and walk away with you, meek as a lamb. I'll forsake my deal with Vaylan and leave the Priests to figure it out while I stay hidden and safe. You can win this right now."

Her mind calculated the ways to hurt him the least while still getting what she wanted. She would find an apothecary and heal any wounds she had caused; then she would hide him deep in the City where Vaylan could never find him, and Wilder would be safe.

Safe, but not her equal.

He saw the hesitation in her eyes and pounced. "Say it, Rose," he whispered fiercely. "Say you trust me like I trust you. Say you believe in the power between us. Say we belong together. That we can defeat Vaylan together. Say we will bring together Priest and Adopted and that we can rebuild this City together."

She was the one holding the blade, and his command was only a whisper, yet she trembled as if she might shatter.

"Say it." His eyes were bright with her reflected fire, and she couldn't look away. "Say you and I will fight and forgive and love each other for the rest of our lives, Rose … Say it."

She drew in a shuddering breath and whispered the words as a promise. "I … surrender."

She barely had time to drop her blade from his throat before he grabbed hold of her, pulling her against him in a passionate kiss. Her blades clattered to the stage floor, and she pressed herself closer to him, crushing him into the honeysuckle with abandon. Her flames combined with his Gift, creating a greenhouse, and every plant on stage began blooming furiously. Vats of water backstage bubbled, and steam poured across the stage in rivers.

Rose was only vaguely aware of such things. She was more aware of Wilder's lips on hers, one of his arms wrapped firmly around her waist, the other hand gently twisted in her hair. The hair pin weapons clicked quietly as they hit the stage floor.

Neither of them noticed her heat combined with his Gift and melted the stone lighting trusses, causing crystalline to flare as it followed the path of the stone back to the orchestra pit floor. Crystalline shimmered dangerously in overheated pools, inching closer to the flammable curtains and wooden stage.

The wolves pounced so fiercely they knocked Wilder and Rose to the ground. When she saw the overheated crystalline, Rose slowly pressed her hands together, dropping the temperature as quickly as she dared. Wilder stretched out his hands and rebuilt the stone trusses, giving the crystalline a smooth grid to flow along. The crystalline flowed upward like slow molasses until it settled into its normal, constant glow.

Rose and Wilder both sank onto the stage in relief.

Wilder looked at the wolves, and a prickle tickled the back of Rose's neck as a conversation she couldn't quite hear was happening between them.

Wilder was kind enough to at least speak his portion out loud. "Yes, I know. We should be careful." He sighed, as if burdened by their mothering. "I'm surprised you didn't stop us earlier. Where were you?"

Storm Fang and Pickles both swung their heads to stare at Rose.

She didn't back down under their accusing glares. "I saw them on the way in and told them I needed to talk to you alone. I warned them not to interfere." She gave them a haughty look. "I guess I will allow your interference this time."

Again, she felt the prickle of unheard language. Wilder bit back a smile but was wise enough not to repeat what they said.

Wilder stood, then held out a hand for Rose. "Let me walk you back to the temple. You need to get some sleep." He grinned. "You'll be back here onstage tomorrow night."

The Pageant

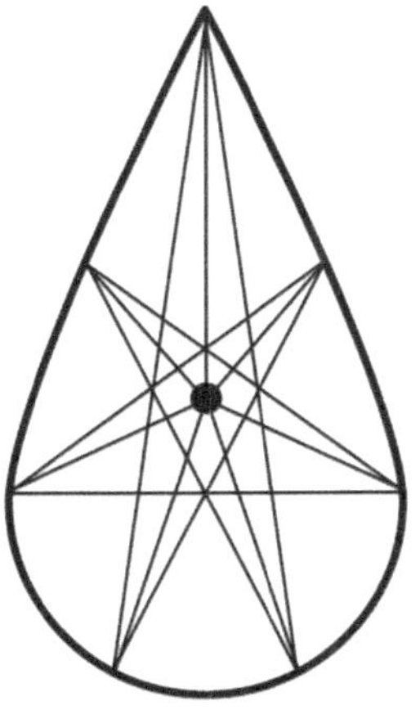

44

Rose's eyes shot open when the Sentinel plopped onto her bed. Before her panic could fully set in, Dany removed her mask and shook out her golden curls.

"You've slept long enough," said Dany. "Wake up and tell me all about that kiss with Wilder."

Rose's chest clenched in fear. She knew Dany suspected her of sneaking out of her room, but Rose was always careful to make sure she wasn't followed. Had Dany guessed she would go to the amphitheater? Did Dany see her fight with Wilder? Did she know Rose could summon fire?

Rose was terrified of all those answers, so she asked, "What kiss?"

Dany snorted a laugh. "That kiss outside the bar down the street. Elise and I snuck out of the temple, and as we left the bar, we saw you kissing." She leaned closer and whispered, "Seriously Rose, that kiss was so hot the two of us giggled about it all night."

"Oh ..." Rose touched her lips at the memory. "That kiss ..."

She had fought with Wilder their entire trip back to the

temple about whether she would perform alongside him in the Pageant. She absolutely refused to humiliate herself by attempting to sing the role. In rare moments, she could admit to herself that she was jealous of Ylena for many things, one of them being her beautiful voice. There was no way that Rose would perform in the Pageant to be compared to Ylena. It wasn't going to happen.

However, Wilder believed differently. He thought it didn't matter to the Goddess how well Rose sang. The Goddess had said Rose reminded her of herself. What could be a better tribute? Plus, the entire City had now seen Rose darken each crystal. If she was on stage when they relit, imagine how powerful that would be? Besides, he sang so beautifully that he'd make up for any of her shortcomings.

It was his last prideful boast that provoked her. She flew at him, but he sidestepped her, trapping her against the wall outside the bar they had just passed. He pressed against her like she had held him against the honeysuckle wall. He reminded her in a low rumbling voice that she had surrendered to him once and should surrender to him again by agreeing to sing.

She fiercely disagreed but pulled him into a kiss just the same.

"Yes, that kiss!" said Dany. "Wait … are you saying there were others like that?" She bounced on the bed. "Tell me! Tell me!"

Rose pushed Dany out of the way and dug through her wardrobe to find something to wear, but also to hide the satisfied grin she couldn't wipe off her face.

"I'm not telling you anything, Dany. Just forget what you saw."

Dany groaned, flopping back on the bed. Rose tried to process the strangeness of a Sentinel lying in her bed, begging to hear juicy secrets about Rose's love life. But despite the armor, Dany was just a girl slightly younger than Rose. A girl who'd been trapped in a Warden's Den her whole life. A girl used by power-hungry Wardens and used again by power-hungry Vaylan. Rose was glad Dany snuck out of the temple and gossiped about kissing boys. It was probably the most normal part of her life.

Dany was still pouting by the time Rose finished dressing in her training outfit. Since Rose refused to be in the Pageant, she needed a distraction to keep her busy all day. Thinking about Wilder onstage, in clear view of Vaylan, caused a pit of anxiety deep in her gut, despite her agreement to trust him. Using sparring as anxiety relief was the only solution she had.

Dany put her mask on to walk Rose down to the training room, then removed it again once they were inside. While Rose sparred with different partners, Dany stood in the corner with the other Sentinels from dance class. They all had their masks removed and stood in a huddle, whispering. Rose found it very suspicious.

And when she heard the giggles, she grew even more suspicious.

"What are you talking about?" asked Rose sharply.

Latham, her first dance student, straightened sharply, then bowed. "Good morning, Marked One. We are discussing prophecies and things."

Rose raised her eyebrow as she studied him. Latham was very chatty, so she knew she could get the information out of him.

She drew herself up taller to look imposing. "Prophecies make you giggle?"

He shrank under the weight of her stare. He murmured, "I said prophecies ... and things ..."

She was about to interrogate him about what *things* that might be when Dany jumped to his defense.

"We heard the Adopted speculating about prophecies this morning, Marked One," said Dany smoothly. "It's caused a lot of discussion among the Sentinels."

Rose gave her a wry look. She was sure that Dany was the source of the giggling, so she called her bluff. "Really? What was this prophecy?"

Dany's Sentinel friend, Elise, cleared her throat, then quoted the words:

Forged in secret
Wielded with silence
The one who grants freedom
Is the one who controls the light

"It's about us," said Latham. "At least, that's what the Adopted believe. We were 'forged in secret, wielded with silence.'"

Elise nodded. "The second part about 'the one who controls the light' is what they were discussing this morning. They always believed it meant Vaylan, but today, they wondered if there could be another interpretation."

Rose tried to control her expression and not curse Yasmine out loud.

Dany gave Rose a meaningful look. "The Adopted like to debate the nuances of the prophecies, but as Sentinels, we react on instinct. When we hear the truth, we know it immediately."

Rose looked at each of them, unsure what to do with this conversation. "Your religious convictions are commendable," she said grudgingly. "From your giggling, I assumed you were discussing more frivolous things."

Dany's lips twitched as if holding back a grin. "I only commented that if someone was powerful enough to control the light, she would surely deserve a ruggedly handsome guy with a body that just doesn't quit ..." Dany closed her eyes as if picturing that very body.

Elise sighed wistfully. "Yes, she would deserve a guy who looked at her like she was his whole world, then kissed her within an inch of her life ..." Elise touched her lips as if feeling the kiss herself.

Rose's mouth dropped open as some of the other Sentinels giggled. She cleared her throat and straightened her shoulders as a show of authority. "That's enough of your fanciful interpretations for now. I think you have better things to do than to stand around speculating on prophecy all day."

Dany's dreamy look focused to a sharp point. "This prophecy is very important to us, Ro—Marked One. It says, 'The one who grants freedom is the one who controls the light.' We've been looking for our freedom for a long time. If there is someone who actually grants freedom instead of servitude, we'd love to meet her."

Before Rose could respond, Vaylan swept into the training room.

"Good morning, Marked One!" he said cheerfully. "I thought I would find you in here."

Sentinels scrambled to put their masks on, while those in training clothes bowed low to hide their faces. She got the sense that Vaylan rarely saw the Sentinels unmasked. They all look embarrassed, as if he had caught them undressed.

He seemed unfazed by their discomfort. "I want to invite you to join me for dinner tonight before we head to the amphitheater. Since it will be an eventful evening, we should have a peaceful dinner first."

It wasn't until he smiled, revealing his dimple, that she finally made the decision. She straightened her shoulders and kept her sigh of resignation to herself.

"I'm afraid I must decline your offer, Vaylan. I need to

head to the amphitheater now, since I will perform the role of the Goddess alongside Wilder tonight."

She heard a couple muffled squeals of delight that were quickly stifled.

Vaylan didn't respond to the unusual sound from his Sentinels. Instead, he narrowed his eyes at her. "Now, Rose ... You know Wilder has made a deal with me. The Priests have access to the amphitheater for the Pageant, and in exchange, he will hand himself over to me. I won't tolerate any broken promises. If you decide otherwise, I have access to plenty of people you care about."

"Wilder will not go back on his deal with you, and I have agreed to go along with his plan. I will sing with him, then darken the final crystal in the basin." After that, she wasn't exactly sure what would happen.

Vaylan appeared to be making mental calculations, and Rose suddenly feared he would trap her inside the temple and not let her attend the Pageant. Now that she had finally decided, she didn't want Vaylan to stop her.

She sweetened the deal. "To prove my trustworthiness, how about I take a few Sentinels with me? Some of them are excellent dancers. They can have minor roles in the performance."

She was pretty sure it was Latham who gasped.

Vaylan's lip quirked in a small smile as he considered his Sentinels onstage for the Pageant. But she wasn't sure she had convinced him yet.

She sighed, and her shoulders slumped. She might as well admit it now; he would figure it out as soon as she opened her mouth tonight.

"You might also be interested to know ... I'm a terrible singer."

He raised an eyebrow, trying to determine if she was telling the truth. "But you were the judge at the auditions ..."

"Yes, yes, I know." She waved her hand in dismissal. "It's all very ironic, but the fact remains, I'm no good. Tonight, the Goddess will sound worse than any other Goddess in the history of Pageants. If we were under the rule of the High Priests, they would execute me for stepping foot on stage. There is no reason for me to lie. You will know the truth on the first note. I just thought you might like to know in advance."

He weighed her words, then burst into laughter.

"Thank you, Rose," he said. "I think tonight will be better than I even imagined."

45

Rose caused a disturbance when she arrived at the amphitheater trailed by six Sentinels, although she could have brought a lot more. Almost everyone from her dance class volunteered, but she only chose six, including Dany, Latham, and Elise. She told the others that maybe they could be in the Pageant next year.

The suggestion was completely ludicrous, but they seemed pleased at the possibility.

To keep from disturbing the rest of the cast, Rose decided the Sentinels should get in costume immediately. When Rose led them directly into the costume room, a familiar face greeted her.

Hazel had worked at Ecstasy Theater during Rose's brief stint as a showgirl. The woman appeared to be in her sixties, her graying hair piled atop her head in a messy bun with a pencil shoved through it.

"Rose, dear, it's good to see you. I heard you might be a last-minute substitution. Have a seat while I sort out these special performers you sent me."

Hazel forced the six Sentinels to strip out of their armor, and once they stood only in their underclothes, she measured them with a detached efficiency before handing them costumes she declared would be perfect. After a few minor adjustments, they were soon dressed in traditional costumes and grinning widely at each other. Hazel congratulated herself on a job well done before summoning a cast member to teach them whatever simple dance moves they could manage in a short time.

When they all cleared out, she turned to Rose, looking her up and down as if performing an extreme analysis. The last time Hazel looked at her like that, she had seen through Rose's inner turmoil just by studying the socks she was wearing. This time, Rose was in her long white jacket and white leather pants, so she wasn't sure what Hazel could draw from that.

"Good for you," she said with a smile. "It looks like you're finally comfortable in your own skin again."

"How can you know that by looking at me? I'm wearing all white as if I belong to Vaylan, but I definitely do not."

Hazel looked slightly peeved that Rose would second guess her. "White isn't Vaylan's color. He wears midnight blue, a playful sort of heresy, I assume."

"No, but—"

Hazel spoke over her. "White is the color of the Goddess. It's the color Brother Owyn wore. It's the color of the wolves that follow Wilder."

Rose's eyes widened. She had never considered any of that. "But it's the color of the Adopted."

"They are the ones who believe Brother Owyn's prophecies are real?" At Rose's nod, Hazel gave her a piercing look. "Are you one of them?"

Rose opened her mouth to disagree, but then closed it again to consider. "Maybe I am ..." The thought surprised her.

Hazel shrugged as if it wasn't an identity altering declaration. "And you are adopted, correct? All Priests are."

Rose leaned back against the table filled with costumes with a thump. The Priests were Adopted? How had she never made that connection before? She needed to find Yasmine and the others to find out if this was something they had already recognized. The theological ramifications …

Then her lips curved in a slow smile. Hazel was right. Rose did know who she was. She used to be a Priest but now was Adopted. A follower of the Goddess and a believer in Brother Owyn's Spark. A sister/mother to a pair of wolves and a woman who didn't need to hide in the shadows anymore. She planned to shine bright enough to light the whole City tonight.

Hazel hummed in satisfaction. "The Goddess will wear white this evening." Her face shifted into task mode as she rubbed her hands together. "Time to get undressed."

Hazel soon found the perfect white dress for Rose. The wide neckline stretched all the way to the edge of her shoulders. It revealed her mark, but Rose didn't want to cover it tonight. She was the Marked One, and even though Vaylan wasn't the true cause of her mark, she accepted his fingerprint as a symbol of her identity. The sleeves were long but fitted so they wouldn't get in her way. And Hazel had cut clever slits in the sides of the dress so Rose could still wear her blades under the full skirt. That was a luxury she wished her showgirl costume had.

Hazel declared herself a genius and shoved Rose out of the costume room and into her dressing room.

Where she found Feather.

Feather sat calmly in the chair in front of the makeup mirror but stood when Rose entered. She was dressed in a costume representing the Virtues. She looked Rose up and down without saying a word.

Rose suddenly felt terrible for not first speaking to Feather about how she would assume the role of Goddess. She tried to stammer out an apology.

"I'm sorry, Feather. I should have—This was not my idea."

Feather's voice was feistier than Rose had ever heard it. "No, it was not your idea. Do you remember whose idea it was?"

Rose thought back to their discussion the night before, then said meekly, "It was your idea."

"Yes, it was." She flipped her dark ponytail with a cool hand.

"Feather, I—"

Feather relaxed her posture with a sigh. "Relax, Rose. I'm not here to claw your eyes out. I'm here to help you get ready." She lifted a hairbrush and beckoned Rose to take the seat.

"Oh ..." Rose smoothed out her dress awkwardly. "Thank you," she mumbled as she took her seat.

Feather expertly brushed Rose's hair, pulling it into a smooth twist. Rose found it easier to look at Feather's reflection in the mirror than directly at her.

"Feather, I'm sorry."

"I told you, it was my idea—"

"Not for that." She looked down, unable to even look at her reflection. "For what I said when you performed with Wilder."

Feather didn't respond but kept brushing. Rose risked a glance in the mirror to find Feather's lips drawn in a tight line.

"I overreacted," said Rose. "And I shouldn't have called you a child. We've gone through a lot together, and I don't consider you a child. I was just lashing out at Wilder, and ..." Her voice dropped to a rough whisper. "And I was jealous."

Feather snorted quietly. "That's nothing new."

Rose bit her lip, unable to dispute the retort. "Not jealous of you with Wilder ... well, not *just* that ..." She sighed. "I was jealous of *you.*"

Feather's brushing stuttered slightly before resuming.

Rose continued, "I'm proud that I'm the one who picked you out of hundreds of girls competing for the role of Goddess. There were a lot of wonderful singers out there, but I knew you had something special. I imagined you singing beautifully in the Pageant, and I thought I would get to bask in the reflected glory of your performance."

She sighed again. "I know it's wrong of me to think that ... I'm sure Wilder never considered such a thing ... But it's the closest I thought I'd get to actually being in the Pageant myself." She looked away from the mirror, seeing deeper within. "But that day, when you sang with Wilder, I didn't see my reflected glory. I only saw you. Gorgeous you, with a beautiful voice and so *kind* ... I was jealous of *you.* Combine that with the way Wilder was looking at you, and, well ... I reacted badly. Very badly. And I'm sorry."

Feather had stopped brushing. Rose looked into the mirror to find Feather watching her with a soft expression.

"I forgive you, Rose." Her voice was back to its normally sweet sound. "I appreciate you saying all that. You're really nice when you want to be."

Rose gave a self-deprecating smile. "I just rarely want to be."

Feather tucked one last strand of hair into Rose's twist and smiled warmly at Rose's reflection. "You look like a goddess to me."

Rose studied herself in the mirror, the terror about her upcoming humiliation rising in her throat. She looked back at Feather's sweet face, trying to draw comfort from it.

"I think your strategy is right," said Rose. "I truly believe I have to be on that stage tonight, working with Wilder to defeat Vaylan and bring this City together." She touched her throat, feeling the panic closing her vocal cords already. She gave Feather a rueful look. "Too bad you didn't know I was a terrible singer before you suggested it."

Feather's sweet smile never wavered, but quiet mischief sparkled behind her eyes. "Oh, I knew, Rose ... I knew." She gave Rose the sign of the Goddess before bowing out of the room.

46

Rose sat alone in her dressing room, unsure what to do next. She could go find Wilder, but he was busy with last-minute preparations. He was the only one with Gifts, which meant he was part of the back-stage crew while also playing a starring role. She could find the crew but wasn't sure if they would be glad to see her after her tantrum the night before. Plus, each of them was performing or assisting backstage, so they were likely busy as well.

She tried rehearsing, but every time she began a song, her voice sounded small and weak inside her little dressing room. She tried to imagine her voice filling the amphithe-ater and wanted to laugh. The moment she stood on stage, she feared her throat would close and she wouldn't get out a single note. Eventually, she gave up rehearsing. She already knew the songs by heart, and there was no way she could practice enough to suddenly become good.

She considered looking for the Sentinels—they might be the only people in the amphitheater truly happy to see her—but they were rehearsing backstage, and she didn't want to keep them from doing something they were excited about just because she was lonely.

She half-heartedly applied more eyeliner but had already finished her makeup long ago. The extra eyeliner was just her nervous hands looking for something else to do. She reached for a small jar of glitter but was distracted by Yasmine entering the room.

Yasmine stared at Rose in awe. "Marked One," she breathed, forgetting she was supposed to use Rose's name. "You look beautiful."

Rose always appreciated someone calling her beautiful, but she was even more grateful to see a friendly face. "Come in and have a seat, Yasmine. I'm desperate for company."

Yasmine moved makeup off a small footstool and took a seat. "I can't believe you're doing this." Her face lit up in delight. "It's just so perfect!"

Rose could barely contain the panic in her voice. "I'm having second thoughts. The longer I sit here, the more I realize how terrible this decision is. I don't know what I was thinking."

Yasmine clasped Rose's hand comfortingly. "It's going to be okay, Rose. Everyone is going to be so happy seeing you and Wilder together onstage together that they won't care how good you can sing."

Rose's panic subsided into confusion. "Wait ... how do you know I'm a terrible singer? You weren't there when I told Vaylan."

Yasmine bit her lip and wouldn't meet Rose's eyes. "Vaylan told all the Sentinels and Adopted that you're terrible. He's rounding up everyone from the Upstairs and Underneath to come to the Pageant, whether they wanted to or not. And when the amphitheater opens, everyone from the Heart will come up the staircase under the stage." She gave Rose a pitying look. "It's going to be a full house."

Rose groaned, burying her face in her hands.

"I have some other news that might cheer you up!" Yasmine's bubbly voice was forced, but Rose looked up, happy to take what she could get.

Yasmine pulled out Walter's notebook. "We've done a lot of studying." Her face was entirely too thrilled for a topic other people found boring, but Rose perked up at the news.

"What did you find?"

Yasmine scooted her stool closer to Rose's chair and lowered her voice. "Brother Owyn spoke a lot about the world he imagined. He wrote such beautiful words about how to create a fair and thriving City." Her face hardened. "It's not the City Vaylan preaches."

Rose was surprised at her angry tone but didn't blame her. It had taken Rose a long time to uncover Vaylan's depravity since he hid everything questionable behind a warm smile. For the Adopted who spent even less time with him, Rose thought the discovery must be even more shocking.

"Vaylan hid the prophecies that went against what he commanded." Yasmine flipped through Walter's notebook, looking for a passage. "Brother Owyn often said, 'Seek the light,' which Vaylan used as a sign of his right to rule. But that's not all he said about light." Yasmine found the page she wanted and traced the single line with a gentle finger. "*Don't let the darkness win.* These are Brother Owyn's words, and Vaylan hid them from us."

Rose cocked her head as she considered Vaylan's plan to darken every crystal and eliminate the crystalline. "Vaylan's mission is to let the darkness win. He would find those words very dangerous."

Yasmine's face turned thoughtful. "Even among the prophecies we had, there were passages that didn't align with what he taught. But he could always rationalize them to make them fit into the rest of his teachings. But in light of these new prophecies, we have to reexamine those questionable passages to see what we missed."

Rose looked at her in surprise. "You are really taking this seriously. I knew those prophecies were important to Vaylan since he killed to keep them secret, but I wasn't sure they would be that valuable to anyone else."

Yasmine held the notebook to her chest. "Sian died for this knowledge!" She caught her breath on a sob before continuing. "Don't you realize these prophecies are the only reason we follow Vaylan? We all have different reasons for joining the Adopted— some were hurt by the High Priests, some were hurt by the Wardens, some were rejected by family or friends, and some just never found a place to truly belong. But there was one thing that drew us together— Brother Owyn's words. Most of us were blessed enough to hear him speak when he was alive, but some only know him through the prophecies. The life he spoke about and his vision for the future gave us hope when the world turned upside down. These words are all we have left of him." Her voice turned fierce. "Vaylan knows that and used the prophecies as leverage to get what he wanted. But no longer. His reign is almost over." Her eyes glittered like steel.

"*The Founder's life will be cut short*," Rose quoted. She looked at Yasmine as if seeing her for the first time. Rose dropped her voice to a whisper. "Are you thinking about taking this prophecy into your own hands?"

Yasmine shook her head, as if coming out of a daze. "No, of course not. The prophecy says it will be someone else."

"What? Who will it be?"

Yasmine opened the notebook, flipping to a page she had bookmarked. "Here ... 'The Founder will perish at the hands of one he loves.'" Yasmine shrugged. "He doesn't even know me, so it has to be someone else."

Rose gripped her makeup table for support. "He's desperate to keep those words hidden because he's afraid they're true."

Yasmine huffed in irritation. "If he were a true follower of prophecy, he wouldn't be afraid of it. He would just accept it as his time."

Rose wondered if Yasmine would feel differently if the prophecy was about her.

"There are differing opinions among our group about who will actually kill him."

Her matter-of-fact tone shocked Rose, but then she remembered their group loved to debate theoretical ideas, so perhaps this was only a theory to them.

"The most common opinion is that it will be Wilder."

Rose's eyes fixed on her. "Wilder? You think Wilder will kill Vaylan?"

"It makes the most sense. Vaylan doesn't have close relationships, not close enough for him to love anyone, but surely he loves his son."

Rose snorted. Vaylan had a funny way to express love.

Yasmine tapped her finger absently on the notebook. "It also makes sense why Vaylan is so concerned about the prophecy about the Scion. It says the Scion will either be converted or destroyed. Perhaps Vaylan believes that prophecy will counteract the other and cancel it out."

"Cancel it out? Is that a thing?" asked Rose.

Yasmine huffed. "No, I don't think so. However, Hunter's latest theory is that it's possible." She shook her head and sighed. "I love Hunter, but sometimes his conjectures are unsound."

Rose wasn't sure what to say about that, but Yasmine continued without waiting for a response. "The second most popular opinion is that you will kill him."

Rose nearly choked. "Me?" Not that she hadn't imagined

it over and over, but it felt wrong to admit that to an Adopted, even one so casually discussing Vaylan's death.

"You are the only other person Vaylan is close to."

Rose whispered, "You think he loves me?"

Yasmine shrugged. "Who can say? I've seen him smile at you in a condescending, paternal way. Maybe that counts as love to him?"

"It sounds like you don't care whether Vaylan lives or dies." Not that Rose cared if he died, but it still seemed odd for Yasmine to say it out loud.

"Of course I care," she said quickly. "It's just ..." She shrugged. "Prophecy." As if that was all the proof she needed for Vaylan to die.

"I guess we will see what happens," said Rose noncommittally.

"Maybe Wilder will do it tonight?" said Yasmine. "We haven't discovered a timeline, but I'll keep looking." She opened the notebook as if she planned to look right now.

Rose imagined Wilder killing Vaylan, then sighed. "I don't think it will be Wilder. He said that even if he had the chance, he wouldn't be able to kill Vaylan. It's just not in his nature."

Yasmine looked up and nodded her head thoughtfully. "So, maybe killing Vaylan is what destroys the Scion ... Interesting theory."

She went back to studying her notebook, leaving Rose to consider that terrifying idea in silence.

47

Rose wandered out of her dressing room in a daze. She found Yasmine's casual observation deeply unsettling. Even though Yasmine usually expressed care for Wilder's safety, when talking about prophecies, the Adopted got a little ... weird. Rose tried to shake off the words, but the looming dread about Wilder's safety and her upcoming humiliation melded together until she had a churning storm in her gut. She stepped from the wings onto the stage, now covered by the closed curtains, and her stomach fluttered in an entirely different way.

Wilder stood in the middle of the cast, giving last-minute directions. Though he was playing the role of the Companion, Hazel had seen fit to dress him in black. His suit was clearly tailored by an expert, one who took delight in Wilder's stunning form. His velvet jacket had a soft sheen, and she wondered what it would feel like against her skin. He waved a hand absently, causing the backstage lights to brighten, and that's when he saw her.

The look he gave her froze time. She was only vaguely aware of the people who continued making their preparations around them. All she could see was Wilder's face, full of love

303

and trust and desire. His eyes traced her body, and she felt a tingling shiver as when he had blown across her flame. She rubbed her fingertips together, feeling the fire lurking within, but a voice disrupted her accidental summoning of a firestorm.

"I guess you're my Goddess."

She turned to find the silver-haired director watching her, his arms crossed over his fur-draped chest.

"I'm not my first choice either," she said drily.

"The rest of the cast has practiced for a few days at least … Still not enough, in my opinion," he grumbled. "Hopefully, you're good enough to just walk on stage and sing the part."

She gave him a weak smile. "I know all the words."

He merely blinked at her, unsure if she was kidding.

"Um … maybe you could drop the aria a couple steps? Not that any of my notes are very good, but the high ones are especially rough."

The awful truth began to dawn on his face. "We could have rehearsed this before now!" he hissed.

She shrugged apologetically. "It's probably best if no one has to hear me more than once."

Wilder chose that moment to approach, preventing her murder.

"The musicians are looking for you, Maestro. You can tell them about the key change."

Maestro had his own barely restrained fire behind his eyes, but he said calmly, "Of course, Wilder. We're professionals who can handle anything." As he walked away, Rose heard him grumbling, "We can handle changing keys right before curtains, cast members attempting to murder one another on stage, accompanying a song we've never heard, someone sabotaging the performance …"

Wilder smiled as he watched him go. "Maestro has had

to deal with several complicated performances in his life. I hope next year's Pageant goes much more smoothly."

She looked at his hopeful face in wonder. "You really believe that, don't you? That there will be a Pageant next year and all will be well."

"Yes, I do." He smiled and took her hand. "I have something for you. Close your eyes."

She gave him a curious look but closed her eyes obediently.

He placed a thin circle of cool metal in her hands. Her eyes sprang open at the familiar shape.

"A circlet?" She hadn't worn a traditional Priest's circlet since the Wardens attacked. They had taken the High Priests' crowns and the Priests' circlets and melted them down on their first day in charge.

Wilder's hands held hers as she held the circlet. "Even if you decide not to call yourself a Priest again, I wanted to give you something that honored your past while also embracing your future."

Her previous circlet had been a simple braided twist of silver that hung just above her brow. This circlet was a warm gold with fingers of flame imprinted along the edges. She stared at it, unable to form words.

"Do you like it?" he asked hesitantly. "I hoped you would, but—"

She grabbed him by both lapels, careful not to drop her circlet, and pulled him into a kiss. She felt him smile against her lips and tried to pull him even closer, but he politely leaned away.

He rubbed a gentle finger across her lips. "It's too close to show time to ruin our makeup, dear." He grinned. "After the show, you can ruin it all you like."

She gave him a pouty look but knew he was right. "Fine.

I'll find Feather so she can help me work this circlet into my hair."

He gave her a tentative look. "You and Feather are okay now?"

"Yes, we made up." Rose grinned. "And after our conversation, I respect her even more than I did before."

Rose's costume was perfect. Her makeup was perfect. And thanks to Feather's help, the circlet in her hair was perfect. Yet as she stood at center stage, waiting for the curtain to go up, she was a trembling wreck. She stared at the curtain, hearing the waiting crowd on the other side, and wondered if it was too late to cancel the show.

She flinched when the orchestra started the prelude, and the backstage lights dimmed slowly. She looked into the wings to see Wilder commanding the lighting. The Companion didn't appear until late in Act One. Until then, it was only the Goddess.

Rose thought she might vomit.

Wilder noticed her expression and hurried on stage. "Rose, you're going to be fine. Just breathe. The rest of the crew is here with you."

Since Feather and Kieran were the best singers in the crew, they had actual roles and were already waiting in their position onstage. Feather gave Rose an encouraging smile, and Kieran gave her his usual ironic salute. Rev and Kai were in the chorus along with the Sentinels, and they waited stage left for their cue. Quinn and Fitz were stage right, wrangling animals for Act Two. Tayeh stood at the edge of the curtain line, looking out at the crowd. Rose guessed she had her eyes on Vaylan in the front row.

"This first part is easy," Wilder said. "Stand here, look

pretty, and let them sing about your Virtues. Just smile, and everything will be okay."

"Oh, that's all?" she said, her voice rising in panic. "Just look pretty? Wilder, these people usually listen to singers who train their entire lives for this role. I'm going to make a fool of myself. The Goddess's power won't return because the crowd will be too busy laughing at me for any of the magic to work!"

Wilder merely smoothed back her perfectly smooth hair with gentle fingers. "Rose, you underestimate how much these people care for you. Priests all over this City watched you beg Vaylan to spare their lives over and over. The Adopted believe you are the one who brings true freedom. And the Sentinels would follow you anywhere, as long as they don't giggle every time I look at you."

"Why should they follow me? I'm a mess! And this performance will prove it. Everyone already knows I'm bossy and mean and have a bad temper, and now they'll know I'm a fraud judge who can't even sing." The overture was coming to a close, and her throat clenched in panic, so her words came out as a strangled whisper. "I've hurt you, the crew, and everyone around me so many times. I don't deserve to be here. I'm just too broken."

Wilder took her hand in his. "Yes, Rose, you are broken. So am I. Even the Goddess is broken. That hasn't stopped me from being devoted to her, and it doesn't stop me from loving you." He raised her hand to his lips. "I believe in you, Rose. I always have."

He pressed his lips softly to her knuckles, prompting a quiet tittering backstage.

Wilder winked, then raised his hand, dropping the stage to full dark as the curtain rose.

～

Rose prayed a desperate prayer that somehow her Spark would suddenly give her the ability to sing as beautifully as Ylena.

But that was not the case.

Rose struggled through Act One, only keeping up with the dance steps through sheer determination and the number of times she had seen the Pageant. But every time she had to open her mouth to sing, it was awful. She was just good enough to recognize how good she wasn't. The songs felt interminable. There were moments when she wanted to stop singing in the middle of the song. Just close her mouth, walk offstage, and never look back. But she couldn't bring herself to do it. She knew how important this was, so she forced herself to keep singing.

She tried to avoid looking at the audience, but when she did, they met her with looks of encouragement and pity. She wanted to melt into a puddle of shame. The only person safe to look at was Vaylan. He appeared to be having the time of his life, savoring each terrible note she hit. He infuriated her, and that bit of fire in her belly was the only thing that kept her going.

That, and Wilder. Once the Companion arrived onstage, the entire audience seemed to sigh in relief. Despite her previous irritation at his cocky statement, he really was good enough for both of them. His smile was enough to distract any critic, and every time he gathered Rose in his arms or spun her across the stage, the crowd cooed in delight.

A few of her notes threatened to veer off course, but when Wilder was onstage, they were more likely to land in the right place. And if occasionally her voice sounded stronger than before, reverberating gently in the wind, he was too much of a gentleman to take any credit.

They made it to the last scene of Act Two, where they carried the Vessel of Tears to the front of the stage. The

Priests had painstakingly collected their tears, hoping that pouring them into the basin would be what returned the Goddess's Gifts. Rose and Wilder sang their final note and poured in the tears.

The light in the crystal basin flickered, then went out.

48

———

Thee crowd gasped. The musicians cut their note short. Everyone on stage froze in place. Everyone held their breath, waiting ... hoping ...

An icy blast of air shot across the stage, sending a shiver across Rose's skin. Only then did she realize that though the amphitheater had been cold, it wasn't as cold as it should have been.

Until now.

Wilder had let go of the Vessel and simply stared at his hands.

As if he had lost something.

She hurriedly set the Vessel on the stage and took Wilder's hands in her own.

"Are you okay?" she whispered.

The wind rushing past threatened to steal his quiet whisper. "I didn't realize I would lose my Gifts before the Goddess returned everything ..."

His voice was more uncertain than she had ever heard. Wilder was the picture of confidence, so his doubt rattled her.

Vaylan's soft laugh from the front row chilled her more than the freezing wind.

"The two of you have put on a magnificent performance this evening!" Vaylan stood slowly from one of the tall thrones that formerly belonged to the High Priests. "It's been beautiful, tragic, and hilarious … A real treat!"

Despite the cold, Rose's fire still burned in her gut. "The show isn't over yet, Vaylan. You need to wait until the end."

He grinned. "Come now, Marked One. This is what we've been working toward all along." He raised his arms to encompass the entire City. "The City is no longer under the control of the Goddess. We are free, just as Brother Owyn promised."

"How dare you say his name!" she hissed.

Darkness glittered in Vaylan's eyes. "I am the one who knew Brother Owyn best. I listened to his prophecies for over a decade in the High Priests' prison." He took a few steps closer to the stage. "Now you will do as foretold … You will deliver the Chosen into my hands. Right now."

"I will do no such thing," she growled.

Then she called the fire.

Flames burst from her fingers and dripped down to form little fires around her feet. The crowd gasped, and a few cried out in fear. Vaylan looked at her, completely dumbfounded. He couldn't comprehend what he saw. His expression brought her a small amount of glee before she returned to the task at hand.

She spun in a slow circle, drawing a ring of flames around her and Wilder and the basin at her feet. When Vaylan sent a group of Sentinels onto the stage to stop her, she raised her hands and drew the flames higher until the two of them were enclosed in a dome of fire.

"What are you doing?" asked Wilder. He had shaken

himself from his surprise and pulled out two blades she didn't realize he had.

"It will not end this way." She looked through the flames and saw Vaylan summoning Sentinels to break through her fire. She looked at Wilder's blades with concern. "Please, don't kill Vaylan."

He shook his head in confusion. "Don't kill him? Isn't that what you've been dreaming about this whole time?"

"Yes, but ... you should let me do it. Just trust me, okay?"

He shrugged. "Fine. I can handle the Sentinels."

"No! Don't kill them either! Some of them are my friends, and you won't know which is which."

He gave her an exasperated look. "Then what exactly should I do?"

"Just stand here and look pretty until I get back."

"Get back from where?"

"You know how Ylena sang so beautifully that she roused the Goddess from her sanctuary on the mountain? Well, I don't have the gift of song, so instead, I'm barging into the Goddess's hideout and dragging her out whether she wants to come or not."

She pulled Wilder into a rough kiss, then slammed her hands against the crystal basin.

Rose blinked her eyes open inside the Goddess's cave. It seemed smaller than the last time, with dark corners and deep shadows pressing in. Rose edged toward the tiny candle flickering on the table and found the Goddess with her head in her hands. She lifted her face when Rose sat down in the chair across from her.

"Goddess, we need your help. Wilder lost his Gifts, and Vaylan wants to take him. We need you to do something."

The Goddess stared at her with lifeless eyes. "You were the one who was supposed to do something, Rose. Can't you see? I can do nothing from here."

"Well, come out! ... Somehow ... I don't know. You're the Goddess. Do something!"

"It was different back then. I had an actual body. I gave it up to join the Companion ... and now I've lost him again." The Goddess's eyes stared into the distance. "I've lived more years apart from him than with him ... You'd think I was used to being alone ..."

"Snap out of it!" said Rose harshly. "Vaylan will break through my fire at any moment. He's probably using crystalline to hurt Wilder right now!"

The Goddess's eyes didn't even flicker at Vaylan's heretical Spark of manipulating crystalline.

Rose slammed her fists down on the table, causing the little candle to flicker wildly. "Listen to me! We don't have time for this. Stop crying, and come help me fight!"

The Goddess's eyes slowly focused on Rose. "Stop crying?" She laughed bitterly. "If only I could ... Except for a few brief moments of clarity, sadness has consumed me for over a thousand years. My grief built this City, and the tears of my Priests sustained it. Sorrow is our core theology, Rose."

Rose ground her teeth together. "But if you stay in here, things will get worse. It will lead to more sadness. We have to do something. Now!"

"You and I are the same, Rose. Your grief is mine. It just appears in different ways. Mine comes like a wave, threatening to drown me. Yours comes like fire, burning you up from within. Eventually, it will consume you, as it has consumed me."

Rose twitched, disturbed by the cryptic words. The Goddess's breathing slowed, and the candle dimmed. The dark shadows began creeping closer and Rose felt her panic rising.

"Goddess, please," she begged. "Come for Wilder's sake. He's devoted to you. He's your Chosen."

"Wilder ..." The Goddess's dull green eyes blinked slowly, and her voice was lethargic. "He's a beautiful singer."

"Yes! You heard him sing as a little boy. You *chose* him!"

"He noticed me when I was sad ..." The Goddess's eyes continued their slow blink. "I didn't choose him ... He chose me."

The Goddess closed her eyes, and the candle snuffed out.

49

Rose opened her eyes back in the amphitheater with a gasp. After the darkness of the Goddess's cave, the brightness of the fire dome was overwhelming. Wilder was suddenly at her side, helping her to her feet.

"Did it work?" he asked.

From his expression, she guessed her conversation with the Goddess had happened in the blink of an eye. She didn't have time to explain all the thoughts rushing through her head.

"Do you trust me, Wilder?"

"Of course," he said with no reservation.

"Surrender to me," she whispered.

He immediately bared his neck, as if waiting for her blade or as if she were a wolf.

She wanted to tell him how much she loved him for that, but she snapped her fist closed, snuffing out all the flames. Then she grabbed Wilder by the neck, dropping him to his knees.

Wilder sat meekly at her feet, one hand in his lap, the other resting on the basin. The Sentinels Vaylan had summoned stood at silent attention, watching for the flames to return. She heard murmurs from cast members behind her, and she prayed the crew trusted her as much as Wilder did. The last thing she needed was Tayeh knocking her out for apparent betrayal.

She turned her attention to Vaylan, who stood watching her from his place in the front row. "The prophecies are right, Vaylan. I will deliver the Chosen into your hands. But if that's what you want, you must come up here yourself."

Vaylan studied her warily, knowing her sudden change of heart couldn't be trusted. He nodded his head at the Sentinels, and they crept forward.

Rose looked at each Sentinel, trying to figure out who each of them were beneath the mask, but there were too many of them. Instead, she held out her hand, and a small flame appeared.

"I am the one who controls the light," she said. "Grant me my freedom, and I will grant you yours."

The Sentinels paused their slow approach and moved to watchful attention.

Rose turned back to Vaylan. "Now is the time to prove if you truly believe the prophecies. If you believe I will deliver the Chosen to you, then come up here and prove it. Or admit to everyone that you have doubts. Admit there are some prophecies you hope never come true."

Rose knew it was a risk. The prophecies hidden in his room proved he had doubts. But above all that, Rose knew the truth.

Vaylan was a true believer.

He squared his shoulders and walked regally up the stairs onto the stage. He passed the watchful Sentinels with a confused expression, then stood just out of Rose's reach.

"This is a trick," he whispered.

She held out her hand. "It's only a trick if prophecy isn't true."

Vaylan took a deep breath, then grabbed her hand.

Rose closed her eyes and slammed her Spark through Wilder and into the basin. If anyone was strong enough to handle the ordeal, it was Wilder. He had experienced both the Goddess's glory and Rose's fire before. She had to trust that he was strong enough again.

With her other hand, she pulled Vaylan with her into the Goddess's sanctuary. They both stumbled, and when Rose straightened, she saw two images overlaid. She stood on stage, one hand on Wilder's neck, the other hand in Vaylan's. And she also stood inside the Goddess's sanctuary, both of Vaylan's hands clutched by the Goddess.

The Goddess's sanctuary was still the small dark cave, but the Goddess stood in her long, flowing white dress, her hair pulled back in an elegant braid. Rose was glad to see she was vain enough to dress up for the occasion. This wouldn't have had quite the same effect if the Goddess was in her ripped sweater.

"Hello, Vaylan. I didn't expect you to enter my domain."

"Where am I?" Vaylan looked around the cave in wild confusion. He tried to pull his hands away from the Goddess, but she held him tight. If he weren't a ruthless murderer who would have unapologetically killed his own son, Rose might have felt sorry for him.

The Goddess's green eyes bore into him. "Here in my realm, my vision is much clearer. Here, I can see you, down to the core."

Vaylan's eyes widened, and he tried to pull his hands away again, unsuccessfully.

"Who are you?" The Goddess's voice rang like a gong, and Rose's own voice echoed the words for the crowd to hear.

Vaylan's tentative voice was heard both in the cave and on stage. "I'm Vaylan." He straightened his shoulders, trying to regain his dignity. "I'm the Lord Founder."

The Goddess looked at him with narrowed eyes. "You are not the Founder."

Vaylan sucked in a breath. "Yes, I—"

"You are not the Founder," declared the Goddess. "You founded nothing. Who is the Founder?"

Vaylan's mouth moved, but no sound came out. Rose saw realization dawn on his face the moment it dawned on her own.

"Brother Owyn was the Founder?" he whispered.

"He was the one with the sight. He was the one with the vision of a better world." The Goddess's voice echoed with cold justice. "And you killed him."

The part of Rose that remained in the amphitheater heard the crowd gasp, and Vaylan in both locations tried to explain.

"The prophecy—"

"He was with you through your long years in prison. When the darkness threatened to consume you and you broke, giving rise to your Spark, Brother Owyn was the rock that kept you sane ... And you killed him. *The Founder perished ...*"

"*... at the hands of one he loved.*" Vaylan finished quoting the prophecy in a rough whisper.

"He gave you the prophecies to teach you, to form you into the leader he dreamed you could become. He loved you like a son. He saw you as his legacy, his lineage ... So again, I ask ... Who are you?"

Vaylan's shoulders slumped as the prophecy clicked into place. "I am the Scion."

"Brother Owyn hoped he would convert you to his ways, but you chose destruction. You are the one who saw death in the eyes of the Goddess's own, expecting your own son to kill you, when all along, Brother Owyn's blood was on your hands."

Rose watched Vaylan's world crumble around him and saw something within him break. He *was* a true believer, and when faced with the truth of his sins, he was forced to believe that as well.

The Goddess looked at him with hard eyes. "You are the cause of the Companion's death, and if I hadn't sworn to never kill one of my own again, I would incinerate you for what you have done. Instead, I will only take back what is mine. This City, the Companion's blood and bone, it all belongs to me. You will control it no more."

She let go of one of his hands and placed a palm on his forehead. He swayed under her touch, and when she drew her hand back, he gasped. He looked at free hand in the same lost way that Wilder had.

The Goddess's expression held no remorse. "If you hadn't been so determined to have the Chosen delivered into your hands, I never would have reached you, and you could have escaped with your Spark intact."

He looked up at her in a mixture of awe and fear. "You are the Chosen ... You will suffer at the hands of the Marked before disappearing into the dark ..."

The Goddess's voice no longer rang through the amphitheater. It was for Vaylan and Rose alone.

"I have suffered plenty. And now, all I want is to disappear into the dark, never to return."

The Goddess closed her eyes, plunging the cave into darkness.

Rose blinked and found herself suddenly back in the amphitheater. She swayed on her feet, and Wilder stood quickly, grabbing her waist to steady her. She sucked in a sharp breath as her eyes shot to Vaylan, but he offered no resistance. He sank to the ground, blinking slowly as he looked around in confusion. The Sentinels at his back watched in silence.

Rose straightened her shoulders and called forth her natural bossiness to put things in their proper order.

She turned to the Sentinels. "Dany, please escort Vaylan somewhere safe. We will deal with him when we finish the Pageant."

The second Sentinel on the left bowed, signaling the other Sentinels to follow. Wilder raised an eyebrow but didn't ask her how she knew which Sentinel was which.

Then she turned to Feather, who was staring at her with wide eyes, along with the rest of the cast. "I might need you to fill in as the Goddess if I'm gone too long. We need to finish this Pageant. Quickly." Feather didn't respond, but just kept staring at her in shock.

Then Rose turned to Maestro in the orchestra pit. He had his hand over his mouth and was gawking as if watching a fascinating play.

"You can go back to the original key for the aria. Feather and Wilder can handle it as is."

She turned to Wilder. "Hopefully you won't even notice I'm gone."

"And where are you going?" he asked with an amused grin.

"I convinced the Goddess to save us. Now I'm going to save her."

50

Rose touched the basin again and found herself in the dark. She had been in small rooms with no light and even in the Grotto when the crystal's light went out, but never had she been in such complete darkness. She tried calling a flame to her hand, but the darkness was so absolute there was nothing to summon.

Fear stole the air from her lungs, and she had to crouch down to catch her breath. But crouching made it worse. She felt like the cave was suddenly that much smaller, so she stood quickly, then swayed on her feet, unable to find her balance with no frame of reference. She closed her eyes and pretended it was just her closed eyes that made it so dark. The illusion was enough to get her breathing under control so she could think.

She knew the Goddess still lived. The Goddess had said she was cursed to never die, and Rose believed her. Rose just had to find where she was hiding and bring her back.

She strained her ears for the slightest sound. There was no hint of dripping water like in an actual cave. No animal noises. No sign of airflow. There was simply a ... void. An emptiness. Nothing that could bring pleasure, but also nothing that could bring pain.

She thought about the sad woman from young Wilder's vision. She seemed numb to everything, unaware of the world. Nothing roused her until Wilder sang the saddest song he knew, trying to relate to her. Rose thought her terrible voice might cause the Goddess to burrow deeper, so she found another way to communicate.

"I lost them when I was fourteen." She thought her voice might echo as if she were in a giant cavern, but it sounded like she was in a narrow tunnel. She tried not to panic thinking just how narrow and instead strained her ears to hear.

The faintest whisper came from somewhere on her left, so she took a single step in that direction.

"My oldest sister's name was Ginger. She had red hair like me. Even though we were both adopted, I felt a special connection to her. She was strong. Opinionated. Fierce. I wanted to be just like her when I grew up."

Rose paused again to listen. The noise was quiet, like the faint rustle of fabric, and Rose took another step toward it.

"My brothers Liam and Zain were a mystery to me. They were grown men by the time I was a teenager, and we found it hard to relate to each other. All I knew about them was that they were some of the most skilled fighters in Temple Discipline and that they were completely devoted, heart and soul, to the Goddess ... to you."

She waited for the rustle of sound before taking the next step.

"I knew they had secret meetings ... meetings I wasn't allowed to attend. I heard their whispers about righting the City's wrongs and defending those too small to defend themselves, but I was never sure what they actually planned to do."

A soft sigh. A single step forward.

"I wish I would have known when they were planning to make their move, because maybe I would have had time to prepare ... Or maybe there is no way to be prepared ... All I know is that one day, I was training with Caed and Kai, and Mims pulled us from the training room. She didn't say what was wrong, just dragged us out of the temple to a friend's house. We didn't ask questions ... not when we saw the terror in her eyes. She exchanged a meaningful look with the woman who owned the house, then shoved the three of us into a hole cut into the floorboards. After she covered it with a rug, it was completely dark ... Only slightly less dark than this ..."

A sniffle. Two steps forward.

"We didn't talk. The three of us just clutched each other, waiting for it to be over ... waiting for some explanation ... I don't know how long we were down there. I had never liked the dark, but that day, I felt like the walls were closing in, like the house would topple in on us, like I would be lost in the darkness and no one would ever find me."

A gentle exhale. A slow step forward.

"That must be when I gained my Spark, though I didn't know it. All I knew is that when Mims came back for us, I was huddled in a tight ball, with Caed and Kai trying to comfort me. It wasn't until we were back in our rooms at the temple that she whispered the story of what had happened. Ginger, Liam, and Zain had gone with a group of others to confront the High Priest of Purpose. They knew what he did to children—everyone knew—but they were actually willing to do something about it ... But they weren't successful. All of them died in the attempt."

Rose heard the direction of the shaking inhale, but she couldn't take the step yet.

"It was such a waste." Her voice caught on a sob. "The

three of them trained their whole lives. They were devoted to you. They could have done so much to make this City a better place, but they were just gone. They left that day without even telling me goodbye."

The tears rolled down her cheeks and landed quietly on her dress.

The Goddess's voice floated up to her from the ground a few steps ahead.

"Before he was my Companion, he was just Nelson. He was a simple bard, but his music rescued me when I was in one of my darkest moments. After I lost him, I avoided all music. It reminded me too much of him. I spent centuries in my cave on the mountain. Then one day, I wandered back into the City, just to be close to him. I made my way into a healing center and lived there for several decades. Amidst people yet alone. That's where I heard Ylena's mother sing."

Rose sank down to her knees, closer to the sound of the Goddess's voice.

"Her song revived me for a time. It held the promise of something new. A child born to Priests ... born from the Goddess's love ... It brought me a measure of hope." She sighed. "But like most times in my life, periods of hope are often followed by periods of despair."

Rose inched closer and thought she was close enough to touch her.

"I was in one of those periods of despair when young Wilder saw me. So many other people just passed me by, another sad face in a City of sad people, yet Wilder saw me, truly saw me. When I heard my aria sung in his sweet, clear voice, a tiny piece of my soul mended."

Rose reached out and took hold of the Goddess's hand. A soft sob escaped from the Goddess's mouth, but she squeezed Rose's hand back.

Rose spoke gently, trying not to scare her away. "I know

you have grief beyond what I can imagine. But will you please let me help you out of here?" Rose's voice was the barest whisper as she pleaded using Brother Owyn's words. "Don't let the darkness win."

The Goddess drew in a shaking breath, then allowed Rose to lift her to her feet. Rose tried again to summon a flame, but there was nothing for her to grasp hold of. Nothing but darkness surrounded them, and Rose couldn't even tell which direction she had come from. She wanted to lead the Goddess out but had no idea which direction to go.

Then she heard him sing.

Wilder's voice was quieter than the softest sigh of the Goddess, yet Rose clung to it as her lifeline. He was singing the Goddess's Aria himself. She followed each note as it wound through the darkness, step by tentative step, the Goddess clinging to her arm. She couldn't stop herself from blinking, hoping it would help her eyes adjust to the darkness, but not a single sliver of light appeared.

The dark path seemed endless, but Wilder's voice grew louder. Rose hurried, pulling the Goddess along faster, hoping to see a light up ahead.

Then suddenly, the darkness changed.

There was still no light, only the faint sound of Wilder's voice in the distance, yet something about the texture of the darkness was different. Rose thought she could sense the edges of the room, as if she were now in a clearly defined place.

She held out her hand and summoned a flame.

The small flicker of light was bright in the dark cave. Rose and the Goddess blinked their eyes, trying to focus. The Goddess still wore the long white dress from her confrontation with Vaylan, though it was crumpled from sitting on the ground. Her awareness seemed distant, as if she was only one step away from melting back into the darkness.

Rose brightened the flame in her hand and walked around the empty cave but couldn't find what she was looking for.

She turned to the Goddess and spoke as gently as she could. "Where is he?"

The Goddess turned her head to the right, and suddenly the Companion was there. He was lying on a stone slab, his body as rigid as a statue. Rose led the Goddess to him and placed the Goddess's hand on his.

Rose tried to get the Goddess to listen, but she only stared at the Companion. "I need you to stay here, okay? Please don't fall back into the darkness." Rose flared the light a little brighter, then left the flame to hover next to the Goddess's hand. "Stay here in the light." Rose touched the Companion's icy hand and shivered. "I'm going to try. Please don't leave until I try."

The Goddess didn't look up, but she nodded slowly, and Rose took that as the only agreement she would get. So, she listened closely to Wilder's voice and followed it the rest of the way out of the dark.

51

———

Rose heard his voice before she could feel her body. She had gone from one place of darkness to another, but this time, the darkness was familiar. This darkness was of night behind closed eyelids. It was almost bright compared to the darkness of before. She savored the lightness of this darkness, listening to the words of Wilder's song. It was the Goddess's song of love lost, of a broken heart, of grief beyond imagining.

Wilder sang it too well.

Her eyes popped open, and she found herself cradled in his arms as he sang, a single tear running down his cheek. She huffed in indignation. "Wilder, you said you trusted me. Did you seriously think I would die on you like that?"

He paused his singing, a smirk spreading on his lips. "It's called acting, Rose. I told you, I'm very good at it."

Rose heard gasps from the crowd as Wilder pulled her to her feet. She wasn't sure how much the audience really understood was going on, but they appeared to still be enjoying the show.

She leaned closer to the orchestra pit and whispered, "Maestro, let's just skip to the end, okay?"

Maestro rubbed his forehead as if it was exhausting to work with fools, but at least he complied and cued the orchestra to begin the last song—the newest song, the song of the Wedding of the Goddess and Companion.

Rose still felt raw from her conversation with the Goddess. That was the first time she had told someone the full story about the loss of her siblings. The story had unearthed sadness that she had kept buried for years beneath anger. She didn't like how weak the sadness made her feel. But she also felt a lightness within her, as if her tears had washed away a sliver of her frozen anger.

As the music of the song swelled, she was filled with such a bittersweet sense of love. She opened her mouth to sing and instead produced a sobbing laugh ... or a laughing sob ... she wasn't sure which.

Maestro gave her an irritated look and signaled the orchestra to vamp on the intro again, and Wilder took her hand and whispered, "Are you okay?"

She took a deep breath and instead of burying the strange bittersweet sadness, she held it close to keep it safe. Then she began to sing.

Her voice was no more beautiful this time. In fact, it was even shakier from crying. And without Wilder's Gift manipulating the wind, she didn't have any fancy tricks to help. It was just Rose ... broken, angry, jealous, bad-singing Rose.

Just Rose pledging her love to Wilder and Wilder pledging his love to her.

Wilder's worried look faded as she sang. He wasn't concerned about the skill of her voice or whether she knew what to do with the strange sadness still lingering in her chest. He loved *her*, despite all else. She leaned into that love, letting it fill her and warm her from within.

Wilder spun her around the stage, leading her expertly through each of the steps. She let go of the words of the song and let the chorus sing her part. She focused on dancing with Wilder and being alive. The City was dark and cold and running out of food, but Rose and Wilder were alive and in love. She took every sweet note sung by the chorus, each sigh of the crowd, each heartbeat she felt through her hand on Wilder's chest, and she bundled it up into a fiery whirlwind in her soul.

The fire sprang to life through her fingertips on Wilder's chest but didn't burn him. The white flames twinkled in his eyes, an echo of the love that always sparkled deep within his gaze. His gentle hands didn't leave her waist as she pressed her hands together, wrapping her love for Wilder, the Goddess, and the City into the heart of her flame.

Then she flung the firestorm outward, toward the seven crystal spires at the edges of the City.

The bright white fire hit the crystals, dripping down their surface until they shimmered. The crowd gasped and began to cheer, but Rose didn't celebrate yet. The fire only clung to the outside of the still dark crystals. She frowned at them, her place in the song forgotten.

Wilder took her hand, twirling her around until he was the only one she could see. His eyes reflected the white fire burning on the crystals, but all she noticed was the slow blink of his long lashes. A tendril of hair had fallen from underneath her circlet, and he lifted the curl in gentle fingers, tucking it behind her ear. His fingertip traced a slow line behind her ear and down her neck, causing her to shiver despite the warmth of him so close. He leaned even closer, and his lips hovered right above her own. She felt his whisper more than heard it.

"Don't you remember, Rose? Your flames are always much more magnificent when we kiss."

His lips were already so close, but when he kissed her, they collided with the force of the mountain. She clung to him, feeling the powerful muscles of his back through his soft velvet jacket. His hands twisted through her hair, accidentally pulling out hairpins and knocking her circlet askew.

Fire and energy and power coursed through her, and she smiled against his lips as she savored it. Wilder made her feel powerful and alive, and that was the Gift she would offer the City.

She tore her lips away from Wilder, flinging her hands out wide. She gathered up every bit of power and strength and life she had within and then *pushed* it inside each of the fiery crystals.

White flames shot from the crystals, straight into the sky, then sped back down, slamming into the spires.

The dark crystals flickered, then relit in a steady glow.

The crowd erupted in cheers as the orchestra continued to play. Wilder grabbed Rose, hugging her and spinning her around.

"I knew you could do it!" He kissed her over and over, dropping dozens of little kisses all over her face as she stared at the crystals in awe.

"Does this mean ... he's alive?" she asked.

They looked at the basin, the only crystal that had not relit. Rose bit her lip. "Maybe we should check on her one more time, to be sure?"

Wilder walked with her to the basin, and they touched it together.

They blinked in the bright light of the glowing sanctuary and found the Goddess and Companion kissing passionately. Rose had the sudden feeling that this must be how it felt to see your parents kiss.

Wilder whispered, "They seem fine. Maybe we should just go?"

The Companion pulled away from the kiss and said to

the Goddess, "Erenne, darling, you should welcome your guests."

The Goddess grudgingly disconnected herself from the Companion but didn't let go of his hand. She gave Rose a warm smile. "Rose, I can never repay you for saving his life ... or mine."

Rose bowed her head, slightly embarrassed. "I'm honored, Goddess."

"But one more request ... please, look after Walter, will you?" said the Goddess. "I want him to find a place where people can appreciate him."

"I'm sure we can find him a place with someone who can appreciate his strange stories," said Rose with a smile. "The other day, he mentioned having a conversation about his Spark, but he couldn't remember if he was talking to a calico cat or a tabby." Rose laughed.

The Goddess tapped her lips in thought. "I've been both, depending on the occasion. I'm not sure which I was for that specific conversation."

Rose stared at her in shock. "What? You mean Walter's not crazy? He's actually talked to a cat before?"

The Goddess smirked. "And a butterfly at least once ... Walter's always been a little odd, but he's not crazy. Find him a safe place with people who won't take advantage of him." The Goddess stepped closer to Rose and Wilder but pulled the Companion with her, unwilling to let him go.

"I see a future for the City, Upstairs and Underneath, bound together as one. I believe the two of you will be at the core. Lead it well. You have my blessing." She placed her hands on their foreheads and said, "You are my children from above and below. Unite my City with a kiss."

Rose and Wilder blinked and found themselves back at center stage, only a heartbeat later than the moment they left.

The Goddess's blessing burned on Rose's forehead, and she looked at Wilder with a gleam in her eye. "I'm not sure if the Goddess realizes exactly how many times we've kissed tonight—"

Wilder grabbed her by the waist and pulled her into a kiss. Rose wrapped her hands around his neck, drawing him closer, savoring the joy of the City united and her heart at peace.

The crystal basin relit, flickering to life at their feet. Honeysuckle and jasmine and lilies exploded as blooming vines sprang to life from the simple backdrop, streaming across the stage, through the wings, over the rafters, and along the proscenium overhead. A warm wind tickled the flowers until they dropped their delicate petals in a steady rhythm, as gentle as snow.

As the petals softly landed on their shoulders, Rose withdrew her lips from Wilder's and arched an eyebrow. "You really are quite a show-off, aren't you?"

He grinned. "I have plenty more to show you, dear."

She laughed as he spun her, dancing across the stage strewn with petals.

A WEDDING

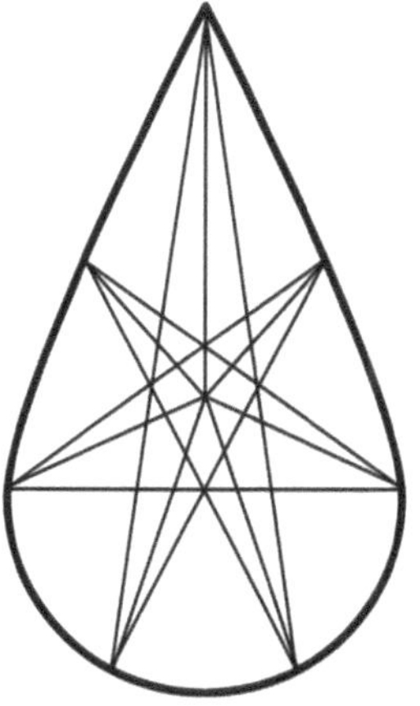

52

Loud music rang through the Library. Rose recognized the band from the nightclub in Grotto Chaos. Dozens of people thrashed around the open space in front of the makeshift stage, and their laughter and shouts added to the completely unusual noise in the massive Library. Rose watched the dancing crowd in fascination but didn't move from her seat at the table with most of the crew.

"It really was a beautiful wedding," said Feather with a wistful sigh. "Pledging to love one another forever during a ceremony inside the Goddess's holy Library ... it's just so romantic." Her cheeks glowed even brighter than usual because of her time out in the fields the last three months. The feast spread out on the table directly resulted from Feather and the others whose Gift of Order had returned.

Tayeh scooped another helping of mashed potatoes onto her plate. "You sound as love-struck as most of the Sentinels. I couldn't keep them focused on training this morning, with all the giggling and dramatic sighing."

Rose glimpsed Latham and Elise on the dance floor, happily bouncing along with the crowd. Dany stood at the

Library doorway in an official capacity as Sentinel. Not that anyone was worried about needing a Sentinel to keep guard, but Tayeh had convinced Rose to give the Sentinels meaningful jobs. As a result, Dany stood guard in her Sentinel uniform, but since they had destroyed the faceless masks, Rose could clearly see Dany's dreamy expression.

"I don't blame them for being overly sentimental," said Rev with a warm smile. "I do hope they're working in shifts. It would be a shame if they don't have time to try out their dancing skills today."

Along with the Sentinels training with Tayeh, Rose had happily handed off their dance instruction to teachers with more skill. She often grumbled when Sentinels followed her around as a permanent honor guard, but secretly, she was quite proud to have her own squad of dance fighters.

"I'm surprised you and Wilder aren't out there dancing," said Kieran with a wave of his wineglass toward the dance floor. "The two of you always like to be the center of attention." He hid his teasing smile as he took a sip.

Rose followed the invisible thread that connected her heart to Wilder's and found him crouched down at the table next to Mims, who sat telling a story to a group of Priests. Wilder's black suit was perfectly tailored to his exquisite form, and his lips curled in a grin that set Rose's heart fluttering. She resisted the familiar urge to scoff at the silly emotion and instead let herself savor her reckless heartbeat.

Fitz laughed. "Looks like Priests dragged Wilder into a conversation. He might be there a while." Besides Wilder, Fitz was the only one in their crew currently dressed in black, since he now embraced the title of Priest.

Rose wondered how long it would take for the City to sort out what it meant to be a Priest. After the Goddess returned her Gifts the night of the Pageant, it was clear the Gifts would be given differently from now on.

First off, she hadn't returned her Gifts to any children. Some of the older Sentinels had seen their Gifts return, but they were the youngest people with Gifts in the City.

Second, it wasn't only Priests who received Gifts. Some people weren't her followers at all. The Priests who had Gifts, and those who considered themselves Priests despite their lack of Gifts, weren't sure what to do with Gifted people who didn't worship the Goddess. Were they Priests or something different?

Fitz had wisely said that the Goddess gave Gifts as she saw fit and had plenty of scripture to back it up. Rose decided to trust him on that but was secretly glad the Goddess had seen fit to return the Gifts to all the crew. Something about her crew representing the Goddess's Virtues filled Rose with joy.

Wilder's warm hand touched her bare shoulder. She looked up to find him looking at her with such love she couldn't speak around the lump in her throat.

He offered her his hand. "I think it's time we danced, don't you?"

She took his hand and surrendered without a word.

He didn't take a straight path to the dance floor, instead walking slow so he could give her a lingering glance up and down. "Have I mentioned how good you look in red?"

"You mentioned it." She swished the fabric of the long scarlet gown playfully. "But you can mention it again."

He grinned, and his eyes trailed down her neck. His sultry gaze slipped into a familiar look of concern as he focused on her collarbone, clearly on display in the strapless gown.

"It doesn't hurt?" he asked.

Her fingers unconsciously floated to the fingerprint mark. "Not since the night in the amphitheater. I think the Goddess healed it somehow." Rose had lived with the pain of Vaylan's mark on her skin for so long that it still surprised her it didn't hurt anymore.

"I'm glad she didn't remove the scar, though," said Rose. Even though Vaylan was locked in prison, she didn't want to forget all she had been through.

Wilder brushed a gentle finger across the scar. "Marked One ..." he whispered. His touch and whisper sent a delighted shiver through Rose.

"Marked One!" Yasmine's urgent voice quickly smothered the moment.

Yasmine wore a pale lavender dress that highlighted the crown of violets wrapped in her hair. She clutched a notebook to her chest, and her face was lit in a religious fervor Rose had seen many times.

Yasmine's voice was breathless with excitement. "I didn't want to bother you earlier, Marked One, but I just have to tell you what we recently discovered."

Almost every day, one of the Adopted came to Rose with something new they uncovered in Brother Owyn's prophecies. Rose considered herself one of the Adopted, so she was interested in their discoveries, although she thought some of them were a bit too devout in their studies of prophecy.

Rose put on a patient smile. "What did you discover today?"

"It's about your daughter. We believe she will do something great!"

Rose could barely choke out the words. "My daughter?"

"Yes," said Yasmine with glee. "Yours and Wilder's, of course."

Rose merely blinked at her stupidly, but Wilder looked fascinated. "I know some Priests have already become pregnant, but I hadn't yet considered the possibilities for us ... We will have a child someday ..." He looked at Rose in awe.

"Yes, at least one." Yasmine's voice had returned to the

matter-of-fact tone she adopted when discussing prophecies. "Hunter believes the prophecies say you will have three, but honestly, I think he is reading too much into the prophecy about the Triad." She rolled her eyes as if it was a common disagreement. "It's just too literal to interpret that as triplets."

"Triplets?" Rose's voice was barely a squeak.

Wilder bit his lips to hide his grin and spoke in a solemn voice. "Thank you for this information, Yasmine. You have once again blessed us with your devotion to the prophecies."

Her face returned to its zealous glow, and she bowed to them before running off.

Rose's mind had stuck in a loop of a single word. "Triplets?" she whispered.

"Don't worry about that today, Marked One," he said with a mischievous grin. "Let's just enjoy this beautiful wedding."

He pulled her closer to dance, though they still hadn't made it all the way to the dance floor yet. Rose allowed herself to be distracted by the music and Wilder holding her close, by the smell of the food and the abundance of flowers dripping over every surface in the Library.

Her eyes drifted to the dance floor, where she saw Kai and Quinn dancing and smiling. They were easy to spot in their bright white suits—the wedding couple the only ones dressed in white, as tradition required.

"I still can't believe they convinced the librarian Priests to let them have their wedding here." Rose shook her head in amazement as she watched some of the black-clad librarians dance.

Wilder laughed. "The Knowledge Priests love Quinn so much they would give him anything he asked. I wouldn't be surprised if they ask Quinn and Kai to move into the Library."

Rose smiled. "Since the librarians already let Walter live here, I guess they could be neighbors."

Wilder gave her a serious look. "Don't get any ideas about having our own wedding here, Rose."

The two of them had been so busy working with the Priests, Adopted, Sentinels, and other people in the City both Upstairs and Underneath that they hadn't discussed wedding plans at all.

"The idea never occurred to me," she said haughtily. Rose had no intention of revealing that during Quinn and Kai's ceremony, she had indeed imagined her and Wilder exchanging vows in exactly the same patch of sunshine but surrounded by roses instead of blue hydrangeas.

Wilder's knowing grin implied he knew she was lying. "Good. Because the Library is entirely too small."

"Too small?" Rose looked up at the seven stories of open balconies filled with tables of people.

"We will have to get married in the amphitheater. It's the only place big enough for the entire City to attend." Rose's mouth dropped open, but he kept talking. "Obviously, everyone who saw us in the Pageant that night will want to come. Plus all the other Priests and Adopted who couldn't attend before. Along with everyone who has expressed their support for us leading the rebuilding efforts in the City ... It's going to be quite a large crowd."

She imagined standing on the stage again, and despite how wonderful everything turned out, she only remembered her embarrassing performance.

She grabbed the lapel of Wilder's black suit and pulled him close. "If you think I am stepping foot on that stage again, you are mistaken," she growled.

"Really?" His voice was a warm purr. "So, you're prepared to fight me over our wedding venue?"

"You bet I am," she said fiercely.

"I'm afraid we'll have to save that fight for later," he whispered. "I don't want to see you murdered by librarians for burning down the Library."

His twinkling eyes caused her lips to form a grin without her permission. He was her match in ferocity and passion, her equal in strength and devotion. She was ready to fight him and to love him for the rest of her life.

She grinned. "Fine. We'll burn down the City tomorrow. But tonight, we'll just dance."

∼

The End

ABOUT THE AUTHOR

Susannah Welch lives in sunny South Florida with her brilliant husband and a magically hypoallergenic cat. She enjoys singing and dancing and showing off. She likes her stories with a little bit of drama, and a whole lot of sparkle.

f facebook.com/susannah.welch.author

instagram.com/susannahwelchauthor

www.ingramcontent.com/pod-product-compliance
Lightning Source LLC
Chambersburg PA
CBHW061047190726

48286CB00006B/1638